Jessica Watkins Presents

CHASING DESIRES

by KASEY MARTIN

Copyright © 2017 by Kasey Martin
Published by Jessica Watkins Presents

All rights reserved, including the right of reproduction in whole or in part in any form. Without limiting the right under copyright reserved above, no part of this publication may be reproduced, stored in or introduced into a retrieval system, or transmitted, in any form by means (electronic, mechanical, photocopying, recording, or otherwise), without the prior written permission of the copyright owner.

This is a work of fiction. Names, characters, places and incidents are either the product of the author's imagination or are used fictitiously, and any resemblance to actual persons, living or dead, business establishments, events, or locales, is entirely coincidental.

CHASING DESIRES
by Kasey Martin

Prologue

CHASE

Chase gasped as her body jerked upright with awareness. A cold sheen of sweat covered her from foot to head as her body trembled. The scene was the same every time her lids closed. She was reluctant to go to sleep because of the nightmares of a phone call that plagued her unconscious mind.

That phone call would be the last time she spoke with him. The partner that treated her like family, the most important person in her life, and the man that was there when nobody else was. Daniel Reyes.

The memories assailed her, so she sat back and let them take over…

"Chase, don't worry. I have everything under control." The heavy exasperated sigh that left her partner could be heard loud and clear over the phone.

Chase gave a sigh of her own. "Look, you're the one who taught me to never go in without back-up. Now, you just want me to ignore your cardinal rule because you're too impatient to wait for me?"

"It's not about me being impatient. You know better than anybody how long I've worked to take these guys down!" Daniel's voice was ragged and hard. Chase knew that he felt

Chasing Desires
by Kasey Martin

passionate about his case, but she'd never heard him sound so desperate before.

"Listen, you need to go to Worthington, so we can get the reinforcements that you need for an operation of this magnitude. Use your head!" Chase pleaded. She was desperate for her partner to come to his senses.

"I'm using my head. Just have my fucking back! I never thought I would have to beg you for that, partner." Daniel growled hatefully.

His words hurt Chase, but she had to convince him that he was making a mistake. The one time she'd taken time for herself and gone on a weekend trip, just so happened to be when her partner got a break in his case and decided to go into a dangerous situation without her. She just needed him to wait until morning, so she would have time to get back to town and have his back.

"You know I got you, Danny," Chase dejectedly replied. "But I can't have your back from Florida. I can be on the next thing smoking and help you handle Angeletti."

"I'm sorry, Sis. The deal goes down tonight. I can't wait for you to ride in on your white horse." She knew that Daniel was smiling wide at the savior reference. They always joked that Chase had a hero complex; she had the need to save any, and everyone she thought had the slightest problem.

CHASING DESIRES
by Kasey Martin

"Don't be sorry. Just call Worthington." She pleaded once more.

"Fine. I'll call Worthington." He stated dismissively before continuing, "Listen, I have some things that I need you to keep for me."

"What things?" Chase asked curiously letting go of the fact that he changed the subject.

"Just some things I need to put in a safe place. You know I don't like people snooping around in my shit." Daniel laughed tightly.

Chase knew that he was trying to lighten the mood, but she also knew that things had been heavy between him and his latest fling. A fling that she had yet to meet. Daniel was such a good guy, but the company he chose to keep was questionable at best.

"Yeah, just leave it at the apartment. You still got the key?" Chase would just pretend that her friend wasn't hiding things from his girlfriend at her house for whatever reason. That would be a conversation they would have later.

"Yeah, I got it. I'll just stick in the closet."

"Okay. Daniel, be careful, and I'll see you when I get back."

CHASING DESIRES
by Kasey Martin

"Of course. Have a safe flight back." She could hear the smile in his voice, but she would never get to see it spread over his lightly tanned handsome face.

Chase would never get to have that conversation with her best friend. She still didn't have the balls to thoroughly look through the bag that he left in her closet. She dared to open it once when they told her he died, but when she opened up the black duffel bag, all she saw were clothes that still held a faint scent of his cologne. After she had broken down in despair, she'd closed the bag and put it into a storage unit never to open it again. Chase vowed then and there that she would avenge her partner…if it was the last thing she did.

***

Daniel

Daniel pulled up to the red light. His head swiveled from left to right as he cautiously checked his surroundings. The area was familiar with the bank branch that sat on the corner across the street from a fast food restaurant that the local thugs known as the ninth street gang hung out.

Tonight must've been slow for the drug trade because it was almost midnight and the streets were bare. Daniel had just come from dropping his bag off at Chase's apartment. He felt the contents were much safer at her house especially if he was unable to pull off this plan of his tonight.

Chasing Desires
by Kasey Martin

Daniel pulled up to the eerily quiet warehouse. He overheard earlier that an important deal was going down, and this was his chance to close his case against the Angeletti family for good. Daniel had been undercover for so long that he just wanted to get out and live a healthy life. There was nobody he could talk to that would understand the pressure he was under to succeed. His father was an immigrant who worked himself into an early grave, so Daniel put the pressure on himself to be a man that his father could be proud of. However, the longer he stayed undercover the harder it was to distinguish the real Daniel from the criminal persona he acquired.

Daniel looked at his watch and noted there was movement in the window of the top floor of the warehouse. He smoothly exited his car, his walk confident and full of swagger. His long legs quickly ate up the distance from the car to a side door. He easily snuck into the warehouse undetected. He was making his way to a back office when he heard a familiar voice.

"I knew I couldn't trust you. What the fuck are you doing here?" The man's voice was hollow and Daniel knew he had to play his cards right or this would be his last conversation.

"Of course I can be trusted." Daniel held his hands up in a sign of surrender.

"What kind of fool do you take me for?"

Chasing Desires
by Kasey Martin

"Hey man, you know me," Daniel responded trying to calm the situation. He had never been a fast talker, but at the moment he wished that he would've taken the time to learn the skill.

"You're right I do know you." The man pulled out a gun with a silencer attached. Daniel knew then that his plan would go up in flames if he didn't think fast.

"Listen. I'm here because I'm supposed to be here. It's my job." Daniel was undercover as one of the go-to enforcers of the Angeletti family.

"No. You're here sticking your nose into business that doesn't concern you."

"Everything concerns me," Daniel responded darkly. "As a matter of fact, I have knowledge of something that will bring down everyone. Especially you."

"What the hell are you talking about?" He pointed the gun directly at Daniel's head. "You little shit! You stole the fucking ledger! Where the fuck is it?" He seethed still pointing the gun.

"We can both get what we need," Daniel responded his hands still raised.

The sound of the gun being cocked echoed in the silence. "Or you could die right here?"

Chasing Desires
by Kasey Martin

Daniel should've been nervous, he should've been scared, but this was his chance to get out of this life, one way or another. "Or... we can make a deal."

CHASING DESIRES
by Kasey Martin

CHAPTER 1
LORENZO

Lorenzo awoke disoriented. The last thing he remembered was fighting with Justin Russo. *That asshole shot me!* As soon as the thought crossed his mind, he clutched at his chest feeling the deep ache there.

His arm was sore and it felt like an elephant had been sitting on his torso. The continuous beeping noise seemed to get louder and faster until he felt a small, soft hand gently caress his cheek and then down to rub his arm in a comforting motion. He instantly relaxed and he felt the effects of her soothing touch. The sensation immediately calmed him. He looked up into the comforting chocolate brown eyes that he couldn't forget even if he tried. But that calmness left him completely at the mention of one-word...*Agent*.

As soon as he heard the doctor call her *Agent*, he couldn't stop the loud distressed choke that escaped him. *What the fuck is he talking about?* Lorenzo's brain just couldn't wrap around what he'd just heard. *There is no way in hell that my Chase could be a fucking cop!* His heart wanted to reject the betrayal, but in his head, he knew it had to be true.

After what seemed like ages, she slowly turned to meet his gaze. Her bright, almond shaped eyes were filled with guilt and what appeared to be regret. Lorenzo's heart broke at the sight, but he couldn't turn his head away. *Why would she do this? Who is this woman and what does she want from me? Why is she here?* There were so many questions and things he couldn't comprehend.

Lorenzo narrowed his eyes at the beautiful woman standing in front of him. He was completely shocked, disappointed, and angry. He thought he was getting to know her, but he didn't know who the hell this woman was. "Agent? What. The. Hell."

"Lorenzo, let me explain."

"Let you explain?" he mocked in an angry, raspy tone.

The heart monitor was going crazy, and the ache in his chest increased exponentially. *How could I have been so stupid?* He'd mistakenly taken all her questions and concerns to be her method of getting to know him better. *What a joke!* He thought as he looked into her sorrowful yet beautiful face.

"Why?" The one-word question came out harsh and full of pain.

The lanky doctor chose that moment to step in. "Sir, you need to calm down. You've had a traumatic experience, and this isn't good for your recovery."

# Chasing Desires
by Kasey Martin

Lorenzo felt like his chest was about to cave in. He struggled to inhale air in his lungs, and the shallow breaths were excruciatingly painful.

"Agent, I'm going to have to ask you to step out please," the doctor said with a stern voice filled with authority. "Mr. Moretti, try and calm down."

Lorenzo watched Chase hesitate before backing toward the door as a petite nurse rushed past her. His eyes followed her tall, svelte figure as it disappeared behind the steel door. The nurse labored over him, taking his blood pressure and checking monitors. It didn't matter what she did because the cause and the cure for his stress had just walked away.

***

Several weeks later, Lorenzo sat in his home office trying to get some work done. He'd been released from the hospital, but his recovery from the severe gunshot wound he'd sustained had been a long and tedious process. Although he had once lived a dangerous life as a part of one of the most notorious mob families on the east coast, not once had he ever ended up in the hospital. Of course, he had been shot before, but it was nothing the good "family" doctor couldn't just stitch up. It took him going straight to almost get taken out.

While he was in the hospital, he'd learned that Jan and Justin had pleaded guilty and received time in prison, but he

Chasing Desires
by Kasey Martin

wasn't satisfied. The gangster in him didn't want that kind of justice. He wanted revenge. However, he'd left that life in the past along with the connections to get to someone in prison. Of course, he could call in a favor, but the last thing he wanted was to owe anyone anything.

Lorenzo had worked too hard to get out of the criminal world, and there was no way in hell he was going back. He vowed after his younger brother was killed trying to follow in his footsteps that he would go straight. There was no need for a legal businessman to carry a gun around. Little did he know that he would wind up on the wrong end of a bullet.

But the worst part in all this, besides being shot and almost dying, was the woman that he was falling for had betrayed him. Lorenzo thought he could trust her, but she'd been lying to him since the moment they met. He never thought he would be the sucker to fall for a pretty face and a nice ass, but a sucker was exactly what he'd ended up being.

Chase had played him like a fiddle. She had batted those long lashes, whispered in that raspy tone, and smiled seductively. Lorenzo was a goner every time. She was there when he woke up in the hospital. He was so happy to see her sitting there. She looked like a ray of sunshine, her smile lighting up the dreary hospital room. Her sheer presence had

Chasing Desires
by Kasey Martin

had a calming effect on him until the doctor called her *Agent*. After that, his world all but shattered.

Lorenzo's ringing cell phone snatched him out of his musings. "Moretti," he answered curtly.

"Moretti, it's Chase. I need to talk to you. It could be a matter of life or death."

"Speak of the devil," he mumbled.

He didn't want to care about what she had to say. He swore to himself that he would *never* speak to her conniving ass again. But he knew the invisible pull that caused him to constantly want her, wouldn't just go away. He would have to face Chase and his feelings for her head-on. At least now he could go into this with his eyes open. However, the words, life and death, made him sit up and respond immediately.

"You can come to my place. It's more convenient for me." Lorenzo's voice came out hard, and he was thankful he didn't sound as weak as he felt.

There was a heavy sigh on the other end of the phone. "Okay. I can be over in an hour if that's alright."

"Yeah. An hour is fine," Lorenzo answered gruffly.

"Alright. See you soon." Chase disconnected before he had a chance to tell her to come alone.

The last thing he needed was a bunch of Feds in his place. Lorenzo was now aware that Chase was working with

CHASING DESIRES
by Kasey Martin

Jake Cameron on a federal investigation. However, all the information he had received confirmed that he was no longer the primary subject of their case. And since Lorenzo was out of commission and focused on recovering, he wasn't up to speed on everything that was going on around him. So he had no idea what Chase was actually doing.

It didn't take long to prove that he wasn't involved in anything illegal, but his business was left without its owner and a manager. And even though Charlie was now married and very pregnant, she still managed to continue to work at Premier. As a matter of fact, she was the main reason why Lorenzo's club was still up and running.

Charlie and his personal assistant, Amber, had been a blessing to him while he was in the hospital, and he was glad to have them on his team. He was even grateful to Charlie's big caveman of a husband, Jake, for catching that weasel, Justin, before he got away. They had even been somewhat cordial to one another since Lorenzo's release from the hospital.

He sighed heavily as the pain in his chest from the gunshot wound resurfaced. The last thing Lorenzo needed to deal with was a life and death situation. He was barely at forty percent, so if anything were to go down, he would definitely be a liability. The stress of the fallout at Premier had him popping more meds than he should, sleeping less, and worrying more. A

Chasing Desires
by Kasey Martin

part of what made him the man that he was, was his ability to deal with problems. He was a fixer, a doer, a general to men who needed to be led. Now he was at his weakest, and the most beautiful woman he had ever laid eyes on needed him. *Or so she said.*

An hour later, on the dot, Lorenzo's doorbell chimed letting him know that Chase had arrived. He hadn't seen her since a week after he was discharged from the hospital, and she had also made sure that Lorenzo was aware of the appeals that Justin and Jan had filed. *But what could possibly be life or death?*

Lorenzo moved slowly to open his door. His eyes ate up the sight before him. Chase stood in a casual pair of ripped blue jeans and a lightweight purple sweater. Her hair hung loose around her shoulders, and her brown eyes although weary, were still beautiful. It reminded him of the very first time he'd laid eyes on her. She was in a bar of a popular hotel, and when their eyes connected, he thought he saw a look of recognition in them. He ruled out that he may have met her in passing because there was no way in hell he would forget a woman like Chase. And he was right. He hadn't met her before, but she had indeed recognized him.

CHASING DESIRES
by Kasey Martin

"Agent, come on in." Lorenzo could only address her gruffly; otherwise he would pull her into his arms and devour her sexy, pouty lips.

He noticed that she frowned slightly before covering her facial features with a blank expression.

"Thank you, *Mr. Moretti*. Like I said, this situation is extremely dangerous and I need your help."

Lorenzo led Chase to his spacious living area where they sat uncomfortably before she cleared her throat and began to tell him the reason for her visit.

"Look, I know you feel some type of way about me right now and I'm really sorry about that. But I had a job to do, and you just happened to land right smack in the middle of my case."

Lorenzo's nostrils flared and his eyes filled with fire. "What do you mean you had a job to do? So I was just part of your job, Chase?!"

"That's not what I meant, and you know it," Chase answered curtly.

The audacity of this woman. How could she be mad when I was the one who was deceived over and over again? Lorenzo's thoughts made his face contort with anger.

"Well, that's what you said, *Agent*," Lorenzo spat with a sneer on his face.

Chasing Desires
by Kasey Martin

He watched as Chase's eyes narrowed. Her chest heaved up and down in what he guessed was frustration. Her full, pouty, kissable lips were pressed together in a line. She was so beautiful even in her anger. How could he both hate and want to fuck a woman at the same time so desperately? *It must be the meds.* Lorenzo smirked to himself as he continued to watch Chase react to him. He knew it was probably sick to get turned on by making her so angry, but he couldn't help *his* reaction to her.

Lorenzo kept his eyes on her until she seemed to regain control of her anger. She took a deep breath, and her face went completely blank. He knew that look; it was the professional mask she wore that he hated so much.

However, there was no maybe about the fire he could see blazing in her eyes. She might've been able to show no emotion on her face, but those beautiful eyes told on her every time.

"Look, I know your cousin, Tommy, set up my partner to be killed," Chase stated, pulling Lorenzo back into the conversation.

He stared at her blankly without a response. He didn't know what her partner had to do with anything, but he would sit silently. He had learned that sometimes staying quiet could be more beneficial.

Chasing Desires
by Kasey Martin

"I don't have any solid proof, but your cousin has been getting away with a lot of illegal activities for a long time. I'm sure you're aware of the Angeletti family since you once played a large role in it."

Lorenzo stared at her, unblinking. If she thought he was a rat bastard, or was stupid enough to tell on his family and himself, she was crazy.

Lorenzo frowned before asking, "Agent, are you questioning me under an official capacity?"

"No, I'm here as a *friend* and like I said, this could potentially be a life and death situation."

Lorenzo chuckled without humor. "A *friend*? You lie to me for months and now you're here to accuse me of illegal activities. With friends like you…" Lorenzo shook his head as he let his words hang in the tension-filled air.

"I didn't accuse you of anything. You're just twisting my words because you're upset. And I get it! But dammit, Lorenzo, this is a serious situation, and I need you to listen to me!"

Lorenzo saw the crack in her armor. The mask had started to slip, and the anger and frustration were beginning to look more like desperation. Although he would never be accused of having a big heart, he wasn't a complete asshole.

Chasing Desires
by Kasey Martin

She shook her head and tried to get rid of the strange feeling she got whenever she was around Lorenzo. She had to regain her focus. *Remember your job, Chase,* she silently coached herself.

Chase cleared her throat before she continued. "I know that you're not close to your family back in Jersey and I'm also aware that you weren't working with Tommy when he showed up in Dallas. I know that his visits to your club were unwelcome."

She watched as he nodded his head, but he still didn't respond.

"Tommy has been lying low and staying out of sight. However, I know that he is up to no good."

"So what? Tommy is always up to no good. How does this have anything to do with being life or death, or the death of your partner?" Lorenzo questioned as his lips turned down into a frown.

"I told you about my partner so you could understand why I am investigating Tommy."

"Oh, I get it. This is some type of revenge thing for you," Lorenzo said, a smug look returning to his face.

Chase recognized that he was pushing her buttons on purpose. She was genuinely trying her best to be a professional, but this man was really, *really* pissing her off.

CHASING DESIRES
by Kasey Martin

"This is about *justice*. My partner deserves for the man who is responsible for his death to be held accountable."

"Hmmm...still sounds like revenge to me."

Bastard, Chase thought. *Maybe this is a waste of time. Obviously, he isn't over me being an agent.*

Chase took a deep breath and prayed for patience before she continued. "The intel I received has Tommy targeting some high-profile clubs in Dallas. It's suspected that he has been running drugs, girls, and even guns through them. And while you've been out of commission, he's been trying to invade your club as well."

"What?! I thought you were working with Jake? How could he let a scumbag like my cousin near Charlie?" Lorenzo's voice was raised and his face started to turn a dark shade of red.

Chase didn't like the way he looked. This was clearly stressing him out, but she had to let him know. "Jake is the reason why we know he's trying to run his business through your club."

"So why is this life or death?" Lorenzo asked. "I'm well enough to put a stop to his bullshit."

Chase sighed. "We don't want you to stop him. I need *evidence*—solid evidence. And I have never been able to get this close to him. I need for you to please let him into your clubs."

Chasing Desires
by Kasey Martin

"Why in the actual fuck would I do that?" Lorenzo seethed, his voice growing increasingly louder.

"Because this is a win-win for both of us. I get the solid proof I need to put Tommy away, and you get your family out of your life for good," Chase explained as calmly as she could.

"How do you figure that? What I see is, I look like a fuckin' snitch and my family puts a hit out on me."

"Well actually, you would stay out of commission, and I would be your um...*girlfriend* helping you to get back on your feet."

"Wait. *What?*"

"If I was your girlfriend, there wouldn't have to be an explanation of why I was with you or at your club so much."

"I've already been made to look like a fucking fool behind this Jan and Justin bullshit, and now you want me to let my cousin run around doing whatever the fuck he wants in *my* clubs?"

"I know I'm asking a lot of you, Lorenzo, but Tommy needs to go down. So I really need your help," Chase pleaded with him. She was sure that she could find another way to get evidence on Tommy, but she didn't have the time to start over.

Chase no longer had her superiors breathing down her neck because after Lorenzo was shot, it gave her a short reprieve from their persistent questioning.

CHASING DESIRES
by Kasey Martin

"Why should I help you?"

Lorenzo's question brought Chase out of her thoughts. He really didn't have a reason to help her. She had betrayed his trust in her, but it had been a consequence of the job. She'd done whatever she had to do as always. Sometimes that meant hurting people and using them.

"I know you think that you don't have any reason to help me, but you know as well as I do that Tommy Angeletti is a dangerous man who shouldn't be walking around freely. He needs to be stopped."

"And you want *me* to stop him?" Lorenzo pointed to himself with his mouth set in a grim line.

"No, I want you to help *me* to stop him."

"So you want to continue to use me? Am I right?"

"Yes," she answered honestly. She wouldn't lie to him about that. She needed his help. "I want to use your connection to your cousin to get to him. I need your help to close my case."

She watched as several emotions flashed in the ocean blue depths of Lorenzo's eyes. He ran his fingers through his long hair and down the stubble on his face. "I'm sorry, Chase. Although there's no love between my cousin and me, I'm not a snitch, so I can't be involved with setting him up."

After a minute of thought, Chase simply responded, "Alright."

Chasing Desires
by Kasey Martin

What else could she say? She knew that securing Lorenzo's help would be a long shot, but she still had to try anyway.

"Just *alright*?" he questioned, his eyes holding a glint of suspicion.

"Yes." She nodded. "I just ask that you keep my identity to yourself and please do not interfere with my case."

He nodded. "I'll keep your identity to myself. Like I said, I'm not a snitch. But if Tommy keeps trying to close in on my business, I want to know about it."

"This is an on-going investigation, Moretti—"

"We're past formalities, Chase," Lorenzo cut Chase off. "You know that I have way more information about your case than the normal bystander would."

As much as she hated to admit it, he was right. But she didn't have to like it. "Fine, I'll keep you in the loop." She paused to take in Lorenzo's smug expression before adding, "As much as I can."

Although some of the smugness disappeared from his face, a smirk remained. "Okay, I'll settle for as much as you can."

Chase saw an opening in Lorenzo's words. Maybe she could wear him down and talk him into helping her, especially if she could plant a seed of doubt.

Chasing Desires
by Kasey Martin

"I just need to ask you something before I go."

"Okay, ask."

"Do you have a will?"

"*A will*? What does that have to do with anything?" Lorenzo's face was perplexed, which was exactly what Chase wanted.

"Yes. Do you have a will? Remember, I said this was a life and death situation."

"How could I forget? Yes, I have a will."

"So who does everything go to? You know, if you meet an untimely end?"

"Well, my mother is my primary beneficiary, but since she's…" His words trailed off.

Chase knew that Lorenzo had come to the same conclusion she had. "Your mother isn't well, so that means everything would go to your next of kin or to her next of kin because of her dementia."

Chase had done a lot of research on Lorenzo and she'd discovered that his elderly mother was in an upscale home in Jersey. And although she had mostly good days, she was still suffering from diminishing memory.

Lorenzo's eyes were blazing, and Chase knew that her seed of doubt had been planted.

CHASING DESIRES
by Kasey Martin

"Justin didn't shoot you by accident. We already know that. And you also know that he was meeting with Tommy before he shot you."

Chase knew that Lorenzo was a smart man, and he could put two and two together. His father was dead, and his mother was in a home. He only had his uncle and cousin left. His uncle rarely left Jersey, but he was a smart businessman. There was no way that he would let Lorenzo's fortune and clubs go unclaimed. He would simply put someone in charge. *Tommy Angeletti.*

With that thought hanging in the air, Chase left Lorenzo to think about everything they had discussed.

***

Chase was trying to relax in her newly-rented apartment. Although her superiors didn't support her investigating Angeletti, they backed off because of her reputation for being a good agent. Their lack of assistance had her placing all of her faith into J.C. Incorporated and herself.

When Chase came to Texas, her superiors told her to make do with what she could, so she did. However, when they kept insisting that she needed to run everything by them and do a daily check-in report, she became increasingly suspicious. Her reports were vague, and she knew that her time to close her case was decreasing by the minute. Chase was well aware that she

CHASING DESIRES
by Kasey Martin

had placed all of her eggs in one basket, but she couldn't turn back now. She had to get Lorenzo to agree to help her.

Chase knew that her feelings for Lorenzo weren't completely altruistic, but she couldn't stop herself from wanting to get closer to him. What she wanted was to make Tommy Angeletti pay no matter what the cost. And in order to do that, she had to get next to Lorenzo, despite knowing better. It was a consequence she was willing to pay. She thought back to one of their first official dates.

Chase picked up the call on the second ring. "Hello?" Her voice was husky even to her own ears.

"Hello there, Miss..." Lorenzo's sentence died off.

Chase remembered that she hadn't given him a last name yet. She wanted to stick to her cover so she gave him a fake name.

"Sanders," she lied easily. Chase always used her real first name because anyone from her past could pop up and recognize her. But a different last name could always be explained away.

"Well, hello there, Miss Sanders. I hope I didn't catch you at a bad time."

Lorenzo's deep voice was like smooth silk to Chase's ears. She needed to get a hold of herself. This was her job. He

Chasing Desires
by Kasey Martin

was her job. "No, I'm just online looking for a place. Can't live out of a suitcase forever."

"No, I guess you can't. So since you're looking for a place, does that mean you decided to stay in Dallas?" Lorenzo questioned.

She thought she heard a bit of eagerness in his voice, but she couldn't be sure. "Yes, I'm going to stay here for as long as I need to," she vaguely responded. She would stay in Texas for as long as it took to catch Tommy Angeletti, no matter what her superiors said.

"Well, I'm, certainly glad you decided to grace the great state of Texas with your presence."

Chase heard the smile in Lorenzo's voice and she could tell that he was being genuine. That fact made her wince. For the first time in her career, she almost felt bad for lying to someone. She giggled, hoping that it would hide the distress in her voice. "I don't know about all that."

"I do," he responded in a serious tone. "I'm glad you're going to be here. Now, maybe you will go out on an official date with me."

"Umm... Okay. When would you like to go out?" She had been waiting for weeks for him to ask her out because she needed to get close to him.

CHASING DESIRES
by Kasey Martin

"Are you free right now?" Lorenzo got straight to the point.

Chase liked his straightforwardness. She laughed before answering. "Like I said, I'm just browsing for places, so yeah, I guess I can free up some time for you."

"I'll pick you up in an hour."

An hour later, Chase met Lorenzo in the lobby of her hotel. When she stepped off the elevator, she knew that she looked good by the glimmer in his eyes. She was wearing a wine-colored jumpsuit with a halter upper bodice and neckline. Her ebony skin held a shimmer as if she were dusted with glitter. Her hair was pulled away from her face and tucked behind both ears. Her deep chocolate brown eyes were bright, and she noticed that he couldn't tear his eyes away from her.

"Hey, gorgeous, aren't you a sight for sore eyes?" Lorenzo whistled as Chase seductively approached him, putting an extra sway in her hips.

She couldn't help but blush at his compliment. However, he wasn't the only one impressed because he absolutely took her breath away. He was wearing a dark suit with a matching crew neck shirt underneath. It was both casual and dressy at the same time. His dark brown hair was long on the top and shorter on the sides, and his gorgeous face was clean shaven. But as always, it was his eyes that caused her pulse to race.

CHASING DESIRES
by Kasey Martin

"Hey, yourself, handsome. Are you ready to go?" she finally responded after her perusal.

"Absolutely!" Lorenzo smiled deviously as he grabbed her soft hand in his to lead her to his car.

When they touched, she felt a connection like she never had before and she knew that if she wasn't careful she could be in real trouble.

They drove for about twenty minutes before Lorenzo pulled into the parking lot of Al Biernat's, an upscale restaurant located in uptown Dallas.

"I hope you like surf and turf."

"Al Biernat's is more than a little surf and turf, Lorenzo," Chase stated in awe. She knew this wasn't your run-of-the-mill place and she was thoroughly impressed even though she knew she shouldn't be. She had to keep reminding herself that he was a gangster, a bad guy, a means to an end, and this wasn't really a date. It was her job.

Lorenzo pulled up to the valet and walked around to the passenger's side to help Chase. She placed her hand in his and for the second time that night she felt the pulse of electricity when they touched. The feeling was addictive, and even though she didn't want to let him go, she knew that she had to.

She slid her hand from his, and placed both hands around her clutch purse. He frowned slightly before placing his

CHASING DESIRES
by Kasey Martin

hand on her lower back and leading her through the restaurant. She could barely concentrate on walking because his touch felt like fire. She was shocked that she made it through the restaurant without stumbling. Once they were seated at their table, they ordered their drinks and settled into a comfortable conversation.

Lorenzo kept the conversation mainly on Chase although he answered some questions about his past. Then he quickly turned the subject back to her. No matter how hard she tried, he would not let his guard down. So she kept talking about herself, hoping that he would soften his walls enough for her to break through. Chase kept the conversation light and neutral enough for him not to get suspicious, but she could tell he was starting to relax.

The conversation became easier and easier, and before she knew it, they had talked for so long that the restaurant was closing. Since neither of them felt like going home, they decided to go to a nearby lounge. When they arrived, they quickly got drinks and found a comfortable sofa nestled in a corner. They laughed and talked as they fell into a comfort with one another. When the D.J switched the music to slow hip-hop, the dance floor slowly began to fill up.

"Dance with me." Lorenzo held out his hand with a quirked brow in challenge.

Chasing Desires
by Kasey Martin

"You want to dance to this?" Chase asked incredulously.

"What? You think I don't know who The PARTYNEXTDOOR is?" Lorenzo questioned with a smirk. "I'll give you some advice."

"Uh huh. What advice is that?" Chase questioned.

"Never underestimate a man like me. I am full of all kinds of surprises."

"I just bet you are." Chase laughed as he pulled her onto the floor. She knew that she was playing with fire. But she couldn't seem to stop herself.

He pressed his body against hers as close as he could get. He inhaled a deep breath as he bent down and tucked his head into the side of her neck, wrapping both arms around her tiny waist. They were so close, but she didn't step back to put distance between them. No, she didn't want to. So she wrapped her arms around his neck and swayed to the mellow groove.

Doesn't make sense now
Shit just got real, things are getting intense now
I hear you talkin' 'bout we a lot, oh, you speak French now?
Giving me the signs so I gotta take a hint now
I hit you up like "Do you wanna hang right now?"
On the East Side and you know I'm with the gang right now
You say do I own a watch, do I know what time it is right now

CHASING DESIRES
by Kasey Martin

It's after 2AM and that's asking a lot of you right now

All she talkin' bout is come and see me for once
Come and see me for once
You don't ever come to me, you don't ever come to me
All she ever say is come and see me for once
Come and see me for once
You don't ever come to me, you don't ever come to me.

They kept holding on to one another tight, and the longer their bodies swayed together to the music, the more their hearts beat in sync. Chase knew that she was no longer just playing with fire, she was standing in the middle of the damn inferno.

CHAPTER 3
LORENZO

After Chase left, Lorenzo came to the conclusion that he would have to make a call that he'd tried to avoid making for a very long time. He realized that the questions Chase had asked him were just another one of her manipulation tactics, but she was right, and he needed to find out if Tommy had indeed tried to kill him. The only person who knew everything about everything was the Don.

"Hello, my boy." His voice was gruff like he'd been sleeping, but Lorenzo knew that wasn't the case at all. The man hardly ever slept even at his age.

"Uncle Sal, I need some information," Lorenzo replied without any preamble.

"I've been waiting for this call for a while, son."

"I figured as much." Lorenzo sighed.

"Well, spit it out. What information do you need?"

"Is there business here in Texas that I need to know about?" Lorenzo questioned.

"No. There's no business that *you* need to concern yourself with. But our business is ever expanding. You know that."

CHASING DESIRES
by Kasey Martin

Lorenzo was very aware that the "family business" was continuously growing and apparently, it was expanding to Texas. Lorenzo had already figured as much since Tommy was there trying to convince him that using his business for the family was a good idea. Lorenzo couldn't figure out why the family would even want to be in Texas. He never would have thought that his Uncle Sal would be in favor of that and whatever bullshit Tommy was spewing.

"So it was *your* idea for Tommy to come here?"

"No, son, it was *his* idea to come to Texas. But I must admit that I do agree with his reasoning now, although I didn't see the benefits in the beginning."

"I see." It was the only response Lorenzo could think of that wouldn't show any disrespect for his uncle. He couldn't understand why his uncle, a man who was so intelligent, would put so much faith in his dumb-ass cousin. Lorenzo understood that Tommy was his uncle's only child, but damn, even he had to see that Tommy was an idiot.

"So enough of this talk," Uncle Sal stated, effectively changing the subject. "How are you doing, my son? I'm sorry I couldn't get down to Texas after your misfortune, but my sources said you were alright, so I didn't think it was wise to travel to you."

Chasing Desires
by Kasey Martin

He knew that his uncle had meant what he said because he had people all over the place, so he didn't take offense to him not coming to the hospital. Hell, he'd been unconscious anyways.

"I've been better, Uncle," Lorenzo said honestly.

"I'm sure you have, son. I'm sure you have. So with your current predicament, I'm sure you need help, and as your family, *we're* always up for anything that you may need."

No fuckin' way! Lorenzo thought. There wasn't a chance in hell that he would get mixed up with the family again after he had worked so hard to break away. He thought his uncle understood that and that's why he never questioned him on why he had left. But maybe he was wrong. Maybe his uncle didn't understand why leaving that life was what he'd had to do. Maybe just maybe his Uncle *had* sent Tommy to Texas.

"No, thank you, Uncle. With all due respect, I have all the help I need." The thought of Chase's offer ran through his mind. He hated the thought of getting mixed up with her again, but he needed answers, and there was a very strong possibility that she could help him get them.

"Okay, son, but just know family will always be family no matter where you are."

"Yes, sir. I know."

CHASING DESIRES
by Kasey Martin

"You were always smart, my boy." Sal chuckled and disconnected the call.

His Uncle Sal always did say a whole lot by using as little words as possible. It was a skill he'd acquired from living so long in the crime world. Lorenzo knew that they were speaking on secure lines, but they would never talk about anything in detail unless they were face to face. It was just the way things were. Lorenzo ended the call with a better understanding of what was going on, and he had a lot of things to take care of. The first thing on his agenda was updating his will.

***

SAL

"What the hell is going on in Dallas?" Sal questioned as soon as his call was connected.

"What, no hello?"

"Don't fuck with me! I have no tolerance for bullshit. Now tell me what I need to know!" Sal yelled into the receiver.

"Look, I have had some minor setbacks, but I'm handling it now."

"I don't have time for delays, minor or otherwise," Sal growled. His pleasant demeanor from talking to Lorenzo was long gone.

"It's will be handled. Don't worry."

CHASING DESIRES
by Kasey Martin

"I just brought my guys back from watching my idiot son because you said you had a better solution." Sal's frustration was starting to get the best of him, and he was a man that did not handle failures well. He was a man used to getting what he wanted, when he wanted, and this mess with Tommy was getting out of hand.

"I said I would handle it. Tommy is up to his old ways, but his little plan won't see the light of day. I just have to use other resources."

"These resources better do their fucking job! I don't know what my son is doing, but if Lorenzo is calling and asking me questions, then he's bound to get himself into something that will bring me down. And I just can't have that."

Sal knew that his son was power hungry. After all, Sal had raised him to be. But there was no way in hell Sal was giving up his power. He had worked too hard and for too long to get it, and the only way Tommy or anyone else would take his place was if he was six feet in the ground.

***

LORENZO

After a few days, and setting up a meeting with his lawyer, Lorenzo had to decide just who he would leave everything to in his will. He had worked too hard for everything to go to his scumbag cousin, Tommy, even by default. So after

CHASING DESIRES
by Kasey Martin

some thought, he decided who he would leave his clubs to and where his money would go. He just needed to convince them to take it.

The knock at the door came quicker than he'd expected. He groaned as he pushed himself up out of the comfortable chair he was resting in. Lorenzo slowly made his way to the door. He felt way older than his 37 years, but the blame was placed squarely on the shoulders of his near-death experience. Normally, he was in excellent shape and prided himself on being healthy. Every time he thought about his predicament, it pissed him off.

Lorenzo opened the door to a gruff, burly, sour face giant, and his sweet hazel-eyed wife.

"Hi, Lorenzo. You look so good." Charlie smiled, showing her dimples. She moved to hug him, but her huge pregnant belly got in the way. She giggled and moved to give him a side hug.

Lorenzo chuckled. Charlie had always been an attractive woman to him, but her pregnancy and happiness glow made her absolutely beautiful. "Hey, Charlie."

"Moretti," Jake grumbled.

"Cameron." Lorenzo smirked.

Jake and Lorenzo's encounters were always the same. Jake grumbling and grunting, doing his best impression of a

Chasing Desires
by Kasey Martin

caveman, and Lorenzo smirking and doing his best to get under Jake's skin. They both had come a long way from when they first met. They still weren't best friends, but they did tolerate each other.

"You guys come on in and have a seat."

The couple followed Lorenzo into his living room where Jake helped a wobbling Charlie onto the large, overstuffed sofa. Lorenzo could see the love radiating between the two of them as Jake was reduced to fussing and swooning over his stunning wife. He never thought he would see the day when Jacob Cameron would act like anything but a jackass. But he was wrong. Although he hated to admit it, he could see that Jake was good for Charlie.

"Alright, Moretti, what's so urgent that I had to bring my pregnant wife all the way out here?"

Still a jackass, but straight to the point. Alright then, here goes nothing. Lorenzo took a deep breath and tried to prepare himself for what could possibly be a very difficult conversation. "It has been brought to my attention that my current will does not really reflect what I want to happen after I pass away. And with my recent hospital stay, I figured I needed to update everything, including a new executor to my estate before I die."

Chasing Desires
by Kasey Martin

Charlie's hazel eyes widened and then became glossy with unshed tears. Her emotions spread all over her gorgeous, ebony face. "Oh, Lorenzo, but you're fine now. You being shot isn't a normal occurrence. You don't live that life anymore."

Lorenzo and Charlie had become quite close in the months since the shooting. They talked about all kinds of things, including business, their personal lives, and their families. And although he didn't ever go into great details about his past, Charlie was an intelligent person and she could read between the lines. He had told her enough for her to know about the lifestyle he used to live, which he had left behind.

Charlie also played a huge part in the reason why his clubs were still up and running without his physical presence. Lorenzo had a lot to thank her and Jake for. It was because of them that he was even alive. They had literally saved his life.

"No, I don't live that life anymore." Lorenzo sighed. "But sometimes that life has a way of coming back on you no matter what." He looked at them both, hoping that his serious expression would convey the deeper meaning in his words.

"Okay, so what do you need from us?" Jake sat up and Lorenzo could see when his expression changed from annoyance to serious that Jake understood exactly what he'd meant.

Chasing Desires
by Kasey Martin

"I want to name Charlie and you the executors of my will." He looked between the couple, trying to gauge their reactions. Both of their faces held a look of shock.

Jake started to interrupt, but Lorenzo held his hand up to stop his disagreement. "Charlie runs my business anyway. If something were to happen to me, she would be the one to continue to run it or sell it. Whatever you decided to do, it won't matter to me because I'll be dead."

Charlie locked eyes with Lorenzo, and he smiled to try and lighten the mood. He hated talking about all this doom and gloom shit, but it needed to be said.

"Lorenzo, I'm honored, but are you sure about this?" Charlie questioned, her large doe-shaped eyes roaming over his face.

"Yes. I only ask that *nobody* from my family gets anything." He looked directly at Jake. Lorenzo knew that he would understand what he was saying.

"Okay, so that takes care of the business. What about everything else?"

"I want the money to be invested into a scholarship fund to assist kids with their college tuitions. Make sure it goes to underprivileged kids. I want it to go to smart students who don't see a way out of their neighborhoods or off the streets."

Chasing Desires
by Kasey Martin

Charlie's eyes twinkled in understanding. Lorenzo had confided in her about his brother, Sergio, and how smart he was. He wanted the kid to go to college and go legit. He didn't want his brother to follow in his footsteps, living a life of crime, but in the end it didn't matter what Lorenzo had wanted.

"If you're sure about all this, Lorenzo, we'll be happy to do this for you," Charlie replied.

Lorenzo released a sigh of relief. He thought that this conversation was going to be much harder. "I really appreciate you two for agreeing to do this for me."

"No problem, Moretti. Just remember I'm always here to save your ass."

Lorenzo smirked. *Asshole.* But he had to admit at least to himself that the big jerk was right.

"Yeah, whatever," he finally replied to Jake.

"Guys, if you'll excuse me I need to go to the bathroom." Charlie pointed to her belly. "My giant baby is sitting on my bladder again."

Jake helped Charlie to her feet and as soon as she was out of sight, he narrowed his eyes at Lorenzo.

Here we go. I knew his ass wouldn't be silent for long, Lorenzo thought when he saw the change in Jake's expression.

"So I heard you've talked to Chase. Are you really *not* going to help her?" Jake questioned with his brows furrowed. "I mean your douche of a cousin tried to kill you, and he's still trying to push in on your business while you're recovering."

"First of all, nobody knows if he tried to kill me, and secondly, I'm not a snitch."

"Man, listen. Even if he didn't directly give the order to Justin to kill you, I'm pretty sure he knew what Justin was up to yet he did nothing to warn you about it. So while you're protecting him, he sure as hell wasn't tryin' to protect your ass. And fuck that snitch shit because that shit is for kids. We are talking about your life. And let's be real. He tried to take your fuckin' life. You don't owe that motherfucker anything," Jake damn near growled.

Lorenzo puffed out a frustrated breath. Nobody on the outside would understand his reasoning, and he wasn't about to try to make anybody understand. He didn't give a fuck whether people understood him or not. You lived and died by the code, and whether you were active in the family or not, it didn't give you a pass.

"I've made my mind up about this, Jake," Lorenzo finally answered.

"I know you're smarter than this, Moretti. Don't let your past dictate what the fuck is going on in your present. You are not the same man you were in Jersey, and your slime ball of a cousin is banking on the fact that you are."

Chasing Desires
by Kasey Martin

Lorenzo could understand what Jake was saying, but he was raised in a world different from Jake's. Jake was freakin' Captain America with his military background, and his perfect life. He didn't know shit about growing up on the streets, fighting for power, money, and respect. Lorenzo couldn't imagine what it was like to grow up *normal*. "We're different people, Jake. We live in two different worlds, and in my world, no matter what the situation, you don't rat. I'm not a rat."

"Man, like I said. Fuck that! That man tried to kill your ass, and if you think that he won't take the opportunity to try that shit again, think twice. So while you're setting up your will, you think about what the hell that snake of a cousin of yours is doing."

Lorenzo smoothed a hand down his face in frustration. Everything Jake was saying was true, but he just couldn't seem to bring himself to help set his cousin up. *Shit! What the hell am I going to do!*

"I hear what you're saying, man," Lorenzo responded.

"Yeah, but are you *listening*?" Jake questioned with his brow cocked.

The silence was loud as they stared each other down. The only thing that broke the tension was Charlie returning to the room, looking at both men with a questioning gaze.

Chasing Desires
by Kasey Martin

"Um…fellas, is everything okay?" she asked with a perfectly arched eyebrow raised.

"Fine. Everything is fine, Heart. You ready to go, baby?" Jake's tone had softened considerably when he spoke to his wife.

"Sure," she said slowly as she continued to look from one man to the other. "I'll talk to you later this week, Lorenzo, okay?"

"Okay, Charlie." He walked them to the door, kissed her cheek, and shook Jake's hand.

"Think about what I said," Jake commented before they left.

Lorenzo was getting real sick and tired of people coming to his house and dropping their little bombs for him to think about, but dammit if it wasn't on his mind.

CHAPTER 4
CHASE

Chase was sitting on her cozy sofa with her laptop and case files. She was going over the Angeletti files. She'd looked at this same information for what seemed like the thousandth time, but she couldn't help the feeling that she was missing something. Her mentor had always told her to go with her gut because that was what made a good agent. And Agent Worthington had always given her good advice.

John Worthington was an old army buddy of her father's, and when her dad died, he stepped in as an unofficial surrogate. Chase didn't have any other family because her mother had passed when she was a baby, and her father had never remarried. So when Chase was fresh out of the academy and Daniel Reyes took her under his wing and treated her like a sister, she would be forever grateful. She felt like Worthington and Reyes were the only family she had and she didn't want to let either of them down. She owed it to Danny to put his killer away.

She sat for hours on end as she tried to find evidence that would convict his killer. She looked at old files and some new ones. She searched through her laptop over and over again,

Chasing Desires
by Kasey Martin

trying to find a clue on how to get Tommy Angeletti on something that would stick, especially since Lorenzo was being difficult and unwilling to help her.

"Why are you here?" Chase asked herself out loud as she scanned the pictures of Tommy Angeletti. She knew that he was trying to move in on Lorenzo's clubs, but she didn't understand why. He was doing his usual activities like running drugs, and girls, but she couldn't prove it. There was still no reason for him to move his operation here to Dallas because he was doing all of that in Jersey, and she knew that he wasn't being investigated there. Hell, she did everything in her power to get that scumbag investigated, but she always came up empty-handed. So there had to be another reason why he was here besides his low-level criminal activity.

Maybe it's another crime family that he somehow double crossed, Chase thought.

She pulled up another search of known crime families on her computer. She meticulously went over her notes on which families would have enough power to threaten or even had a reason to threaten anybody from the Angeletti clan.

After an hour, she came up empty-handed. There weren't any other families powerful enough to threaten Tommy no matter what he was into.

CHASING DESIRES
by Kasey Martin

Chase tapped her manicured nails on the table. "Why are you here?" she asked herself again. She made sure that Angeletti had been watched closely, especially since the shooting. She was bound by her job, but legalities weren't really her concern at the moment. As a matter of fact, all she was concerned about was getting Angeletti by any means necessary.

And although Tommy had been in Texas for months, he was limiting his actions and he seemed to be oddly focused on Lorenzo's clubs for some reason. The Angeletti family had a slew of different types of businesses, but none of them were clubs or restaurants, so maybe they were venturing out and extending their portfolio. *That has to be it!* Chase thought excitedly.

The Angeletti's had the stereotypical "mob" businesses consisting of real estate, construction, unions, and imports. Their import business was huge, and the Angeletti's had the Jersey ports on lock. Chase long since had suspected that they made most of their money by controlling the port authority. That was how they got all of their drugs and guns. But why would Tommy come to the Dallas area? There sure weren't any ports here, and he didn't seem to be doing any *new* business, so Chase was truly stumped. Nothing made sense to her about why he was in Texas at all.

Chasing Desires
by Kasey Martin

She sighed as she shut her laptop. This was getting her nowhere. She wanted to bring down the killer of her partner, Daniel Reyes, so she'd been following Tommy for years. His moves, as reckless as they may have been, Chase could always understand why he made them. In the past, Tommy did things that he would benefit from no matter what. He was selfish, arrogant, and super conceited, but whatever he did, it never seemed to go against anything that his father wanted. So the real question was: Why Sal Angeletti would want to bring his business to Texas? Chase had to be missing a vital piece of information somewhere.

Her cell phone rang, and she wasn't surprised to see the name that displayed on the Caller ID. She swiped the screen and answered. "Hello?"

"Hello there, Agent Johnson. Have you made any headway on the case yet?" the deep voice grumbled through the line.

She knew she couldn't avoid his call forever, but she was holding out hope that he would give her more time. "Hello, sir. It's been a tough road, but I'm making progress."

"Uh-huh," he grunted. "I know you, Chase. You're still putting your all into a nonexistent case."

"With all due respect, sir, my case is not nonexistent. It's just taking longer than expected."

CHASING DESIRES
by Kasey Martin

"Chase, I've told you a thousand times that you're wasting your time. Why won't you listen? I can only hold off my bosses for so long. You have to give me something if you're going to stay in Dallas."

"There's no reason for you to be concerned, sir. I will have what I need soon."

"I have every reason to be concerned. One of my best agents goes gallivanting off to Texas against my advice without hardly any resources or back-up. Your reports are vague at best, and you haven't sent in any new evidence. I have every reason to be concerned. This isn't like you."

Chase heard a hint of worry in Worthington's tone, and she felt a small amount of guilt for holding back the little evidence she did have. But she had to stay focused and get what she needed for Daniel. There was a leak at the office in Jersey, and she just couldn't risk it.

"The agency put me in this position. I have to do what I need to do to close my case. There was no concern for me when they allowed me to come here chasing a lead without any backup or resources."

"You know that the Bureau doesn't have the funds for every half-cocked hunch that an agent wants to run down," Worthington responded dismissively.

CHASING DESIRES
by Kasey Martin

"The Bureau may not want to fund my hunch. However, they still want to dictate to me what I can and can't do even though they refuse to help me, sir," Chase responded with malice laced words because the guilt had officially left the building.

Worthington breathed heavily. "Chase, you know our hands are tied when it comes to certain people and cases. You've worked at the Bureau long enough to know how it is. Let's not be naïve—"

"The last thing I am is naïve, and just who are our hands tied by?" Chase interrupted, not liking the implication. She didn't wait for a response before she continued. "Maybe I've worked at the Bureau too long if we can't put in resources to investigate people who we know are criminals because of some invisible binding."

"You know there are politics involved in everything we do, but this goes beyond that. You're obsessed with Angeletti, and there are some things you just have to let go of, if not for the job, then for your own sanity."

"How can you say that to me?" Chase asked exasperatedly. "How can you tell me to let go of getting this maniac off the street? You know what he's capable of?!"

"Listen, I know Reyes meant a lot to you, but sometimes if the proof isn't there, you've got to let it go. There hasn't been anything to back up your claims that Angeletti killed Reyes, and you still have nothing."

"You know if Angeletti didn't kill him, he set him up to be killed. You know he's responsible. I mean, he was undercover with their damn family!" Chase shouted, no longer caring that she was talking to her superior.

"Look, Agent Johnson," Worthington said, slipping into Senior Special Agent role and out of surrogate father with his formal speech. "Going in undercover is a risky job, and there are absolutely no guarantees that you'll come out alive. Reyes knew that, and you know it too."

"This isn't just about Reyes. It's bigger than that. You know that these people are the dregs of humanity and they have pillaged and plundered the East Coast long enough. They have gotten away with murder, and it's time they pay for all of the havoc and chaos they've caused!" Chase's impassioned plea came from the heart. She had to make Worthington understand that these people needed to be brought down.

"I've indulged you for too long on this. You have four weeks; after that I'm pulling the plug." Worthington said with finality.

"Four weeks? But that's not enough time!"

"It is, Agent Johnson. Take this time to get all your ducks in order before it's time for you to come back to Jersey because, without the evidence to back up your claims, you're going to have to let this thing go once and for all."

Chase realized in that moment that she would do everything in her power to catch Angeletti. And once she was done, she wasn't sure if she even wanted to be an FBI agent anymore.

***

MIKE

Mike had been digging into Lorenzo Moretti ever since he saw just how close Chase was to him at the hospital. He didn't care what she said; she was in over her head, and as her friend he was not going to let her fall. She came to him for help, and that was exactly what he planned to do, whether she liked it or not.

Mike pulled some strings with the connections he had with some government agencies, and found out all of the information he could about Moretti. Although Moretti didn't have any major criminal records, it was suspected that he was involved with plenty of criminal activity up and down the East Coast. However, just like Chase had explained, he seemed as untouchable as the Angeletti's.

With Lorenzo being shot, it seemed to push Chase closer to him. Well, that was until he found out she was really an agent. Mike wasn't happy that her cover had been blown

Chasing Desires
by Kasey Martin

because that could've turned out to be really bad and could've potentially gotten her killed. However, he was extremely happy that it resulted in finally putting a wedge between them.

Mike recognized that Chase was entirely too close to this situation. But no matter what he said to her, she would vehemently deny it. And he could tell, in the weeks since Moretti had found out about her being an agent, she tried her best to get back close to him. No matter what piss poor excuse she used about needing him to get to Angeletti.

Mike didn't just use his connections to investigate Lorenzo Moretti. He also used them to find out about the root cause of all of this—Daniel Reyes and who he truly was. According to Chase, the man was practically a saint. He had taken her under his wing and looked out for her when she was a new agent straight out of the academy.

He found out that Reyes had been working undercover in the Angeletti family. He had been deep under for almost four years before he was at a deal gone bad and was killed. It was never suspected that anyone knew that he was an agent.

His body along with several others was burned beyond recognition in a warehouse by the docks in Jersey. He was labeled a John Doe, and his actual identity was successfully buried under a bunch of red tape. Reyes didn't have any living immediate family, or any other relatives. Not even a girlfriend came looking for him.

Mike was determined to find out just why Agent Reyes was at the dock that night and why he'd been killed. He couldn't tell Chase that he suspected her beloved partner wasn't who she thought he was, so he would just keep his findings to himself for the time being.

Mike sighed. *The things I do to help the people I care about.* His cell phone rang and brought him out of his musings.

"Thatcher," Mike answered curtly without looking at the Caller ID.

"Thatch, buddy, we got some new developments with Moretti that you need to know about," Jake stated without so much as a hello.

"Okay, what's going on with him now?" Mike asked as he narrowed his eyes. He could admit that Moretti wasn't responsible for the shit show that was going on in his club. But he would never ever trust the man because he was a criminal, born and raised.

"You need to come to the house because I need to debrief the team and I don't want to leave Heart by herself."

"Alright. I can be there in thirty minutes. Is Charlie okay?"

Chasing Desires
by Kasey Martin

"She's fine. She's just tired. My son is kicking her ass from the inside out," Jake chuckled proudly. "He's a rambunctious little shit, and he's not even here yet."

Mike smiled at his friend's words. Jake was a totally different person now that he was married with a baby on the way. He could see that he was finally happy even though he was still gruff like a big grizzly bear; his softer side came through more often these days.

"Well, I'm glad she's doing okay. I will see you guys in a few."

"Copy that, buddy."

On the way to his car, Mike wondered what was so important about Lorenzo Moretti that Jake had to call an emergency meeting. He wasn't the type of man to wish bad on any human being, but he really hoped that Moretti finally did something that made everyone see what he already saw: Lorenzo Moretti was not a good guy. He was a bad man…a very bad man.

***

DALLAS AGENT

"Hello, I'm in need of some assistance from you." The agent looked at his phone with a frown. If this man was calling for a favor, nothing good would come of it.

Chasing Desires
by Kasey Martin

"And just what assistance would you need from me?" The agent questioned, still frowning.

"I need you to keep an eye on some people for me."

"I'm undercover right now, and I shouldn't even be having this conversation with you." The agent responded, his voice full of agitation.

"You owe me."

The agent knew that he was between a rock and a hard place, but he owed the man his career. He knew that it was in his best interest to appease the man so that he could keep climbing the ladder to success.

"Who do you need me to watch?" he asked after a beat.

"Tommy Angeletti and Lorenzo Moretti."

The agent sighed. He knew that his past would come back to haunt him, and now he was face to face with his consequences. Tommy Angeletti was a well-known gangster, and Lorenzo Moretti had rarely been seen since he was shot.

"I've seen Angeletti around, but I'm pretty sure Moretti is laying low."

"Pretty sure isn't good enough. I need some positive intel on the situation. You need to get closer to them without raising any suspicions."

"I have a cover that will get me closer, but the arrest is mine when I make it."

Chasing Desires
by Kasey Martin

"Just get me what I need, and the arrest is yours."

The line disconnected without the agent being able to respond. He would do what needed to be done so that he could make the arrest of a notorious gangster. He would finally get his power, and maybe then he would be done being an errand boy.

CHAPTER 5
JAKE

Once Jake disconnected the call with Mike, he called the rest of his team, including Chase. After he and Charlie met with Lorenzo, he'd felt a little out of sorts. Jake could understand why Lorenzo wouldn't want his family to get their hands on his estate. He could even understand why he wanted Charlie to be his executor, but what he couldn't comprehend was why he wouldn't just put his sleaze ball cousin in the fucking ground.

Jake understood loyalty, but Lorenzo was taking it a step too far. There was no way in hell he would let someone get away with trying to kill him whether it was family or not. Loyalty was good to have, but misplaced loyalty was not only dumb, but it was tremendously dangerous. *Stupid mobster shit.* Jake ran his hand over his beard in frustration.

Jake and half of his team had just finished working a case for his good friend, Camedon Price. Someone tried to break into Camedon's business to obtain a very private client list that would have exposed a lot of high-profile people's exceptionally adventurous sex lives, but they caught the guy and closed the assignment quickly, so now the team was back at full capacity, and they could finally put all their resources into helping Chase close her case.

Jake was surprised when Chase told him that she was holding back evidence from the Bureau because they wouldn't help her investigation or give her any resources. He knew her to be a very thorough and professional agent. They really needed to get down to the business of who had killed her partner now that she had been put under time constraints.

The doorbell echoed loudly through the house bringing Jake back to the present. He jogged to get the door even though Charlie was closer, but it would take her an hour to wobble through the house. He just loved to see her so full with his baby. Jake didn't have the right words to explain how much he loved his wife. She was his *Heart* and he didn't want to think about where he would be without her.

"I got it, babe," Jake called out as he opened the door.

Marcus stood with a wide smile on his dark brown face. They hadn't seen much of each other since they were working on separate cases, but his best friend was hardly ever without a smile.

"Hey, buddy. What's going on? Where's my girl?" Marcus questioned as he pushed his way past a scowling Jake.

"Don't make me body slam your big ass," Jake threatened his friend jokingly.

Chasing Desires
by Kasey Martin

Marcus chuckled. "I missed you too, big guy."

They made their way to the living room where Charlie was flipping through bridal magazines. She had been helping their cousins with planning their wedding, and it was getting closer every day.

"There's my girl," Marcus sang as he walked toward Charlie with his massive arms spread wide.

"Hey, Marc! You're back. I missed you!" Charlie giggled excitedly as she teetered toward Marcus with her belly leading the way.

After they embraced, they all settled in comfortably to wait for the rest of the team. They kept the conversation light while they waited for the other guys to arrive. Charlie talked about weddings and how Korri was getting on her very last nerve, and Marcus talked about his last job. He had just returned from a three-week long assignment where he worked head of security for an up and coming pop star. He regaled them with hilarious stories of groupies that would do any and everything to try to get close to the handsome young singer.

"Listen, these chicks were certifiable." Marcus chuckled. "I caught one trying to climb up the side of the hotel."

"You're full of shit!" Jake laughed. "Nobody was climbin' up no damn building."

CHASING DESIRES
by Kasey Martin

"Hey, man, I shit you not. I thought this heffa was kin to Spiderman or some shit. Now, granted we were only on the second floor and it was a small boutique hotel, but still. Can't nobody sing that damn good that I'm trying to climb up walls and shit."

They all laughed loudly. Marcus could always tell a good story. He was one of the most entertaining guys Jake knew. But he was fairly certain that Marcus was exaggerating about this particular incident. At least he hoped he was. If not, women were crazier than he thought.

An hour later, Jake's basement, which doubled as a tricked-out home office, was full with his team. The long oak table with large leather chairs was surrounded by different types of monitors. On the largest monitor, there were images of some of the important people in the case: Tommy Angeletti, Sal Angeletti, Justin Russo, Lorenzo Moretti, and Daniel Reyes.

Jake turned the floor over to Chase. She explained in detail all the new developments they had in the case which wasn't very much, considering how long they'd worked on getting Angeletti.

"We know that Tommy has been lying extremely low since Lorenzo's shooting. But we also know he's still trying to muscle in on Premier. In the last couple of weeks, one of his known associates was seen at Premier several times." Chase flipped the screen, and a picture of an average-looking Latino man appeared.

He was someone that could easily blend in anywhere. He stood at an average weight, height, medium build, and had no visible tattoos, or facial hair. His dark brown hair was swept away from his deep set dark brown eyes, and he wore an off-the-rack suit.

Chase explained the times he'd been in Premier, he'd escorted three to four different women each time he arrived. However, the women never left with him, and he was always seen having conversations with other men before the girl was seen leaving with the guy. Chase relayed to the team that the women were prostitutes, but she didn't know if the man was the pimp, or Tommy's representative. After watching him a few days, she had her answer.

"Luis Castillo is definitely working with Tommy Angeletti."

"So who is this Castillo guy? Is he a bit player or is he an important part in all this?" Joe, one of the team members asked.

"He definitely plays an important role. In fact, he has ties to the Salazar Cartel out of Mexico."

At that news, all the men and the few women sat up in their chairs. The Salazar Cartel was one of the deadliest Cartels out of Mexico, and they were one of the oldest. In recent years, they had expanded from California and New Mexico, and they migrated to South Texas. Now, it looked as if they were moving to North Texas with the influence of the Angeletti family.

***

Jake listened to all the information Chase had. He had some ideas of what might be going on, but he would investigate his suspicions before he voiced them. He also thought he might have an idea of how to get Lorenzo to cooperate. But first thing's first.

"So we have another development with Moretti," Jake grumbled as he ran his hand through his beard, something he did when he was deep in thought.

"Yeah. What now?" Mike asked, his voice dripping with sarcasm.

"He wants to make Heart—"

"And you…" Charlie interrupted as she came into the room carrying snacks for everyone.

Jake cleared his throat. "Yes, he wants to make Heart and me executors of his will."

"What. The. Fuck?!" Mike snarled. "Has everyone lost their damn minds? This guy is one of the worst kinds of criminals. A murderer!" Mike yelled as his face turned a shade of red that Jake had never seen before.

Chasing Desires
by Kasey Martin

Mike was known as a laid-back tech guy. He never took anything too serious and he always had an easy-going smile and attitude. But ever since they started working on the case with Chase, he seemed to be wound tighter than a whore in the front pew of a Southern Baptist church.

"Thatch, man, calm the hell down," Marcus warned, his tone more serious than Jake had ever heard it.

"Heart, baby, can you give us a minute please?" Jake leaned down and kissed his wife on her plump cheek. He didn't want her to get stressed out over anything, especially this case.

"Yeah, Bear. You guys try not to kill each other," Charlie replied with furrowed brows as she placed the tray of snacks down and left the basement.

Jake grunted his response as he watched her walk up the stairs and out of the door.

"The rest of you guys have all the information you need for now," Jake addressed the rest of the team. "You can take off, and I'll see you in the office bright and early for your assignments."

The rest of the team nodded their understanding and said their goodbyes. Jake, Marcus, Mike, and Chase along with Joe stayed behind to finish the very heated conversation.

"Thatch, what's your fuckin' problem, man? In all the years I've known you, you have never acted like this." Jake

CHASING DESIRES
by Kasey Martin

looked his longtime friend in the face as he searched for answers.

"You all seem to act like this man is some kind of saint or some shit. You just ignore the fact that he is a part of the Angeletti crime family. Once you belong to them, you don't get out. And he was born in!"

"I understand that, buddy, but Moretti has proved that he isn't part of the family anymore. Just hear me out first, alright?" Jake couldn't understand why Mike was so upset. He might need to get away from the case because he seemed to be taking everything a bit too personal.

"Alright." Mike sighed. He ran his hand through his dirty blond hair and narrowed his blue eyes. "I'll hear you out."

Jake sighed before he continued. "Moretti made us promise that if anything happened to him, we wouldn't let his family get anything. He really doesn't want anything to do with them. People can change, man."

"I never thought I'd see the day that you would defend someone like Lorenzo Moretti," Mike stated, his eyes still narrowed.

"You know me better than that."

"Thatch, I understand your concern, but you know Jake, man. Think about what he's saying. You know none of us trust easy, so if Jake says we can trust him, then we can," Marcus explained.

"I just don't think you guys are thinking clearly. That's all. Everyone is too wrapped up in his bullshit," Mike continued to argue.

"You're right," Joe spoke up for the first time. "All of you are emotionally invested in this one way or another, but as far as I can tell, Moretti hasn't said or done anything that has led us to believe he's still a criminal. We've checked him out six ways to Sunday, and he came out cleaner than a pair of balls dipped in honey."

Everyone stopped and looked at Joe strangely. "Cleaner than what?" Chase asked. "You know what? N…never mind, don't answer that." She put her hand up and turned away from Joe.

"As I was sayin'…" Joe's tanned face held a bright smile that he flashed at Chase. His light brown eyes were full of amusement. "He may have been a mobster in his past, but he's been on the up and up since he moved here."

"Okay, so tell me something. Why is the reason he moved here such a big secret?" Mike smugly asked, his smirking face showed his unwillingness to compromise.

"Because his mother is suffering from dementia, his father died of a heart attack, and shortly afterwards, his younger

Chasing Desires
by Kasey Martin

brother was killed. He blames himself for his death," Charlie answered as she slowly made her way back down the stairs.

"Damn, that's a lot," Marcus grumbled.

"Heart, honey, what are you doing back down here? Goin' up and down these stairs ain't good for you," Jake fussed as he hurried to help her down the rest of the stairs.

She waved him off. "I couldn't hear everything being said from the *other* side of the door."

Jake frowned at her while the others tried to hide their chuckles. He was secretly glad that his nosy wife had chosen then to come down. It helped relieve some of the tension that was swallowing up the room.

"Lorenzo felt obligated to his family, but after his brother died, he went through a really depressing time and he left Jersey. It's not a secret, but he just doesn't talk about it much," Charlie continued.

"But he talked about it with *you*?" Chase questioned with her lips curved into a frown, making the curves of her soft face look hard.

"Yes, he was thankful that Jake and I had saved his life. He told me about a time when he wasn't sure he wanted to keep on living. He didn't go into detail about how his brother died, but he was devastated," Charlie honestly answered.

Chasing Desires
by Kasey Martin

Jake listened to the two women as they conversed, but his eyes remained on Mike, who still didn't look convinced. "All I ask you, as my friend, is to trust me on this, Thatch."

"Fine, but I'm going to keep my eyes open and I suggest you do the same."

"Fair enough," Jake stated with a nod.

With everything that was happening, Jake really hoped that Mike would keep his word and not do anything stupid that they all could come to regret.

CHAPTER 6
CHARLIE

Once Jake ended the meeting, Charlie asked Chase to stay awhile, so she could get better acquainted with her. Charlie had known the woman for a few months, but she still didn't really know much about her. It was time to rectify that.

"Why don't you have a seat." Charlie motioned toward the leather-back stool pushed up next to the granite topped kitchen island.

Chase nodded and sat down gingerly. "So what did you want to talk to me about?"

"Nothing specific," Charlie answered quickly. "I just thought you might need a little girl time, seeing that you're always working around a bunch of Neanderthals." Charlie gave her a small smile. "I mean, I know there are a few ladies on the team, but they are much more accustomed to the guys than I'm sure you are. They've been around awhile."

Chase smiled. "No, I'm pretty used to an all-male work environment. Being one of the few women agents, I kind of had to get used to that sort of thing."

Charlie gave her another smile. She could see that Chase was used to being strong for everyone around her, having to

CHASING DESIRES
by Kasey Martin

prove herself often. But she could also see that she needed a friend.

"That's understandable. But you're from New Jersey and you don't really know anyone here besides the guys, right?"

Chase nodded her head. "Yes, I'm from Jersey and I'm here on my own."

"Well, I'm sure hanging around with those guys all day without any sort of social interaction outside of work has got to be exhausting," Charlie stated, knowingly.

"I won't lie. It has taken its toll on me these last couple of months. That's why I'm really glad you asked me to stay."

Charlie nodded. "I have a knack for seeing a woman in need of a GNO."

"*GNO?*" Chase's beautiful ebony face held a questioning expression.

"Girls. Night. Out!" Charlie exclaimed excitedly. Her pretty face broke into a wide smile that showed her deep dimples.

Chase chuckled. "Yeah, I don't think Jake is going to let you out of the house or even out of his sight for a girl's night out."

Charlie shrugged. Chase did have a good point. Charlie was six and a half months pregnant and she was *huge*. It had to be unnatural for her to be so big, but the doctor just kept telling her that she and the baby were healthy. He just took after his daddy. *I'm giving birth to a giant.*

"You're probably right." Charlie agreed, rubbing her hands together like an evil genius. "Tell you what, instead of a night out, let's have a *night in.*"

Charlie watched Chase's eyebrows rise high on her forehead. "Now, why do I have a feeling that your night in will be far more rowdy than your night out?"

Charlie snickered. "Oh, honey, you have no idea."

***

An hour later, the girl's night in had officially begun. Charlie had invited Korri, Lauren, Brandon, and her newest friends, Eden and Farren, to come over for some quality bonding time.

When the doorbell rang, Charlie waddled as fast as she could to the door. She opened the large wooden door to almost all of her guests. By coincidence, they'd all shown up at the same time.

"Hey, ya'll!"

"Heeeeyy!" They all answered in unison.

They all kissed and hugged as they made their way into the large foyer. Introductions were made all around before they headed to the kitchen to sit down to get the gossip going.

Chasing Desires
by Kasey Martin

Charlie looked around as they all made their way to the kitchen for drinks and snacks. "Where the hell is Lauren?" she questioned Korri and Brandon.

"You know that heffa loves to jet off at the drop of a hat." Brandon waved his well-manicured hand dismissively.

"All I know is her ass better be back here in two weeks for my bridal shower. Ain't nobody got time for her to be sluttin' it up when she's supposed to be one of my bridesmaids," Korri growled with a scowl on her face, her hazel eyes blazing with fire.

"Can you calm down? Damn! Will you get bridezilla a drink and a valium or any type of muscle relaxer please?" Brandon rubbed his hand down his light brown face, addressing Charlie. "Better yet, get this bish some morphine or something because she is wearing me the hell out!" Brandon dramatically rolled his eyes as he headed straight to the bottle of tequila.

Korri narrowed her eyes, pursed her bow shaped lips, put her hands on her narrow hips, and sucked her teeth. "First of all, I don't need drugs to relax!" Korri seethed, her voice rising, showing her frustration and anger.

"Well, you sure as hell need something. Yellin' in my house like you done lost your damn mind." Charlie put her hands on her widening hips. "You know I can't drink. And if you stress me out tonight, I'm tellin' Bear."

CHASING DESIRES
by Kasey Martin

"Ohhh pleeease, don't tell Bear! Whatever would I do?" Korri sarcastically replied as she rolled her eyes heavenward.

Everyone chuckled at the cousins' dramatics.

"Well, I didn't know what to expect, but this is very entertaining," Charlie heard Eden whisper to Farren and Chase as they sipped on their drinks.

"I'm sorry, ladies. My family doesn't know how to behave in front of company, so you might as well know now. Just act like part of the family and join in with the foolishness," Charlie said with a straight face, but her twinkling eyes were dancing with mirth.

Korri sighed. "I'm sorry, guys. I don't mean to bring the drama to the GNO, but I am super stressed right now."

They all nodded and smiled in understanding. "Look none of us had this big massive wedding like you're planning, so I get it," Charlie spoke.

"Yeah, but it's no reason for me to be a bitch," Korri admitted before continuing. "Okay, truth." Korri took a deep breath. "So it was my bright idea to spice up our wedding night by waiting to have sex until we said 'I do.' We haven't been intimate in over a month and right now, I really need some sex."

"Oh, so that's what's wrong with you. It's not the stress of the wedding. You're missing the *D*." Brandon snickered when Korri narrowed her eyes at him with a pout.

CHASING DESIRES
by Kasey Martin

"Why in the hell would you want to do that?" Farren voiced her question with her hand on her voluptuous hips. "I mean, when you got some good D at home, which obviously you do or you wouldn't be acting like an addict going through withdrawals, why the fuck would you suggest not getting it? Please excuse my unladylike language."

"I don't know why the hell I made that decision. But ever since, I've been so *dickstracted*." Korri hung her head and buried her face in her hands.

"Don't you mean *distracted*?" Brandon butted in.

"Shut up, B! No, I mean DICK-stracted. Tony has been walking his fine ass around showing his abs, wearing nothing but basketball shorts and grey sweatpants. And he gets out the shower without drying off! I mean *come on*! Who walks out of the bathroom dripping water all over the damn place?!" Korri huffed, throwing her hands up in exasperation.

"Okay, look, I know we don't know each other well, but I think it's safe to say that I don't think you're going to make it another month until your wedding night," Eden chimed in, unable to hold back her laughter.

"Obviously, I'm not the one to give advice about waiting," Charlie stated, motioning down her body like a Price is Right model.

Chasing Desires
by Kasey Martin

Charlie noticed that Korri's tense shoulders relaxed a bit with her comment. "But baby girl, you are driving yourself crazy for no reason. Get Tony to pound you up against the wall like he usually does, so you can get back to your bubbly, happy, *satisfied* self.

"Yeah, I guess. I just wanted our wedding night to be special."

"It will be special *because* it's your wedding night. You're stressing yourself out for no reason, honey," Brandon chimed in, wrapping Korri in a warm embrace.

"Okay, so now that we've established Korri needs some dick in her life, who else has a problem that we need to solve?" Farren spoke up with a bright smile gracing her caramel colored face.

"Well, I'm too fabulous to have any men problems except these hoes ain't loyal. But hell, what else is new?" Brandon patted his hair, and sipped his drink.

"You, sir, are a hot mess." Chase laughed.

"I'm a hot mess, crazy mess, petty mess, beautiful mess all wrapped in one big loveable package." Brandon winked mischievously.

"You know I always wondered something," Farren spoke up again. "What is it like to date a white guy? I mean I've flirted with all types, but I've never dipped my toe into the swirl pool before."

"Really?" Charlie questioned. As outgoing and open-minded as she knew Farren was, it was very surprising to her that she had never dated a white man before. "Have you ever dated *any* others?"

"I've dated a Puerto Rican guy before, but hell, it took me three dates to figure out he wasn't a light skin brother who spoke Spanish."

"Damn, I'm going to need you to do better," Brandon said, shaking his head.

"Well, as your bestie, you know how I feel. A man is a man, and Camedon's race really doesn't bother me. Plus, he's not the first white guy that I've dated," Eden said as she continued to sip her vodka tonic.

"Yeah, but somehow I feel like I'm giving up on my brothas if I go to the other side."

The women all nodded in understanding. Charlie knew the feeling of being perceived as thinking she was too good for a black man because she was married to Jake. She was used to people making off-handed comments about her being a sellout too. Sometimes being in an interracial relationship could be upsetting if you let it.

Chasing Desires
by Kasey Martin

"Well, while you're waiting on your black brothas, they're off traipsing around the globe with Becky with tha good hair. Girl, bye. You betta get you a Billy Bob and find you some happiness," Brandon responded with all the sass that he could muster.

The ladies all laughed at his comments. Nobody kept it real quite like Brandon.

"I get what you're saying, Farren. We are the foundation of the black family. We are expected to wait on our black man to come to us. We're supposed to remain single and hopeful. Stay loyal and be the ride or die chick. Black women are supposed to stay lonely until one day hopefully a black man will see us as the treasure that we are; something valuable and worth having," Korri responded with fire in her hazel eyes. "Now, don't get me wrong because there are plenty of wonderful black men out there, but just because I'm not marrying one doesn't mean I'm any less of a black woman or that I gave up on the black man. It's ok to fall in love with someone who loves you no matter what his race."

"Right."

"Preach!"

"Amen!"

"Say that!"

Chasing Desires
by Kasey Martin

The responses from everyone in the room were unanimous. Charlie agreed with Korri as black women, a lot was expected of them in general and when dealing with interracial relationships, a lot of shame could be placed upon them. Black women who date outside of their race are often seen as traitors or not proud of being black, and Charlie knew that wasn't the case at all.

"I don't know if I could step out on that ledge. I mean you all have found your Mr. White." Farren snickered at her own joke. "But I'm afraid of being a fetish or some crazy shit."

"You think black men don't have fetishes? I'm sorry to tell you, girlfriend, but *all* men have fetishes," Eden responded.

"Yeah, but you know what I mean," Farren said dismissively. "What about you, Chase? Have you ever dated a white guy before? I mean you're from up North, so maybe it's not as big of a deal as it is down here in the South."

"I have, but nothing serious," Chase responded nonchalantly. "I mean, I've never met the parents or anything, but I do understand what you mean about not wanting to be a fetish."

"Yeah, but I don't want to date a white guy who doesn't know he's white. I don't want someone trying to be down or trying to be something they're not, just to date me."

Chasing Desires
by Kasey Martin

"I think you should just date someone you like. Forget all the other bullshit. Find a person who loves you for you, and if he happens to be white, then so be it," Charlie stated with a smile.

"I guess you all are right. I'm not the one to back down from anything. I am pretty open to damn near everything. In the big scheme of things, dating a white guy is a very small part of my adventurous side." Charlie saw the glint of mischief in the depths of Farren's honey brown eyes. She wondered what Farren meant by *adventurous*.

Although Chase didn't say much throughout the evening, Charlie could tell by the end of the night that she was much more relaxed with the group. She also got to know a little more about the mysterious woman because she'd let her guard down just enough for Charlie to see a glimpse of the lonely woman she had tried so desperately to hide.

CHASING DESIRES

by Kasey Martin

CHAPTER 7

KORRI

Korri had a lot to think about once she left Charlie's. She could see what the girls were saying, and having a different perspective was good. However, she just wanted to make sure her wedding night was special. Korri thought that waiting would make the anticipation of the night more passionate. However, not having that intimate connection with her fiancé, combined with the stress of everything else, was driving her crazy.

Korri didn't want to give up on her idea of no sex before the wedding, but she wanted to make love to her man. It wasn't like she was some virginal bride, after all. However, the idea of the next time they made love, and them being husband and wife, made her feel like she would be starting her marriage off on the right foot.

"Hey, Sweetness! Are you home, baby?" Tony bellowed through the house.

"Yeah, babe. I'm back here in the office," Korri yelled back. She heard him clonking through the penthouse. She looked at the clock and wondered why he was home so early.

Chasing Desires
by Kasey Martin

Korri had spent most of her recent days handling last-minute wedding details instead of designing. She hadn't created a new design in over a month, and it was starting to get to her. She needed to have that creative outlet, but she just didn't have the time. As much as she loved her fiancé and couldn't wait to be his wife, she couldn't wait until the wedding was over and done with. Sometimes she felt like she should've taken a page from Charlie's book and just had something simple and quick. But with the combination of her clients and Tony's, they didn't want to leave anyone out. Now, almost two years later, the wedding was only a couple of weeks away.

"How was your day, Sweetness?" Tony questioned as he sauntered into the room. He was dressed in gray slacks and a crisp baby blue button down dress shirt. The outfit looked tailor-made because it fit every ripple and dip of his body to perfection.

Korri moaned in frustration. "Why do you always have to look so damn delicious?" she asked as she licked her lips, looked him up and down, and smiled mischievously.

Tony gave her his signature smirk. "What do you mean, baby? I always look like this." He held his arms open wide and smiled deviously.

Korri laughed. "Whatever. What are you doing home so early anyway?" she questioned after her laughter died down.

CHASING DESIRES
by Kasey Martin

"A little birdie told me my baby was stressed out. I just came home so that I could take care of her." He strolled closer to her, walking in even, measured steps like a predator stalking his prey.

"I'm going to kill Charlie." Korri rolled her eyes. "I swear that girl doesn't know the meaning of girl talk."

Tony chuckled as he drew closer. "Charlie didn't tell me anything."

"So, *Jake* told you. That's the same thing," Korri drawled.

"Nope, he didn't tell me either," he responded as he closed the short distance between them.

Korri crumpled her brows in confusion. She had no idea who could've told him about her stress other than those two blabber mouths. Well, technically Jake wasn't so much a blabber mouth, but Charlie was and she told her husband everything.

"Alright, I give. Who spilled?" Korri asked curiously.

"First of all, I know you, Sweetness. I've noticed for weeks now that you've been stressed. That's why I've been trying to get you to go to the spa and I've been giving you massages every day."

Korri nodded in agreement. Tony was the perfect fiancé. He was so supportive and attentive. She couldn't ask for a better person to love her or receive her love.

"That's true, but you said a *little birdie* told you, so somebody said something."

Tony further approached and stood right behind Korri's chair. He started massaging her shoulders and neck as he trailed kisses down her jaw. "Are you bothered that somebody told me that you are stressing yourself out over something that I would be more than happy to rectify?"

Korri sighed at his caresses. Even though they hadn't been intimate, he still gave her a lot of affection and she ate up the attention. She loved his touch, which was one of the reasons she was going through withdrawals.

"Baby, you are making me sooo weak right now," Korri whimpered as she tilted her head to give him better access.

"Mmmmm…" Tony moaned as he whirled Korri around in the computer chair and dropped to his knees in front of her.

"You're distracting me, Superman. Who told you about our GNO conversation?"

At this point, Korri really didn't care who had told Tony. She just wanted to know who to thank later.

Chasing Desires
by Kasey Martin

"I must not be doing a good job distracting you if you still have the wherewithal to ask me questions." Tony sighed as he continued his teasing touches.

"W-what?" Korri stuttered incoherently.

Tony chuckled and the deep rumbling sound that vibrated through his chest was so hard, Korri felt it. "Brandon told me, Sweetness."

"Ummm…I'll be sure to thank him later." Korri exhaled. She was surprised that she could get out a coherent sentence.

She moaned again, forgetting any questions she may have wanted to ask. She was so lost in Tony's kisses, feeling more relaxed than she had in weeks. She wasn't about to give up that feeling to have a conversation.

Korri wiggled and squirmed in her seat as Tony attacked her neck and chest with kisses. She forgot whatever reason she had for wanting to wait until their wedding night. This man was going to be her husband and the lack of sexual intimacy was not going to change how special he was.

I was so crazy to think that I could give this up even for a couple of months, Korri thought to herself as Tony picked her up from the chair and carried her to their bedroom.

***

Chasing Desires
by Kasey Martin

The moment Tony reached their bedroom, he placed Korri down on the bed softly and began to undress. His hands were moving painstakingly slow, and Korri thought she was going to scream if he didn't hurry the hell up.

After removing his socks and shoes, Tony took off his slacks and shirt along with his under shirt. He stood there in his boxer briefs, his muscular thighs and abs on full display. Korri bit her bottom lip. She couldn't wait to lick him from head to toe.

He removed his underwear and stood in front of her with his manhood jutting out from his body proudly. Korri hadn't even touched him yet, but he was already rock hard and ready.

"Your turn, Sweetness." Tony smirked as he stalked slowly toward her.

Chills broke out all over Korri's skin. The anticipation of the moment was heightening her arousal. She wanted to rip her T-shirt and jeans to shreds just to have skin to skin contact with him.

Korri quickly stripped off her shirt and jeans. Tony pushed her back on the bed and got on top of her, refusing to let her take off her bra and panties.

"You said it was my turn," Korri huffed, exasperated.

He pinned her hands above her head. "I have an idea, Sweetness. How 'bout I take care of my baby? Let me relieve

Chasing Desires
by Kasey Martin

some of your stress and frustrations without us having intercourse?"

Korri shook her head back and forth rapidly. "No, I want it *all*. We've gone too far to turn back now." Korri thought she was going to die of sexual frustration if she didn't get a release soon.

"I'm not talking about turning back, Sweetness. You will definitely get yours, and I will get mine, but just not with intercourse."

Tony slowly kissed down Korri's body. She moaned in blissful pleasure. He unsnapped her bra and lavished each breast with sucks to her chocolate kiss tips. "Yes, baby…" Korri moaned.

"Keep your hands above your head and don't move," Tony commanded, his voice laced with passion. He kissed his way down to her belly button where he nipped at the skin on her tight belly.

Korri giggled at the ticklish sensation, but she didn't dare move her hands. Tony kissed his way down to the apex of her thighs, but he didn't take off her panties like she wanted him to. Instead, he licked and sucked at her inner thighs, making her squirm.

Chasing Desires
by Kasey Martin

"Now, baby, I promised you the next time we made love we would be husband and wife. And I would never break my promise to you."

Korri started to protest. She wanted to tell him that she took it all back. She wanted to make love to him. Being husband and wife didn't matter as long as they were together. But before she could get a word out, he stopped his teasing and crawled up her body to look her in her hazel eyes.

He kissed her slowly and seductively. He pulled her bottom lip into his mouth, sucking on it until she couldn't help the gasp that left her. He took advantage of her opened mouth, slipping his tongue inside. He licked and tasted every inch of her. Korri groaned at the taste and feel of him. His kisses were intoxicating, and she was quickly reminded why she was so addicted to this man.

He took his time seducing her with his touch, grinding his hardness into her panty clad mound. She was soaking wet and so turned on that she forgot to keep her hands above her head. Korri ran her nails down Tony's broad muscular shoulders and down his back. He stopped kissing her and narrowed his eyes.

"I thought I told you to keep your hands above your head like a good girl. Now, you don't want me to spank you, do you? Because I sure as hell will break my promise if I have to spank that delectable ass of yours."

Korri wanted to disobey his orders just so she could get a spanking, and have him fuck her, but she knew how Tony was about keeping his promises, so she decided she would behave.

She placed her hands back above her head, and licked her lips seductively. When he bent down to give her a kiss for following his directions, she bit his lip playfully. He chuckled at her mischievousness, but he didn't say anything. He just went back to devouring her body, showering her with nips, licks, kisses, and the occasional suck.

"I'm going to eat your pussy until your sweetness fills my mouth and then I'm going to start all over again."

A chill ran down Korri's spine. She absolutely loved when he talked dirty to her. But what really made her excited was the fact that she knew it wasn't just talking. He would definitely follow through on everything he said.

Tony made his way to her drenched center and tugged her little lacy, pink thong to the side. "If I take these off, I won't be able to keep my word so…" He stopped midsentence, pulled her panties to the side, and took a long lick of her dripping wet womanhood.

Korri almost had an orgasm from that alone. "Uhhhmmm…"

Chasing Desires
by Kasey Martin

Tony circled her clit with his tongue, putting just the right amount of pressure on her sensitive nub. He rubbed a strong finger up and down her pulsing center before slipping it deep inside of her. Korri moaned out her pleasure doing her best to keep her hands above her head. She wanted to grab his head so bad. She thrust her pelvis up to get more friction, but he wasn't having it.

Tony wrapped a strong arm around her waist, effectively stopping her movements. "This is my pussy and I'll eat it like *I* want to."

Korri groaned at his crass words. He knew exactly what he was doing to her. She was so worked up, but he kept her right on the edge. Teetering so close, but not letting her go over. He would thrust his thick digit into her heated core and then add another one until she could feel herself beginning to clench around him, but he would slow down his pace and take one finger out.

He continued this torturous routine for what seemed like forever to Korri. She didn't want to be frustrated, but her body felt so good even without having an orgasm that she couldn't complain. All she could do was enjoy the sensations he was creating.

"Sweetness, I need you to do me a favor," Tony said between his long licks.

Chasing Desires
by Kasey Martin

"Anything, Superman! I'll do anything. Just please let me come, baby. Please," Korri pleaded as she tried but failed to work her hips.

"I'm going to let you go, but I need you to touch me. I want to feel your soft hands on my cock. Can you do that for me, Sweetness?"

Korri smiled wickedly and nodded enthusiastically. Tony released her waist from his strong grip, grabbed her hand, and moved it to his hard-as-steel shaft. He wrapped his large, rough hand around her soft, smaller one and guided it up and down his cock in a slow steady motion.

They moaned in unison at the feeling. Tony removed his hand and sat up slightly, so Korri could continue rubbing him as he went back to kissing her treasure. He wasted no time putting his tongue deep into her creamy kitty thrusting it in and out while he rubbed her descended nub in a circular motion.

Korri could feel herself building rapidly, and this time Tony wasn't backing off. He increased the speed and pressure just the way she liked it. In turn, her grip tightened around his large member and she pumped hard and fast.

Their panting and moans became louder with their frenzied movements. They climaxed together, Tony spilling his seed into Korri's hand, and she creamed into his mouth.

"Damn, Sweetness, I needed that."

CHASING DESIRES
by Kasey Martin

"*You?*" Korri giggled. "I thought that was for me?" she questioned breathlessly, a satisfied smile gracing her beautiful face.

"No, baby." Tony smiled. "That definitely was for both of us."

"Thank you, Superman. I love you so much."

"Anything for you, Sweetness. You know that. Next time, you promise to come to me when you're frustrated. You know I will take care of you. And next time I promise not to walk around tempting you on purpose." He chuckled.

Korri slapped his chiseled chest. "I knew you were doing that shit on purpose!"

They both laughed as they snuggled together in their bed. Korri already knew that she was marrying the right man, but his actions tonight just proved that he would go above and beyond for her, and she couldn't wait to become his wife.

CHAPTER 8
LORENZO

Lorenzo had spent the last few weeks trying to come to terms with helping a woman who he knew for a fact had betrayed him. But after Jake let him know that Tommy was working with the Salazar Cartel, he knew that he had to step in and get his cousin as far away from his business as possible. He knew that no matter how much he'd warned Tommy to stay away from his business, he wouldn't. As much of a dumbass as he was, he would never pass up an opportunity to make money. He was like his father in that aspect.

Lorenzo's uncle would never pass up a chance to make money. *Never.* He knew that no matter what he said to try and convince his uncle that whatever Tommy had planned was a bad idea, if they could make a profit and expand the family business while doing so, Sal would never back Lorenzo.

He sighed as he made the call that hopefully he wouldn't come to regret.

"Hello?" Her husky voice always did something to him.

"Hello, Chase. Uhum…" Lorenzo cleared his throat trying to get his thoughts together. "Yeah, I was wondering if you could come over. I have some things I would like to talk to you about."

"Uh, yeah, sure. Give me a couple of hours, and I'll be there," she answered.

"Great. I'll see you then."

Lorenzo disconnected the call. It just wasn't in him to curve his thinking about something that had been engrained in him since birth. Going against family just wasn't something that you ever did no matter what. There was no excuse and no forgiveness. But he just couldn't let go of the nagging feeling that Tommy really did have something to do with him getting shot.

Until he found out for sure, he would keep an eye on his cousin. And what better way to do that than to let Chase into his club to investigate. The only problem with that was, he would be letting her back in his life, and he really truly didn't want to do that. But sometimes it's not about what you want it's about what you need.

***

Lorenzo could feel small delicate touches all over his body. He must've fallen asleep while waiting on Chase. He couldn't figure out what was going on, but his body was on fire. He couldn't help the deep guttural moan that left his lips. He slowly opened his eyes to peer into deep, dark brown sultry

Chasing Desires
by Kasey Martin

ones. The look in her eyes alone had him so turned on, it almost jumbled the rush of thoughts that were crossing his mind…*almost.*

Why didn't I hear the buzzer? And how in the hell did she get into my house? "Chase, what are you doing? How did you get in?" Lorenzo asked with confusion written all over his handsome face.

Chase just smiled without responding to Lorenzo's questions. Her pretty, cocoa brown skin glowed under the dim lighting in the room. She walked seductively toward him, showing off her tiny, sheer white baby doll dress. He could see that she was totally naked underneath the see-through fabric. She straddled his hips, and his heart rate picked up to an unfathomable speed.

"Fuuuuck…." he groaned, his strong hands moving to grip the lush curves of her ass.

Her breasts swayed in this face as she leaned over him. They were perky and tipped with dark brown hard peaks that he couldn't wait to taste. Her body was a dream. It was muscular and toned but still feminine with curves for days. She stood at an average height, but her long legs seemed to go on and on as she wrapped them around his waist.

He slid his hands from her behind to her trim waist and tugged her body closer to him. She moved her hips, grinding

Chasing Desires
by Kasey Martin

her heated center over his hard steel. The feel of her was soft and smooth, and with that small touch he knew he wouldn't be able to get enough. How could he have thought he would be able to stay away from her? The betrayal would always be there, and he would never be able to trust her. But trust didn't have anything to do with claiming her body. Claiming her body and making her bend to his will. *That* he was more than certain he could do.

Lorenzo sat up with her still on his lap and pulled her lips close to his. He devoured her mouth, nipping and sucking from her like a fountain. She moaned and continued to grind her wetness into his hard-as-stone cock. His breathing was labored, but he kept kissing her. She was panting, moaning, and working her hips in a circular motion, continuing to drive him completely insane.

"I need to be inside of you." The hoarse desperation in Lorenzo's voice was unrecognizable to him.

"Not yet. You need to answer that," Chase whispered seductively.

Her raspy tone always had a way of turning him on, so he almost missed what she'd said. Lorenzo was confused. "Wha-what? Answer what?" He couldn't focus on anything except the beautiful woman grinding on his lap.

CHASING DESIRES
by Kasey Martin

Chase chuckled in a raspy tone. Then he heard it. His doorbell was ringing. When Lorenzo opened his eyes, he was alone.

"Shit!" It was a dream...an almost wet one too. Lorenzo dragged his hand over his face and let out a deep breath. He was sporting a massive hard-on and now he had to face the woman who'd indirectly caused it.

He answered the door hoping that Chase wouldn't look down and notice how aroused he was. There wasn't much he could do to hide it now, though.

Chase stood at Lorenzo's door looking beautiful. Her smooth ebony skin always held a glow like her body was wrapped in brown silk. Her succulent, plump, and glossy lips made it hard to focus on anything but her mouth. When his gaze finally moved upward, her bright eyes held an inquisitive stare.

He tried to stop his obvious ogling, but his eyes wouldn't obey. He surveyed her attire, and she was dressed in workout gear. The tight gray yoga pants and equally tight pink tank top were doing absolutely nothing for his current situation. He could imagine himself peeling the pants down her perfect legs.

He ran a frustrated hand through his too-long hair, and down his bearded face. He took a deep breath, trying to reign in his thoughts. If he didn't, he wouldn't be able to stop himself

Chasing Desires
by Kasey Martin

from wrapping his arms around her, pulling her down, and screwing her on his living room floor like a possessive animal.

Damn! First the dream now these thoughts. What the hell is she doing to me? Shit, just focus on what's important.

"Hey, come on in," Lorenzo finally stated as he tried and failed to focus on anything but her thighs in those damn pants.

She gave him a quizzical look, but after she glanced down, he noticed that her cheeks held a hint of a blush, but she made no comment as she nodded and preceded him into the living room.

Guess she noticed. He smirked.

"I was surprised that you called me," Chase commented, ignoring the elephant in the room. He guessed if she could pretend not to see he was aroused, he could pretend right along with her, at least with a little self-adjustment, he could try.

Chase took a seat with a look of both reluctance, and curiosity on her face. She smiled up at him, and he had to admit that it helped to break the tension in the room a little.

"Well, there's no need in beating around the bush. I gave your idea some thought and with the information I recently received, I'm willing to help you."

He saw her expression change from just curious to completely shocked. "Wow, I really didn't expect you to want to help me. But thank you. I understand how hard this must be for you."

"Do you? Do you honestly and truly understand? Because I need you to know that this could potentially be a life and death situation, not just for me, but for the both of us."

"I understand. I'm not naïve, and this is my job. Nothing will come back on you."

"Fine, but I need you to do me one favor…" Lorenzo trailed off to look deep into her eyes.

"What favor is that?" Chase questioned.

"I need you to be honest with me when I ask you any questions about the case. Being in the dark is not something I'm willing to do again. I'm sure as an agent you can understand the importance of having all the facts when you're going into a situation. This is more than a case for me, Chase. More than some job. This is my livelihood, my family, my fucking life." He paused and then added, "And yours too." He had to continuously remind her that his life wasn't the only one affected by their actions.

"I get that. And I understand."

"Good. Now, how are we going to do this?" Lorenzo asked, glad to finally get the awkward initial part of this conversation over.

Chasing Desires
by Kasey Martin

"Well, to be honest, I've been thinking more about that initial plan and how we don't exactly have to go through with it. You were right before."

He sat up, listening more intently to what she had to say. *I was right. Never thought she'd ever say that, at least where I could hear.*

Chase continued, "I have been hanging out with Charlie more these days, so if I started to work at Premier, it wouldn't seem weird or out of the ordinary. If I worked there, I wouldn't need a cover or a story to explain why I'm there all the time. Then I wouldn't have to go undercover as your girlfriend."

"No," he rejected almost too quickly. He wouldn't even entertain any bullshit like that. If any of this came out, it would look like another one of his employees had set him up again. He wasn't going to be made to look like an idiot again.

"I just want to make it easier on you, Lorenzo. I know how you feel about working with me and I'm giving you a way out."

"I don't need a way out. I need you to be honest and forthcoming with me." He was starting to get frustrated, and his chest was beginning to hurt.

Fucking, Justin Russo! He thought, rubbing his throbbing chest. Every single time he got stressed, his chest started to hurt. The doctor said he was healing fine and it was

Chasing Desires
by Kasey Martin

all in his head. So basically the bastard was calling him crazy. And at the moment, his doctor was right because he sure as hell felt crazy.

Lorenzo was going against everything he knew, helping a woman that he didn't trust but wanted so much that it was almost as painful as the shot he'd survived.

"I just thought that if I worked there, you wouldn't have to explain why I'm at Premier all the time," Chase tried to explain again.

"Your story wouldn't work. I know my cousin."

"What does that mean?"

"It means since we have gone out on more than one occasion and he has no doubt seen you with me. At the very least, he knows that we were dating. So you working there won't work for several reasons, but Tommy seeing us together is the major factor."

"Ooo-kay… So again, what does that mean? What should we do?"

"It means that you working at Premier is out of the question. My woman would never work for me." He shook his head. "No, that would be a dead-ass giveaway."

"Alright. So then we go with the original plan?" she questioned again.

"Yes, so that means we will need to be seen together."

CHASING DESIRES
by Kasey Martin

"Right. But we can't be living it up. You have to be my *patient*. Remember? Too sick to go into work, so you sent your dedicated new lover to check on things."

"*Lover*, huh?" Lorenzo couldn't hide the wicked smile that graced his chiseled face. Chase definitely needed to choose her words more carefully, and he needed to think of something other than being her lover before he was sporting another friendly reminder that he hadn't had sex in months.

"Sorry, but you don't look like the type of guy that keeps *girlfriends*," Chase stated coolly, looking him directly in the eyes.

Lorenzo had to admit she was bold. And he liked bold. "You're right. I'm not the type. But in this case, I'm going to have to pretend to be the type. There's no way anyone would believe that I would let some chick I was merely banging help me with anything."

"Alright then. Girlfriend it is," Chase conceded without much of a fight.

Lorenzo was happy that they had finally come to an agreement. They took a couple of hours to hash out Chase's cover, and what exactly she would be looking for while she was at Premier. It sounded like a solid plan, but it also sounded way too easy. And he knew from experience that this situation was anything but easy.

CHAPTER 9
CHASE

Chase was glad that Lorenzo had finally agreed to help her even though she could see how reluctant he was. And although going in undercover as an employee would have worked, she had to admit that going in as Lorenzo's girlfriend was a much better option.

After they discussed how she would infiltrate his club, they decided it would be best if they were seen together gradually. They had already been on several dates, so it wouldn't seem odd if they picked up where they left off. Chase was really glad that they were able to sit down and have a civil conversation.

She wasn't going to lie. The shock of him calling her combined with how he answered the door had her off her game. Chase couldn't keep her eyes from dipping to the low-slung gym shorts he was wearing. And he was wearing the hell out of them. They molded to his body like a second skin, which is why she couldn't help but notice the obvious print of his rather large member.

She couldn't help the heat that rose up her neck and settled in her cheeks. Chase did her damndest to tear her eyes

Chasing Desires
by Kasey Martin

away, but she knew that he saw her because of the smirk that covered his handsome face. Her greedy eyes ate up the sight of his muscular chest, clad in a dark blue T-shirt and up to his smiling, chiseled face.

Chase had to shake her head and remind herself of the reason she was there. *Reyes.* She promised herself that she would avenge her dead partner, and drooling over the one man that could help her get closer than she had ever been before, was not just alarming. It was incredibly stupid.

Once she got her mind focused, the conversation went smoother than she expected. The first time she tried to convince Lorenzo of the idea, he shot her down so fast she was surprised she didn't get dizzy from the rejection. But all the little seeds of doubt she'd planted actually worked in her favor. Now, she had to be smart and make sure all her hard work paid off.

She left Lorenzo's house and decided to go home and call Jake and the boys. She had to let them know of the new developments in the case. She knew that they were just as invested as she was in getting justice for her partner, and they would work long hours right alongside her.

Chase had only been home for twenty minutes when she heard a knock at her door. She answered to the smiling face, and dark brown eyes of Marcus Wright.

Chasing Desires
by Kasey Martin

"Hey there, CJ. How's it hangin'?" Marcus was the only one that talked to her like she was one of the boys. He treated her more like a little sister than a colleague, and she found that she actually liked it.

"Hey, Marc. Everything is hangin' just fine." Chase chuckled at the dark chocolate giant of a man.

He smiled wider and gave her a hug before coming inside her tiny apartment. Usually, Jake would be lead on any debriefings of the case, but Charlie wasn't feeling well, so he'd sent Marcus and a sullen-looking Mike.

"Hi, Mike." Chase timidly smiled at her friend.

Things between the two of them had been strained since a big disagreement on how she should be handling her case or more importantly, how she was handling *Lorenzo*.

After walking her to the elevator, Lorenzo had leaned down and captured her lips in a slow sensual kiss before running his hand down her cheek. She couldn't help but lean into the intimate caress. His kiss was brief, but it stole her breath away just the same. She knew then that she was in trouble, but she had to keep her eye on the prize.

The couple said goodnight, and he turned and left the hotel. She couldn't help but watch him walk away until he was out of sight. Chase knew that she had her team watching her, so

Chasing Desires
by Kasey Martin

she tried to keep her expression as neutral as possible. But she couldn't help the heated feeling Lorenzo had left her with.

As soon as Chase entered the elevator, she knew she wasn't alone. She also knew that she didn't keep the neutral expression on her face as well as she thought she did. When she turned around, another set of familiar blue eyes were staring at her expectantly. She sighed and hit the button to her floor. Even though she was tired, she was well aware from the look on Mike's face that the night was far from over.

They were in the elevator alone, and it was the opening he needed because Mike didn't wait before he started his questioning.

"What was the kiss about?" He asked in a low menacing tone. His fiery sapphire gaze, and the scowl he wore detracted from his handsome face. The low tone he spoke in, told her that this was indeed going to be a very long night.

"You know what it was about, Mike," Chase responded on another heavy sigh.

They exited the elevator not saying another word until they entered her room. The tension in the air was thick and uncomfortable, and the last thing Chase felt like, after having such a wonderful night, was having an argument with her friend.

CHASING DESIRES
by Kasey Martin

"I think you're getting too close to this guy, Chase. I know you're trying to get evidence on his cousin, but I don't know if this is the right way to go about it," Mike stated as soon as he closed the hotel room behind him.

The two of them have had the same conversation many times. Mike was a loyal friend who helped Chase without much explanation. He knew people with the resources to help, and whenever she called him, there was no hesitation on his part. The only thing they didn't agree on was how close she should get to Lorenzo. Mike had told her that he thought she should just get a job at the club and snoop around. He didn't think getting romantically involved with her target was wise.

"I'm going to go get out of this tight-ass dress before we have this conversation yet again." Chase kicked off her heels and walked to the bedroom of her hotel room. She always went the extra mile for one of her dates with Lorenzo. She had to make sure she kept up appearances for her cover. At least that's what she had told herself.

She emerged from the bedroom, changed into yoga pants and a large T-shirt. She sat down next to Mike on the small sofa. "Listen, getting a job at Lorenzo's club won't be enough. It would take too long to learn the ends and outs and gain his trust. He would be suspicious if all of a sudden I went

Chasing Desires
by Kasey Martin

from dating him to wanting a job. Being in a relationship with him is the quickest way to gain his trust."

Mike shook his head, his blond hair flopped in his pale chiseled face. "He's dangerous, Chase. Going out in public is one thing because it's easy to have your back. But what happens when he wants to take you back to his place?" Mike ran his hand through his hair, ruffling it with the movement and trying but failing to get it out of his crystal blue eyes.

Chase couldn't comprehend why Mike was so worried about this. "I've been an agent for well over a decade, Mike. I know how to take care of myself." Chase waved off his comment and his concerns with a flick of her delicate wrist. "I'm also smart enough not to go back to a man's place, especially a man who is an integral part of my investigation."

"Chase, all I'm saying is that you need to be careful," Mike pleaded. The fire in his eyes was now replaced with uncertainty.

"You know me, Mike. I'm always careful. I can't believe you're questioning my judgment on this." Chase was becoming more and more irritated with the conversation. She thought out of everyone here in Dallas, her old friend would trust her, but it seemed like he was the only one not on board with the plan.

Chasing Desires
by Kasey Martin

"I know that you are way too emotionally invested in this particular case to see things clearly. I get it. Reyes was your partner, but you gotta take your emotions out of this."

"I'm a good agent! I have enough pressure without you, my friend, giving me shit for my decisions!" She seethed, staring directly into his face.

"I know that you're a good agent and I'm not giving you shit, Chase. I'm telling you the truth," Mike stated passionately.

His narrowed eyes and the way he held his lips tight in a frown, Chase knew that he was frustrated, but hell, so was she.

Chase blew out a long breath and ran her fingers through her hair. She tried to calm down and make herself relax. She knew Mike was just worried and he was only trying to help. He was her support system and the only one she could count on when she truly needed him.

"You're right. I'm sorry, Mike. But you know me. And you know I got this. Yes, I'm emotionally invested in this case more than I normally would be, but that doesn't mean I'm not going to do everything I possibly can to be safe and to get what I'm after."

"Okay, but I still think that you getting too close to Moretti is a mistake."

"Duly noted. But like I said, getting close to Moretti will gain me his trust. I got this, Mike."

CHASING DESIRES
by *Kasey Martin*

Mike sighed and held his hands up in surrender. "Alright, Chase. Whatever you say."

That last conversation had been haunting her because ever since, she felt like a wedge had been placed between her and her friend and she had no idea what to do about it. Maybe once the case was over and Mike saw that he had nothing to worry about, they could go back to being friends.

Who am I kidding? Chase thought solemnly. Her friendship with Mike may never be the same after this case, especially when he found out she'd taken a leave of absence and had asked Jake not to tell him.

***

They sat down quietly in Chase's small but quaint living area. Even though she had no plans whatsoever to stay in Dallas after her case was over, she had to admit how charming her place was. She found herself feeling more and more comfortable in Texas. Growing up as an army brat, she was used to moving from one city to another, so as an adult she found herself not liking change.

"Alright, so let's get down to business," Mike stated, looking impatient.

"*Okay.*" Chase's upper eyelids raised in a stare, her wide-open eyes glaring at Mike in annoyance. She and Mike were going to have to talk sooner rather than later. She could feel the animosity radiating from him.

Marcus must've picked up on the tension as well because he narrowed his eyes at both of them before he spoke. "So what do you have for us, Chase?" Marcus finally asked after he searched their faces for a few moments.

"Lorenzo agreed to the initial plan of being in a 'relationship' with me as a cover."

"What? I thought we decided you were going in as an employee since Moretti was out of commission. He knows who you are now, so going in as an employee won't be such a big risk as it was before."

Chase inhaled a deep breath. She had been hopeful that Mike would see that Lorenzo cooperating was a good thing. *I guess that was wishful thinking.*

"Hold on, Mike. Let the woman finish. I'm sure this plan can be just as beneficial in the long run," Marcus thoughtfully interjected.

She heard Mike huff like a petulant child, but she didn't look in his direction. She was too afraid that seeing his sulking face right now would piss her off.

"The risk isn't with Lorenzo. It's with *Tommy*. Lorenzo thinks that his cousin had to have been watching him, and if

CHASING DESIRES
by Kasey Martin

that's the case, then he likely knows that we had gone out before the shooting."

Chase went on to explain in detail everything she and Lorenzo talked about. Marcus was on board, and they hashed out more of the plan that would help to keep Chase safe. However, Mike continued to look on in disbelief, uttering his displeasure at the entire idea until it was time for them to leave.

Chase had never seen her friend act this way, and she was beginning to think that maybe she should ask Jake to put him on another assignment because based on his recent behavior, *he* was the one too emotionally involved in the case.

***

A few nights later, Chase was getting ready for her date with Lorenzo. This would be the first time they'd gone out since he found out her true identity, and she had no idea what to expect.

She wore her hair down with a side part. Her make-up, as usual, was minimal, and her lips were glossed with a plum color. She wore high-waist, wide-leg black pants with a slim-fitted plum-colored long sleeve shirt, and black platform stilettos.

Chase felt confident and sexy. And although the date was supposed to be for appearances only, she still wanted to impress Lorenzo. When she heard a knock at her door, she

Chasing Desires
by Kasey Martin

knew that she had to cast her reservations aside and put on her professional mask.

Lorenzo stood at the door looking dapper in his dark charcoal suit with a sharply pressed light grey dress shirt. His strong jaw was still covered in a thick dusting of hair, and his long curly hair was gelled away from his face and tucked behind his ears.

"You ready?" he questioned.

The look in his eyes gave Chase the chills. She wanted to tell him she would never be ready for a man like him, and that they didn't have to go anywhere because it would be better if they could just stay in her apartment and rip each other's clothes off. But her conscience would never let her do that, so she simply answered, "Sure. Let's go."

Even after arriving at the restaurant, the sexual tension was still palpable between Lorenzo and Chase. He was flirting with her nonstop, and instead of being annoyed by his antics, Chase was eating up the attention.

"You look absolutely stunning tonight." Lorenzo's voice was low and deep and it once again gave her chills.

"Thank you. You don't look too bad yourself." Chase grinned mischievously at the indignant look on his face.

Chasing Desires
by Kasey Martin

Lorenzo chuckled. "Damn, I'm going to have to get my game together if that's the best compliment I can get."

Chase laughed. "I wouldn't kick you out of bed for eating crackers."

Lorenzo loudly laughed. "What the hell does that mean?"

"It means you're cute enough not to get kicked out of bed even if you do something annoying like getting crumbs everywhere."

They shared another laugh, and Chase could feel herself starting to relax even more. The chemistry between them was still undeniable, and the looks he continued to give her across the table were heating her core to a boiling point.

Lorenzo excused himself from the table. Chase watched as other women gawked openly at her date. All she could do was smile because Lorenzo was indeed worthy of all the female attention.

Once he returned, he sat beside her instead of across from her where he was previously seated. He smiled playfully then he leaned down and kissed her mouth gently. He barely pressed his firm lips against hers, but Chase felt the previous throb return to her core.

CHASING DESIRES
by Kasey Martin

Lorenzo leaned back and stared intensely into her eyes. Chase had no idea what he was looking for, but the butterflies in her stomach began to flutter uncontrollably. Lorenzo looked at her with the most breathtaking smile she had ever seen, then he leaned in and kissed her softly right behind the ear.

Chase was so lost in the moment that she barely recognized a man had approached their table. She had never seen the guy before, so she instantly went on alert. He stood at an average height with dark blond hair and brown eyes. The smile he graced her with was both devilish and sexy at the same time. Chase couldn't help but return the stranger's smile. When Lorenzo looked at her with a cocked eyebrow, she pointed at the stranger.

When Lorenzo turned around, he nodded his head in acknowledgement.

"Lorenzo Moretti, it's nice to see you out and about again," the man said with a wide smile on his handsome face.

"Lucas Franks." Lorenzo nodded, "It's good to be out." He continued with a small smile.

Lorenzo reached out, and they shook hands before Lucas turned his attention to Chase. The look in his eyes couldn't be mistaken for anything but lust, and Chase could feel a blush coming on. Although she worked around many men, she spent her time trying to blend in without being the center of their attention, so all this interest was new to her.

The sound of Lorenzo clearing his throat brought Chase's attention back to him and away from the brown-eyed hunk staring at her. She gave him a faint smile and pulled at her earlobe, something she did when she was nervous.

"And just who is this lovely lady?" Lucas asked Lorenzo the question, but his gaze never strayed from Chase.

Chase held out her hand. "I'm Chase. It's nice to meet you, Lucas."

"Nice to meet you too, Chase." His deep voice was smooth, and the bright smile on his handsome face was absolutely gorgeous. He held Chase's hand a little longer than necessary, and the wink he gave her was totally inappropriate. She couldn't seem to keep the smile off her face.

"Yes, this is my *girlfriend*, Chase," Lorenzo emphasized in a possessive tone with a stern expression.

"*Girlfriend*, huh? Lucky man." Lucas gave Chase another slow once over from head to toe. That lustful look in his eye had returned full force.

CHASING DESIRES
by Kasey Martin

Chase cleared her throat and slowly turned to face her date. The look in Lorenzo's eyes was not pleasant. In fact, he looked as if he were about to commit a homicide although they were merely pretending to be a couple. She was afraid of what would happen if they were a *real* couple.

"Yeah, *girlfriend*, so if you want to keep your eyes, I suggest you stop staring so hard at *my* woman."

The smile on Lucas' face slowly melted away, and he reluctantly took his eyes off Chase to stare at a stoned-faced Lorenzo. "My mistake."

The atmosphere crackled and popped with a tension so thick it had its own heartbeat. Chase looked back and forth between the two men. They seemed to be in some sort of stare-down contest. She really didn't know what to think about the whole thing. She knew that she and Lorenzo were supposed to be a couple, but she hadn't expected him to take the role so seriously.

Chase looked at both men as she rubbed her earlobe. She shot a wide-eyed look at Lorenzo, hoping to convey that he needed to relax.

He grunted, but he didn't say anything. However, his shoulders relaxed slightly, so Chase knew that he'd gotten the message.

"I see that my party has finally arrived, so I'll leave you two to enjoy the rest of your meal," Lucas said after an awkward beat.

"Thanks. We will." Lorenzo grabbed Chase's hand, kissed it, and gave her a seductive wink and smile.

She instantly blushed. *I've got to get this blushing shit under control. I am not a teenage girl.*

Lucas smiled tightly and left with a nod. As cute as he was, Chase was glad to see him leave because he seemed to take the tension with him.

As soon as he was out of earshot, Chase turned to a blank-faced Lorenzo. "What the hell was that?" she whispered, frustration lacing her tone.

"If we are supposed to be a couple, you can't eye-fuck some stranger in a restaurant while we're on a date."

His words came out so calm that Chase almost missed the malice behind them. She was a little flustered, but she refused to take any bullshit from someone she was simply pretending with. This was a job. "First of all, if you think you're going to talk to me any kind of way, then you have the wrong one." Chase looked Lorenzo up and down like he was crazy. "Secondly, I wasn't eye-fucking anybody. He was eye-fucking me, and he's *your* friend."

After a long moment, Lorenzo replied. "Fine. However, he's an *associate* and not a friend. And as you well know, I *never* have girlfriends, so people are going to come at you for all different reasons, and you have to be prepared. You also need to act like *you're mine*," he stressed.

Chase pursed her lips and grunted in response, but she couldn't help the fluttering of her heart at his words. *You also need to act like you're mine.* She knew what Lorenzo really meant, but she couldn't help her reaction to him.

Lorenzo placed his hand against her cheek and caressed it. Then he tilted her head back so she could look directly into his eyes. "Do you understand? You're mine."

All Chase could do was nod. *Now that definitely didn't sound like a pretend statement.*

***

DALLAS AGENT

Chasing Desires
by Kasey Martin

When he was asked to watch Angeletti and Moretti, the last thing he expected would be to recognize the sultry vixen that was sitting beside Lorenzo at the fancy restaurant.

He had to admit that he was entirely surprised to see Chase Johnson sitting next to Lorenzo Moretti of all people. He was pretty confident that she was working, but did Moretti know that his beautiful dinner companion was a fed? And if he did, why was he with her?

This situation had the potential to get messy, but he would be damned if anybody got in the way of his plans. He dialed the number to a contact that could shed some light on the subject and hoped to God that he wouldn't give him the runaround.

"Hello." His voice was gruff as usual, but he needed information and fast.

"There's a New Jersey agent in Dallas, so why wasn't I informed that there was somebody investigating here in my territory?" The question was bold, but his contact was the only person who could help him, and he had to know what was going on. One slip up and his whole life could be ruined, and he would never let that happen.

"Listen. You know how it works. Need to know basis." The contact vaguely answered.

He took a deep breath to calm himself. He needed to tread lightly to get the information he needed.

"Okay, so *what* can you tell me?"

"Perhaps you need to be more specific, and maybe I can help you."

It was going to be a long conversation, and hopefully, when everything was said and done, he would come out on the winning end of this complicated game of chess.

***

CHASE

The ride back to Chase's apartment was contemplative. After the obvious show of possession from Lorenzo, she was completely thrown off. She told herself that this was a job, but she knew that it was more than that.

Lorenzo's driver pulled up to her building, and parked. Lorenzo insisted on escorting her up to her apartment even though she was more than capable of protecting herself if the need were to arise. However, she didn't argue. She allowed him to accompany her to her front door.

In the back of her mind, Chase knew that she had a team discreetly watching their every move, but when Lorenzo leaned down and placed one of the hottest kisses on her that she had

Chasing Desires
by Kasey Martin

ever had in her entire life, she completely forgot about everything except him.

He sucked her pouty bottom lip into his mouth and bit it teasingly. Chase's eyes remained shut even after she felt Lorenzo pull away from her. The butterflies were back in her stomach in full effect. She slowly opened her eyes and his crystal gaze had drawn her into a trance.

"You really shouldn't look at me like that." His voice held an edge that she had never heard.

"L-like...like what?" Chase stammered slightly. *I need to get a hold of myself.*

"Like you want me to forget this is all for show." Lorenzo eyes gleamed in challenge.

Chase sighed heavily. She'd damn near forgotten herself that it was all for show. "No, I don't want you to forget." She backed up slightly and shook her head to clear her thoughts.

"Well, I guess I'll let you go inside." Lorenzo kissed her one last time, winked, and walked back to his waiting vehicle.

Once Chase was inside her apartment, she knew that this was no longer a job for her. She was falling for Lorenzo

Chasing Desires
by Kasey Martin

Moretti. Her mouth curved into a blissful smile that lit up her entire face, and she sighed with contentment.

As she walked to her bedroom, her doorbell rang. Her smile was impossibly wide as she opened the door expecting to find Lorenzo standing there. However, it was wiped clean off her face when she opened the door to a seething Mike.

CHAPTER 10
TOMMY

"I absolutely hate this fucking waiting game. We have the territory we need, and the girls are making money hand over fist everywhere they work. The drug game is strong, and we have the manpower behind us. At this point, I think the cartel is stalling. If they don't want this deal, I need to know, so that I can come up with something else. My father has backed off for now, but he won't sit back forever."

"Hermano, chill. The cartel will not back out. The deal will go on as planned."

"Look, we don't have time to chill. I don't need my father becoming suspicious again. It took forever for him to trust me enough to pull his goons back to Jersey. We have to move now while we have the territory on lock. There is only so much we can do to prove we're worthy of their backing!" Tommy yelled as he paced back and forth in his penthouse suite.

"Hermano, relax. There's no need to go off the plan. We'll just keep making our money, and when the cartel is ready, they will be here," Luis Castillo responded in his heavily Spanish accented English.

Chasing Desires
by Kasey Martin

Luis knew that Tommy absolutely hated whenever people told him to chill or relax, but he was right. They could keep making money until the cartel showed up to back him. But the last thing he wanted to do was go back to being his father's puppet. He needed the cartel to come through and quick.

Tommy knew that he could trust Luis not to miss anything that was important to their business. They had known each other for over twenty years. His meeting Tommy was coincidental, but their friendship proved to be very profitable. Now that Luis had moved up in the ranks of the Salazar Cartel, their friendship and business had elevated to another level.

Tommy trusted Luis as much as you could trust a criminal like Luis. And Luis was one of the few people who knew who Tommy truly was. Everyone assumed that Tommy was some sort of idiot, but he wasn't. He had just lived in his father's shadow for too long, but it was time that came to an end.

"You know what? You're right. I say we go into the new club, Prime, and set up shop. That way, we can gain even more territory while we wait."

Tommy watched as Luis nodded his head and rubbed his hands together. "We could definitely slip into Prime without any trouble. They are focused on getting Premier's business back to where it was before Lorenzo got shot, so Prime is basically sitting wide open."

Tommy nodded his head. "Yep, and the clientele there is ripe for the picking. We can have the girls moving product *and* turning tricks."

"Right. If we strike while the iron is hot. We can move the product with ease just like we've been doing at Premier."

Tommy had already proven that he could be an asset to the Salazar Cartel, and using mules to transport cocaine and heroin from Mexico directly to the club was ingenious. Everyone always looked for the typical drug dealer to move products. They would never expect a group of party girls to have enough drugs on them to supply the entire state of Texas. They would never suspect that most of the girls' johns were actually members of his crew. The girls would deliver the product to the crew, and the guys would distribute it out to be sold. If the girls were ever suspected of anything, it was hooking.

Tommy was finally able to make plans and follow through with them without his father breathing down his neck. With the cartel's backing, he could finally gain the power he needed to take over the family.

Tommy knew that he would never gain his father's approval or his support. No matter what he did for him, no matter how many times he took the wrap for his bullshit, and no matter how many of his secrets he kept, the old man just would never see Tommy for who he really was. He was way too power hungry and he would never give it up.

When he finally hooked up with the Salazar Cartel, it would give him the power he needed to finally prove to his father that he was worthy of heading the family. If that didn't work, he would have enough power to finally force his ass to retire.

***

LORENZO

Tonight was the night. The staff at Premier had decided to throw Lorenzo a party. And although they had gone on a few dinner dates here and there, Chase would now be introduced as his girlfriend to his employees. After their first heated date, things had cooled down considerably. He wasn't sure what had happened, but she had a frostiness to her demeanor that hadn't been there before. He thought he was making some headway with her after their kiss, but it seemed like he was back to square one.

Lorenzo sat next to Chase in the back of a blacked-out SUV. She looked stunning in a burgundy fitted dress with mesh cut-outs. Her hair was straight with a part down the middle, and a bold burgundy lipstick accentuated her luscious lips.

CHASING DESIRES
by Kasey Martin

She sat silently, scrolling through her cell phone. Although she would have some sort of backup, tonight was really all about establishing her cover. She wasn't really there to work her case although Lorenzo knew that she just wouldn't be able to help herself.

"So you know that you're going to actually have to act like you like me tonight, right?" Lorenzo asked Chase with a lopsided grin on his succulent lips.

He watched her as she placed the phone on her lap and turned to look at him. He searched her eyes and saw determination in them. He couldn't help to get sucked in by the enchanting chocolate color.

"Believe me. I know. I will be sure to play the part well. I won't mess this up because I know what's at stake for both of us."

Lorenzo was well aware that Chase knew what was at stake. He reminded her every chance he got, especially after their first date when they ran into one of his associates. He knew that she was a good agent and he was glad that she took her job so seriously.

"Great. So that means no flinching whenever I touch you and you need to look at me adoringly. Please get rid of the irritated look you have on your face right now."

CHASING DESIRES
by Kasey Martin

Chase actually gave Lorenzo a genuine smile. He tried not to think about why it was so important to him that she gave him one of her rare smiles, but he couldn't help but feel good that she truly looked more relaxed because of him.

"This isn't our first rodeo. I got this. I won't flinch or look at you with irritation." She paused and pointed a manicured finger at him. "I won't as long as you don't irritate me."

"I make no promises, doll face." Lorenzo winked at her and gave her his most charming smile.

He couldn't help but flirt with Chase because after all, she was a beautiful woman. The last time they went out, he felt so much jealousy that he couldn't control the possessiveness he displayed. Lucas Franks was a longtime associate that worked as a promoter for different clubs and restaurants. Lorenzo had worked with him numerous times and not once had they had any problems. But after one flirtatious look at Chase, he was ready to rip the man's head from his body.

Lorenzo knew that he had to keep reminding himself who Chase was. She wasn't his woman for real. She would do anything for her job. He had to remember that she didn't think twice about using him. He was determined not to forget that again. He was only working with her because he needed to find out if his cousin actually tried to kill him. And Chase was the best way to get that done. However, he couldn't ignore the feelings he had for her no matter what he tried to tell himself.

***

Lorenzo got out of the vehicle first, opened Chase's door, and offered his hand to help her out of the tall SUV. Once she was standing beside him, he reached down and grabbed her hand.

"Now or never, *Pumpkin*," Lorenzo whispered in her ear.

"Uh, yeah, I don't think so."

"What?" Lorenzo asked, smiling mischievously.

"You won't be calling me *Pumpkin*. Nope. Not at all," she said vehemently, shaking her head.

He snickered at the cute little scowl she had on her face. "Well, you're my *girlfriend*, so I should have some cutesy nickname for you."

"Well, *Pumpkin* definitely *won't* be the cutesy name you'll be calling me."

"Hmmm," he hummed noncommittally.

"I'm serious, Moretti. I hate cutesy nicknames, and as your girlfriend, you should know that about me." She gave him a sugary sweet smile, but he knew that she was being anything but sweet.

CHASING DESIRES
by Kasey Martin

"Well, since we're on names, you should probably stop calling me Moretti. My girlfriend definitely wouldn't call me by my last name."

"You're right, *Pumpkin*." She bit her lip seductively. "I'll remember that." When she smiled up at him this time, it reached her eyes. They proceeded into Premier hand in hand like a real couple.

The party was happening in a reserved section of the VIP area, but the club was still packed wall to wall with people. Lorenzo was really happy that the shooting, and all of the negative press that followed, hadn't damaged the reputation of the club or the restaurant as badly as it could have. It did take Charlie a couple of months to get the clientele back, but now it was like the shooting had never happened. Even Club Prime was doing pretty well, and Lorenzo couldn't have been prouder.

Walking through the club was bringing back both good and bad memories, but Lorenzo knew that he would have to suck it up and get through tonight without any incidents. The familiarity of everything gave him comfort. The colorful fabric that draped the walls and cascaded from the ceiling to connect to the opulent chandeliers, was something he was glad that he'd kept.

Lorenzo decided to do some remodeling after he was released from the hospital. Of course, his assistant, Amber, was the one who'd executed the changes. He was glad that everything turned out great. The bar had been upgraded from a solid brown oak with dark hardwood floors to a sleek contemporary black hard top with chrome and glass accents. The flooring was replaced with black marble tile that led to plush black carpet in the different VIP areas that were still roped off. Each section still had leather couches, but they'd been exchanged from brown and white to black with pastel throw pillows that matched the fabric that graced the walls and ceiling.

Lorenzo and Chase walked into the party already in progress, still holding hands. The looks they received appeared to be mostly shock, but Lorenzo saw a couple of glares of animosity. It wasn't a practice of his to sleep with his employees, but he was known to flirt with them. He could see by the hateful frowns that Chase was receiving from some of the women that flirting was probably something he should no longer do with them.

Lorenzo was greeted with smiles, hugs, and well wishes. He was glad to see that his employees were loyal and had stuck with him through this difficult time.

After introducing Chase to everyone, they settled in on one of the comfortable couches with a couple of drinks. Lorenzo could tell that Chase wasn't very comfortable. She was sitting with her back rod straight and she looked around stiffly at everyone with a small smile on her face.

"Hey there, *Pumpkin*," Lorenzo whispered into Chase's ear to get her attention. "You need to relax." He leaned back to look at the dazzling features of her face and gave her a reassuring wink.

Her shoulders immediately relaxed, and he smoothed his hand down her back. Chase automatically leaned into Lorenzo's touch, and he smiled inwardly. She probably wasn't even aware that she had relaxed into him.

"Hey, Lorenzo, I'm really glad to see you up and around. You had us scared there for a while," Peter, one of the assistant managers, stated while gazing at Chase with a twinkle in his eye.

Lorenzo didn't like the look he was giving her. He knew that look. It was the same one Lucas had given her and the same one he often wore. Lorenzo wrapped his arm possessively around Chase's waist and pulled her snuggly to his side, kissing her cheek. She gave him a quizzical look, but she didn't say anything.

"Yeah, I'm doing well thanks to my *Pumpkin* here."

Chase rolled her eyes at Lorenzo, but she gave Peter a small smile. "Hi. I'm Chase."

CHASING DESIRES
by Kasey Martin

"Hi, Chase. It's nice to meet you." Peter smiled a little too wide and openly stared at her longer than he should have.

Lorenzo narrowed his eyes at Peter's boldness.

"So, Chase what do you do?" Peter questioned as he sat down on the couch so close to her that their knees bumped.

Lorenzo looked at Chase with a cocked brow. They had never discussed what her job was for her cover. He never even thought to bring up the subject. Hell, he was still getting used to the fact that she was a damn Fed.

"I do consulting work for different business. Usually, security," Chase answered without missing a beat.

Lorenzo was glad that she was prepared, but he didn't expect anything less from her.

"That's nice. Is that how you met the boss man?" Peter asked, leaning in closer than necessary.

Lorenzo could barely contain the sneer that fought to break out on his face. He had to remember she wasn't really his. *He sure is asking a lot of damn questions. What is this? A fucking interview?*

"No. We met at a bar actually." Chase giggled as she leaned away from Peter and into Lorenzo's side. She gazed up at him lovingly and kissed his cheek.

He smiled down at her and gave her another wink. *She was right. She definitely could play the part.*

Chasing Desires
by Kasey Martin

"Oh, surely that was just a coincidence because you don't look like the type of woman who would pick up a guy at a bar," Peter snidely commented as he glared at Chase.

Lorenzo wasn't sure why Peter's demeanor had switched so , and he didn't care. Lorenzo sat up and looked at the little prick in an entirely different light. He must've grown some balls while Lorenzo was gone because there was no way this little weasel would've been so bold in the past.

"I beg your pardon?" Chase narrowed her eyes at Peter as she crossed her arms over her chest and sat up to look at the man directly in his smug face.

That was one of the things Lorenzo liked about Chase. She was bold and she would never back down from a fight. However, this little shit was his problem. And he would deal with him.

"*Pumpkin*, give me a minute, would you?" Lorenzo's statement sounded like a question, but it was anything but.

"Yeah, sure. Okay, Mor—" she stopped midsentence.

Lorenzo knew that she was about to call him by his last name again.

"Sure, sweetie." Chase smiled at him before narrowing her eyes at Peter again. "Excuse me," she said before she grabbed her purse and walked gracefully away.

CHASING DESIRES
by Kasey Martin

Lorenzo watched Peter's beady eyes roam over Chase's swaying curves as she left. He didn't have a reason to feel jealous because he and Chase weren't really together. Plus, Peter was no competition. However, he still felt rage. This asshole had sat across from him and openly ogled what he thought was another man's woman—*his* woman. And on top of that, he'd made rude comments to try and belittle her. There was no way in hell Lorenzo was going to let that shit ride.

"There's no fucking way I've been gone that long."

Lorenzo's comment caught Peter off-guard. He turned and looked at him with his eyes squinted and his nose crinkled in confusion. "Ex-excuse me," he stuttered slightly before clearing his throat. "I don't know what you mean."

"I've only been gone for three or so months. It definitely wasn't long enough for you to forget who the fuck I am." Lorenzo's face held a serious expression that left no room for disagreement.

He watched as the color drained from Peter's face. His pale skin became whiter as he visibly swallowed. His brown eyes grew wide with uncertainty and worry.

"I uh-uh, no. I haven't forgotten who you are. But I still don't understand."

"Then let me clarify it for you. That woman that you tried to disrespect is *mine*. She's not some piece of ass that you

Chasing Desires
by Kasey Martin

can talk to any way you want. That's *my* woman, and if you ever so much as think something crass about her, I will know and I will whoop the dog shit out of you. Got me?" Lorenzo sat back and sipped his drink that he had no business drinking. He knew not to mix alcohol with his pain meds, but he needed to relax.

"Yeah, I got ya. I didn't mean anything by it. I j-just thought she was just one of your *girls*. I didn't know that you had a main chick now."

"She's not my main chick. She's my *only* woman, and you would do best to remember that."

Peter nodded without saying anything else. He sat back with a bewildered look on his face. Lorenzo looked around and noticed that their conversation hadn't been private. Several of his other employees had the same puzzled expressions.

Lorenzo knew that it wasn't the most professional way to handle an employee, but it was his business, so he didn't really give a shit.

Well, at least I don't have to make some big announcement about having a girlfriend.

CHASING DESIRES
by Kasey Martin

CHAPTER 11
CHASE

Chase really didn't like that asshole, Peter. She wasn't sure who the hell he thought he was, but she was definitely about to tell him about himself until Lorenzo asked her to leave. Chase wasn't sure what he was going to say to the beady-eyed little bastard, but if the look on Lorenzo's face was telling, the other man wasn't going to like whatever he said.

Chase decided that she would go to the ladies' room and freshen up her make-up before going to the bar. There was no reason for her to rush back, and maybe by the time she returned Peter would have a better attitude, or maybe he would be gone. *I can only hope.*

Chase was reapplying her lipstick when the restroom door opened and a petite, curvaceous, dark-haired woman sashayed in. Her purple dress was so low cut that her girls were practically spilling over the neckline. The woman sneered at Chase as she locked eyes with her in the mirror.

She had seen the same woman giving her the evil eye when she first walked into the VIP, but she was in a different section, so Chase paid her no mind because she obviously wasn't an employee. Chase continued to primp and stare back at the woman curiously.

"So I guess you're Lorenzo's latest."

It definitely was a statement and not a question, so Chase didn't bother responding.

"Just so you know, he always comes back to me *Mami*, so don't go gettin' your hopes up, sweetheart."

One corner of Chase's mouth turned up. *Meeting in the ladies' room* flitted across her mind, and she almost burst out laughing at the pathetic woman. She was way too grown to be arguing over a man in the bathroom of a club. *I wish the hell I would.*

"Did you hear me?" the woman questioned, putting her hands on her round hips as she cocked her head to the side with way too much attitude.

Chase did laugh then. Loud. "Girl, please, there's no need for you to warn me about anything. If he was yours, you wouldn't be in the bathroom stalking me to stake your claim."

"You must not know who I am?" The woman stepped closer to Chase.

Oh, okay, I'm going to have to show my ass in here tonight, Chase thought as she stepped toward the other woman, closing the gap between them and taking her by surprise. "No, *you* have it wrong. You don't know who the fuck *I* am." Chase

Chasing Desires
by Kasey Martin

wasn't extremely tall; she was average in height, standing five-foot-seven, but in her heels, she stood three inches taller, so she was towering over the other woman who had to be five-four even in heels.

Although the shorter woman took a step back, she still wasn't willing to back down. "Like I said, he will come back to me when he's had enough of you." She grinned wickedly.

"You have it wrong again, *Mami*. If he comes back to you, and I highly doubt that, it will be because *I'm* through with *him*."

The woman's smile faded slightly, but she waved her hand dismissively. "Whatever."

"Pathetic…" Chase laughed again as she snapped her clutch closed and walked around the pouting woman. If she were to continue this stupid conversation, it would only make her want to slap some sense into her, so she just left the bathroom without looking back.

When she emerged from the restroom, she was assaulted with the now familiar ocean blue gaze. Lorenzo was leaning against the wall. His tall, sinewy frame was draped in a tailored black suit with a crisp white shirt that was unbuttoned at the top. His hair was way longer than it had been when they'd first met. His curls were pushed out of his face and tucked behind his ears, but they almost reached the collar of his shirt.

Chasing Desires
by Kasey Martin

The smile he gave her would have taken her breath away if it would've come from any other guy. *Hell, who am I kidding? His smile does more than take my breath away.* Chase pressed her thighs together to try and relieve the now persistent ache Lorenzo had caused.

"What are you doing out here?" she asked.

"What does it look like? I'm waiting on my dear, sweet, *Pumpkin*. I can't stand to be without you for too long." He pulled Chase into a warm hug and nuzzled her neck.

She wasn't sure who he was putting on a show for because there weren't many people who would see them in the darkened hallway, but she felt her resistance slowly fading. Chase wrapped her arms around Lorenzo's neck and leaned back to look into his handsome face.

"What's this—"

The restroom door flung open, interrupting Chase. The same irritating woman from before stormed out.

She leered at Chase and narrowed her eyes before her pretty face brightened. She smiled at Lorenzo. Chase looked between him and the woman. Lorenzo's face remained perfectly impassive as if he had no idea who this person was.

"Hey, *Papi*! Long time. No see," the woman purred before she licked her lips provocatively.

Chasing Desires
by Kasey Martin

Chase removed her arms from around Lorenzo and she tried to take a step back so she could observe what was going on. However, Lorenzo wasn't having it. He pulled her closer to his side, wrapping his arm around her waist.

"Camilla," he said her name as if it put a foul taste in his mouth.

Interesting. Chase thought as she watched the overconfident woman deflate slightly before she regained her bravado. She had to give it to her. She had an uncanny ability to bounce back quickly.

"So that's it? After everything we have between us, you can barely speak to me?" she huffed as she crossed her arms under her ample bosom.

"All we have? Camilla, don't embarrass yourself. You know exactly what we *had*." Lorenzo narrowed his eyes at the brazen woman.

"Why are you acting this way? We have something good. You can't just throw all of this away," Camilla hissed, holding out her arms and waving her hands down her body to show everything she had to offer.

If this wasn't a job, Chase knew that she would've been long gone. She would never in her life had stood by and watched a lovers' quarrel, especially if she was supposed to be on a date. But this was a job, so she would stand there and

CHASING DESIRES
by Kasey Martin

watch this grown-ass woman fawn over a man who obviously didn't want her.

"I haven't dealt with you in almost a year, Camilla. So what game are you playing?"

"I'm not playin' a game, *Papi*. I just—"

"Where were you when I was in the hospital?" Lorenzo interrupted her before she could finish getting her words out.

Camilla looked shocked at first like she hadn't expected for him to ask that question, but she recovered quickly. "Aww, *Papi*, don't be mad that I couldn't visit you. I knew you would be fine. A big strong man like you would never go out like that."

Chase couldn't believe the audacity of some women. Here she was, mean mugging and following her to the bathroom to try and claim a man she didn't even bother to go see on his deathbed. *Damn shame.* Chase continued to watch the scene unfold with newfound disgust for the woman.

"Let me make a few things clear, Camilla," Lorenzo spat her name again. "This woman, *my woman* was by my side the entire time," he clarified, nodding towards Chase. "She is who I *have*, so I don't need what we *had*."

"Y-you don't really mean that, Lorenzo." Camilla actually looked sincerely hurt, but Chase had a feeling that the rejection was hurting her pride more than her feelings for Lorenzo.

"The fuck I don't," Lorenzo stated with finality.

He grabbed Chase's hand and practically dragged her behind him as he stormed past a sulking Camilla. Chase was fully aware that Lorenzo only said those things because of the case, but she couldn't help how hard and fast her heart was beating at his passionate words.

***

The rest of the night was uneventful. There weren't any other rude employees or crazy stalking exes anywhere. As a matter of fact, Chase was finally able to relax a little and actually enjoy herself. Although she was still getting stared down by random women, none of them dared to approach her.

There was also no sign of Tommy or Luis, but some of the girls they'd been seen with were milling around the club. The bouncers acted quickly to escort all of them out as discreetly as possible. Lorenzo seemed to be irritated by the women, but he didn't say much about what had happened.

They did help Chase prove her point that Tommy was making moves inside of Premier while Lorenzo recovered at home. But whatever he thought about the confirmed information, he didn't let it show much. It wasn't like he didn't know what Tommy was up to, but to see it with his own eyes was something totally different.

After the women were gone, Chase could feel a slight shift in Lorenzo's mood. He wasn't as talkative with everyone, and he looked as if he were in deep thought. She would ask him about it later, but for now, she decided she would stay quiet and continue to observe her surroundings.

After a few minutes, Lorenzo smiled with his eyes twinkling in amusement and asked, "Are you ready to go, *Sunshine*?"

"Nope, not that one either." Chase tried to scowl at him, but she couldn't help the smile that graced her face.

"Come on. I like *Sunshine*." He smiled wickedly at her.

She was glad that the mood seemed to lighten back up with their banter. She liked an easy-going Lorenzo. He wasn't this comfortable around her even before, when he'd had no idea that she was an agent. Then he spent weeks damn near cursing her very existence, so this witty word play between them felt nice.

"How 'bout you keep thinking on it and in the meantime, you just call me Chase."

"Nah. No fun in that." He laughed and then nodded toward the offices. "I need to go speak to Amber before we leave. Will you be okay here?"

Chasing Desires
by Kasey Martin

"Yeah, sure. I'm fine. You sure you don't want me to come with you?" she questioned. If he was going to speak to his assistant to check up on his business tonight, it might be some information she could use.

Lorenzo must've read what she was thinking in her expression because his face darkened slightly.

"I'm sure. This isn't about business, *Chase*. I just want to make sure Amber is okay."

He abruptly left, making the mood heavier than before. She knew that he was reminded of the case by her question, but she was ultimately there to take down his cousin. It was probably for the best that the flirting, kissing, and pet names ended for the night. Both of them seemed to have forgotten why they were really there in the first place.

Throughout the night, Chase had slowly forgotten herself again. The touching and teasing between them made her feel like she was on a real date, but she wasn't. She had to constantly remind herself that she was a professional and her fallen partner deserved justice. She had to tell herself she was doing all of this for him—Daniel Reyes.

After the big blow up with Mike after one of her dates with Lorenzo, she had to remember that it wasn't about her feelings. She was an agent first and she had a team depending

Chasing Desires
by Kasey Martin

on her to do a good job. She couldn't get caught up lusting over some man no matter how gorgeous he was.

Mike had been so angry that night and she couldn't believe the things he'd said to her, but in the end, he was partially right. She was getting too close to Lorenzo.

"Mike, what are you doing? You know you aren't supposed to be here so soon after a date, someone could be watching." Chase quickly pulled a red face Mike into her apartment.

"There's nobody watching you but the team, Chase. But I suspect you already know that."

"What the hell is that supposed to mean, Mike?"

"You know what the hell it means, Chase! I told you that you were getting too close to this guy and now you're dry humping him on your front porch! If you're trying to convince Angeletti that you're Moretti's girl, you win a fuckin' Oscar!" Mike shouted.

Chase knew that Mike had his reservations about the whole operation, but him yelling and cursing at her was unacceptable.

"Don't come into my house and fucking yell at me like I'm some child! I've told you before and I'll tell you again, I am an experienced federal agent. I know what the fuck I'm doing.

CHASING DESIRES
by Kasey Martin

I'm undercover and I will do what needs to be done!" Chase shouted, her face heated in anger and frustration.

"Oh yeah? What needs to be done, huh? Does that include sleeping with him?" Mike seethed as he stepped closer to Chase.

Before she knew it, her hand smacked him so hard that his face was blazing with her print. Mike stumbled back in shock, but he didn't say anything.

"Get out." Chase calmly stated. She'd be damned if anybody made her lose herself control.

Mike stormed out without another word, and that was the last time they talked to one another.

Chase sat alone sipping water as she tried to wipe the upsetting memory from her mind. She knew that Mike was there tonight, and it made her slightly worried about how he would react.

Chase casually observed the room around her as she waited for Lorenzo to return. Then out of nowhere, she saw a familiar purple dress. Chase assumed Camilla had left after the little confrontation in the bathroom, but she was wrong. Chase spotted the woman at the bar. She was sitting talking to the bartender when a man walked up behind her and leaned to whisper something in her ear.

Chasing Desires
by Kasey Martin

Chase could tell by Camilla's initial reaction that she didn't know the man. She leaned back and pursed her pink glossed lips and gave him the once over. Chase chuckled to herself. *Leave now, dude while you can. That one's bat-shit crazy.*

The man obviously didn't receive Chase's telepathic warning because he stayed and tried to talk to an unconvinced Camilla. Chase couldn't see the man's face clearly, but she could read by his body language that he wasn't about to give up on his quest.

When he waved the bartender over and flashed a big wad of cash, Camilla's whole demeanor changed. Her eyes lit up like a Christmas tree, she leaned in touching the man's arm, and the biggest Cheshire cat grin adorned her pretty face. The man seemed to be expecting the response as he wrapped an arm around her waist, and leaned in again.

Chase shook her head. *So easy.*

Chase continued to watch the couple in adverse amusement. Then the man handed Camilla a drink and turned to escort her off to God only knew where. When the couple turned and faced her, Chase got a good look at the clueless man she was beginning to feel sorry for. She nearly choked on her water.

Oh shit! Luis Castillo.

# CHASING DESIRES
by Kasey Martin

CHAPTER 12
MIKE

Mike sat back and watched the show Chase and Lorenzo were putting on. He just couldn't understand how somebody as intelligent as Chase could get so wrapped up in a guy like Lorenzo Moretti. He knew that she was supposed to convince everyone that was watching that they were a couple, but in Mike's opinion, she was going above and beyond what was professional. After the blow up at her apartment, he had kept his distance from her and the case. However, tonight they were shorthanded, so he stepped in to help out the team.

Mike knew that his feelings for Chase went beyond friendship, but he didn't want to jeopardize what they had. However, it seemed he did just that whenever he tried to warn her about Moretti. So he took it upon himself to dive deeper into this case. Being the computer genius that he was, he knew information that even Chase wasn't aware of. One thing he had found out was that Chase had taken a leave of absence. Mike could only assume that after she was given only four weeks to close her case, she decided to take matters into her own hands by temporarily leaving the bureau. He just didn't understand why she didn't tell him about it.

CHASING DESIRES
by Kasey Martin

Mike wasn't certain why she was hiding the fact that she wasn't officially working the case for the FBI anymore, but what he was certain of was that she was officially going too far with this whole Lorenzo thing.

After looking through Reyes' files with a fine-toothed comb, he found out some very disturbing information. Daniel Reyes was not who Chase thought he was, and the more he uncovered, the more worried about this whole thing he became.

"Hi there, handsome. You want some company?" a leggy woman with long blonde hair and bright green eyes sat down on the barstool beside him.

Mike gave her a sly once over, and he could tell by the quick glance that she was definitely *working*. "Nah, I'm good."

The blonde didn't seem to want to give up as she continued to stare at Mike without moving along. "If you're not looking for a good time, then why are you at a bar?"

Mike looked directly at the woman then. He thought that they had escorted all of Tommy's girls out of the club earlier, but obviously, they had missed this one. "I don't pay for pussy, sweetheart, so I suggest you move along."

The woman looked taken aback at Mike's bluntness. But he couldn't care less. How could a hooker be appalled by his crass words? Mike made sure to pay close attention to the

Chasing Desires
by Kasey Martin

woman because she was obviously smarter than the others that were tossed out before, if she was still here.

"I didn't ask you to pay for shit, asshole!" The blonde screeched in an annoying voice.

Mike wasn't buying her act. "You didn't have to. You're obviously in here working," Mike stated, looking at the woman's tight, low-cut red dress that left very little to the imagination. All she needed was a "For Sale" sign stamped on her somewhere.

"I'm not working. I'm just here to have a good time. You just looked like a guy that needed some fun. But it's clear why you're sitting by yourself. Dick!" the woman huffed as she gathered her purse, slid from the barstool, and marched off.

Mike chuckled and mumbled to himself, "She's got some spunk. I'll give her that."

Once the annoying woman left, Mike continued to observe Chase. He still didn't understand how being Moretti's girlfriend could get her close to Angeletti, especially if the two didn't have any contact. But nobody wanted to listen to logic, so Mike was here at Premier watching Chase's back even when he thought this was all an exercise in futility.

Mike tried his best to contain the groan that threatened to come out when he watched Moretti lean in and whisper in Chase's ear, and she damn near melted into a puddle against him. *She's so much better than that asshole,* Mike thought as he watched them in disgust.

Moretti eventually left the section and gave Mike a reprieve from having to watch the two of them together. His friend was past making mistakes. She was in too deep and he was going to have to be the one to close this case for her.

Mike watched as Joe, one of his team members, walked by him with a nod. It was protocol when they were in the field in a place like this to check in with one another. There were two more team members there as well.

Joe gave the signal that Chase was ready to move out, and then Mike saw when the plan changed. Luis Castillo walked in and started talking to a woman that was sitting right down the bar from him. After the last debriefing, Mike did some research on Luis Castillo. He was moving up in the Salazar Cartel, and although he and Tommy hadn't been seen together lately, when Tommy first got to Texas, Castillo was stuck to his side like a Siamese twin.

Mike gave the signal for the team to hold their positions. Mike discreetly moved down a couple of barstools to get closer to the conversation.

"Hola, *Mami*, you lookin' real fine tonight. Why would a beautiful woman like you be sittin' all by your lonesome?" Castillo used the lame line on the woman in a tight purple dress.

CHASING DESIRES
by Kasey Martin

Mike had to try extra hard not to groan out loud. *I hate bars.*

The woman looked him up and down, and turned to give the bartender her attention. She definitely wasn't interested in the corny lines he was throwing her way.

"Come on, baby, don't be like that. You too fine to be lookin' so mad," Castillo tried again. "Let me buy you a drink." He leaned in and whispered something that Mike couldn't hear, but whatever it was, she didn't protest. So it must not have been as lame as the other lines he'd thrown her way.

When Castillo pulled out a large wad of cash, Mike could see why the woman's mind changed. She smiled widely and rubbed her small hand down Castillo's arm.

Stupid woman. He'll have you turnin' tricks before the night is over. Mike shook his head. Some women couldn't see past money. He saw when Chase noticed that Luis Castillo was there. She wasn't obvious, but because Mike was watching her, he saw her eyes widen slightly in recognition.

Mike watched as Chase got up from the VIP section and walked to the back offices. He knew that she was going to tell Moretti that they had company. Mike wasn't sure if Angeletti and Castillo were aware that Moretti was there tonight, but he had to assume they knew because of the girls that were put out earlier.

Chasing Desires
by Kasey Martin

He continued to keep an eye on Castillo and his playmate. It didn't take much for him to finesse the woman. After about ten minutes on the dance floor whispering in her ear, he led her off to a VIP section in the back of the club.

Mike waited before he took a stroll around the club and headed in the same direction Castillo had taken the woman in. He knew that his team had his back because they were blending in effortlessly, but they were close enough to the situation if he needed their help.

He stopped when he saw the couple cozying up on a couch in a secluded section. He took a sip of his beer and stood at the perimeter of the dance floor. He saw the same tall blonde approach Castillo and sit down beside him. Castillo scowled at the woman and grabbed her by the upper arm before dragging her away from the section. Another man that Mike had noticed earlier walked up and took the woman's other arm, guiding her away from Castillo and out of the club.

Angeletti and Castillo had more people in Premier than the team was aware of. They would have to pull the surveillance video from tonight to try and get a good look at everyone that might be involved in their little prostitution ring.

***

LUIS

CHASING DESIRES
by Kasey Martin

"Crystal I told you to keep your ass at the bar and wait for Jose." Luis snarled out between clenched teeth as he dragged her out of the VIP section.

"I kn-know what you said, Luis." Crystal stuttered out flipping her long blonde hair over her shoulder. "I just came to warn you that this place is crawling with pigs."

"You think I'm stupid, bitch! I know what the fuck is going on around me." Luis waved over one of his men. He was really tired of dealing with whores that wouldn't do what the fuck they were told.

Luis saw the men walking around the club. They were obviously some sort of law enforcement, but he wasn't concerned. The girls that were escorted out were merely a distraction. Crystal however, was the girl that had the goods, and he couldn't have her getting caught up. He needed her to follow instructions, so they could get the product to his crew for distribution. Having that much cocaine on one person was bound to get somebody caught up, but she was the only girl available for the transport.

Now that he was finally getting the fine *Mami* he'd met earlier to loosen up, maybe he could put her into rotation, and have her moving product right alongside Crystal.

CHASING DESIRES
by Kasey Martin

Luis smiled deviously as he made his way back over to the woman he planned to make one of his best mules in the very near future.

***

MIKE

The next day, everyone was gathered at Jake's house for debriefing. After Mike noticed that there were more people involved that they weren't aware of, they decided it wouldn't be safe to meet in the offices.

Being overly cautious was something they were willing to do to make sure everyone's cover was safe. They knew that Tommy Angeletti knew who Jake was because of his involvement with helping capture Justin Russo, so it would be nothing for someone to stake out the offices and find out all the key players. Their identities were masked by mounds and mounds of fake profiles and paperwork. Anybody looking into J.C. Inc., would get a headache trying to figure out who worked there and what their role in the company actually was.

Jake's house was a super secure location that they often used. The gated community was highly secure, and anybody going in or out of the neighborhood was video recorded. To get into Jake's house was a whole other level of security, so if you weren't invited in, you wouldn't get in.

without his permission. It was now obvious to Sal that Tommy was trying to make up his own rules, and there was no way in hell he was going to let the little ingrate get away with defying his word. He was the head of the Angeletti family, and nobody crossed him, especially not his own son.

The call finally connected after several frustrating rings. "You told me everything would be taken care of in Dallas!" Sal shouted into the phone.

He had never been a man to shout and lose his temper. Before this mess, he'd had the power to just merely look at a man and things would get done. Not anymore.

"Things in Dallas are being taken care of. I told you that your son is up to his old ways. Nothing will come back on you, but you need to be patient.

"Fuck patient. If that little bastard is trying to take my place, I need to know. Immediately."

"Tommy is a lot of things, but I doubt suicidal is one of them. He's just trying to make a name for himself. There's no need to worry. Like I said things are being handled."

Sal slammed the phone down on his desk. He hated working with the smug bastard, but he had to admit that the man was a necessary evil because he was good at what he did. However, if he heard one more rumor about his son trying to take over the family, he would put an end to all of this shit himself. That was a promise.

CHAPTER 13
LORENZO

Lorenzo was happy to have something to focus on besides his recovery. With everything going on at Premier and with Chase's case, he didn't have time to worry about feeling bad. He finally had energy and felt useful for a change. He was starting to feel like his old self again.

He couldn't actually believe it, but Chase was right. Not just about his cousin moving in on his business, but about not settling in the depression that threatened to take him under. In all the weeks he had been recovering, she was the only one to notice that something was off with him. It happened when they were going over the details of her case and what he would be expected to do. She spoke up when she observed that he was hurting not just physically but mentally as well.

Chase looked him in the eyes and point blank asked, "How are you really doing?"

"I'm fine," Lorenzo stated not looking her in those chocolate orbs.

"I hear you saying that you're fine, but I can tell that there's something going on with you, Lorenzo," Chase insisted with worry coloring her features.

CHASING DESIRES
by Kasey Martin

Everyone always asked if he was alright, but not the way that she did. It was like she could see past his tough guy façade, and right into his soul. He needed to talk to someone, so it might as well be her.

"Recovery has been rough for me." Lorenzo sighed. "I just want to get back to how I used to feel and be useful again."

"Recovery can be difficult. Have you talked to anyone?" she asked softly in that raspy voice he loved to hear so much.

"Nah, I'm not a shrink kinda guy."

Chase smiled at him softly. He really liked when she smiled at him like that.

"You know, I had the same frame of mind as you once. I didn't think talking about how I felt was going to get me anywhere either, but it actually helped me. Being able to talk to someone about why I felt so helpless after my partner died helped me to cope. Believe me it's better than being full of rage and hopelessness."

"And now? You're not angry anymore?" he questioned.

"No, I'm still mad as hell." She chuckled. "I just know where to focus that energy now. You should think about seeing someone, but I'm here either way as a friend."

And just like that, he had let his guard down, and she slipped right in, making him forget that trusting her was something he couldn't do. Chase was capable of getting to

CHASING DESIRES
by Kasey Martin

Lorenzo in a way that no other woman ever had before. He was so comfortable around her, and playing the role of her man was something he could do without thought. That was why she was way more dangerous to him than his cousin could ever be.

When they were at Premier it was like they were on a real date. They laughed and talked so effortlessly that it was easy for him to forget the reason they were there. Then she reminded him of who she was by asking about his business. The comment made the fantasy of the evening crash around him in a blink of an eye.

It would do me good if I never forget who I'm dealing with. Lorenzo shook his head at himself. He couldn't believe that he had almost let Chase suck him back into her web. He knew that she was only there for her case. It was a job for her. *He* was a job for her.

Lorenzo understood that he was in too deep to turn back, but he would bide his time and keep his head on straight until he got both her and his good-for-nothing cousin out of his life. But for now, he would do what he had to do, which was take his ass to the doctor. And although he was against it, Chase was going to accompany him there.

He could've gone alone and he didn't think it was necessary for her to go with him. But after she'd spotted Luis Castillo at Premier, she was convinced that he had seen the two of them together. So she was certain that Tommy would be keeping a closer eye on him since he now knew that Lorenzo was well enough to be out and about.

His cell phone chimed, letting him know that Chase was there and on her way upstairs. A short two minutes later, he heard two knocks on the door before he opened it. And there she was, standing there looking lovely as ever.

"Hey, *Honeybunches*." She winked as she sauntered past him and into his house.

"I still like *Pumpkin* better. I think I'll stick with that." He grinned playfully.

"Yeah, well, that's your nickname for me that I still don't like by the way. And anyway, you need a nickname too." She laughed lightheartedly before asking with a smile, "You ready to go?"

"I am. You sure you want to go with me? I mean, you don't really need to."

"I told you Castillo saw us together, Lorenzo, and if he didn't know who I was before, he certainly does now with all the canoodling we were doing the other night."

"Yeah, but this is real life, Chase. You don't have to go to the doctor with me. It wouldn't affect your case or your cover if you weren't seen with me at my appointment."

CHASING DESIRES
by Kasey Martin

"I know this is real life, Lorenzo. I'm a real-life human woman with emotions and feelings, so you don't have to treat me like I'm some robot," she stated on a sigh. "We're working together closely, and I would like for us to at least try to be friends."

He looked at her wearily. He didn't want to trust this woman, but when she said things like that he couldn't help but want to be her friend. *Hell, who am I kidding? I want to be more than friends. I'm definitely going to regret this*, he thought as he ran his hand through his long hair. *I still need a haircut*, he thought absently.

"I like your hair like that."

"What?" Lorenzo questioned, his face twisted in confusion.

"I noticed you keep running your hands through your hair like it bothers you. I like it that length. It looks good on you." She gave him a small smile.

Chase was far too observant, and he would have to remember that about her. He had to constantly remind himself that he wasn't dealing with some ordinary chick. No, Chase was a trained FBI agent, and she was definitely extraordinary.

"Thanks," Lorenzo finally mumbled. "Let me get a jacket, so we can head out."

CHASING DESIRES
by Kasey Martin

She nodded and placed her hands in her back pockets of her tight jeans. He sighed again. She wasn't even aware that that little move thrust her beautiful breasts out so perfectly that he wanted to attack her right there. He would never be able to control his urges around her if he didn't get his head in the game. *This is a job for her. I am a job to her.*

He kept repeating the words over and over again like a mantra, but the more he said them, the less he actually believed them. *Shit! How am I going to do this?*

***

They were seated in the waiting room of the doctor's office when Lorenzo noticed a guy trying way too hard not to be seen. *Amateur*. He couldn't believe his cousin would send a guy that was so obvious about what he was doing. *Tommy's losing his edge being in the South. He would've never sent somebody that stood out so easily if he were still in Jersey.*

Lorenzo leaned over and nuzzled Chase's neck, so that he could whisper in her ear. He was sure that he could've just told her what he'd seen without being so extra, but he had to admit that it was a bonus to get to touch her when he wanted and how he wanted when they were in public at least. He was pretty sure she would slap him if he tried kissing her in private.

Chase arched an eyebrow at him and leaned back to gaze at his face. He loved her beautiful almond shaped eyes and how expressive they were. He knew that she wanted to know what he was up to without asking out loud.

"You were right. We have company," Lorenzo whispered, his lips grazing the shell of her ear. He could've sworn she shuddered, but he could see that she worked hard to hide any reaction to him.

Chase took a small look around the waiting area and cocked her head to the side. She looked at him and winked. "I clocked him ten minutes ago when he followed us in from outside. Tall white guy with the brown jacket?" she whispered back, tickling his ear with her breathy response.

It was Lorenzo's turn to shudder. He quickly took a deep breath to cover his body's response. He had to give it to her; she was a better agent than he initially thought. He nodded. "Yep."

"Mr. Moretti, the doctor will see you now," the nurse called from behind the sliding glass window.

"That's us. Come on, *Pumpkin.*" Lorenzo smiled as he tugged a scowling Chase from her chair and led her through the examination door.

The doctor told them mostly good news. Lorenzo was healing just fine, but the doctor suggested that he start a regular exercise routine and continue his healthy eating to help the process. He also told him that the residual pain he was feeling could be caused by stress, and that he should try to relax more and not rely so much on the pain medication. Other than that, everything seemed to be improving. His range of motion was getting better, and he wasn't experiencing the shortness of breath as often as before.

He observed Chase listening intently to everything the doctor said. She even asked a couple of questions and had a few suggestions that the doctor agreed with her on. He wasn't sure why she was going through all the trouble, but he realized he was grateful that she was there. Yes, he could've come to the doctor on his own, but having someone else there that was concerned for him was a relief.

He caught Chase's eye, and she smiled at him and patted his hand. *Maybe she was right. Maybe we can be friends.* Lorenzo could feel his walls crumbling down even more, and there wasn't much he could do about it.

When they left the doctor's office, their little spy was still there as obvious as ever. *There was no way my cousin hired this fool. He has to be Castillo's man.* Lorenzo shook his head as he held Chase's hand as they walked to the waiting car. Lorenzo hadn't driven since he was released from the hospital because he wanted to make sure that he was completely healed, and the doctor hadn't released him to drive yet.

They slid in the back of the blacked-out SUV, still holding hands. Lorenzo knew that it was for the benefit of whoever was watching, but he couldn't help the comfort he got from holding Chase's soft, delicate hand.

"I'm really glad that you were able to come with me today. Thank you," Lorenzo admitted with a smile.

Chase smiled shyly. "It's really not a big deal, Lorenzo. Like I said, I want us to be friends."

Lorenzo nodded. He decided to stop fighting against his instincts. The betrayal was still there, but he knew what he was getting himself into this time. His eyes were wide open.

He pulled Chase towards him, and she was stiff against his side before she finally sighed and relaxed slightly. She looked up at him with questions covering her face.

"We need to practice to keep up appearances, *Pumpkin*." His mouth twitched into a half smile.

She chuckled. He knew the excuse was lame at best, but he didn't care. He was a man that went all in when he made his mind up about something and his mind was made up about Chase. She wasn't *just* going to be his friend; she was going to be much more than that.

Lorenzo felt like they had something special when they were first getting to know each other. That connection was real and the chemistry they shared wasn't something that could be faked no matter what her job may have been.

Chasing Desires
by Kasey Martin

"You know, at some point, you're going to have to meet with Angeletti." Her statement broke through the quiet cabin of the vehicle.

"I figured," he stated simply.

Chase turned to fully face him. "In order for any of this to be worth it, we have to get Tommy in your club. He has to be around in order for us to get evidence on him. Otherwise, we are doing all of this for nothing."

"I understand what you're saying, Chase, but I can't have hookers running rampant through my establishment. It could damage my reputation beyond repair, and I just can't take that risk."

Before they could finish their conversation, they arrived back at Lorenzo's place. They decided to continue the discussion once they were in the safe confines of his home. As they walked through the lobby of his high-rise complex, he noticed another man discreetly eyeing them. He was much more cautious than the other noticeable guy, but Lorenzo was still able to spot him.

Chase had been right yet again. They were being trailed everywhere even in his building where you had to go through a background check just to get in the damn lobby. He couldn't believe the boldness of Tommy to send someone to his home. It was time to get this ball rolling, and get Chase what she needed. It was time to meet with his cousin.

But first things first. Lorenzo had to get what *he* needed—*Chase*.

CHAPTER 14
CHASE

Chase followed Lorenzo through the lobby and up to his apartment. She felt the shift in their situation in the doctor's office. She could finally admit, at least to herself, that she cared about Lorenzo as more than just a means to an end. He had become a friend, and someone she didn't want to see hurting and in pain. She didn't want to see him going through his recovery alone, and if she could help it, he would no longer have to.

The conversation they'd had in the car just showed that they still needed to get on the same page when it came to how to handle Angeletti, but at least they seemed to be in agreement when it came to their new formed friendship.

However, the heated looks they exchanged and the electricity she felt when they touched made her feel more than friendly toward him. She would have to be blind not to see how handsome he was.

He could make the smallest of movements like running his hands through his curly hair, and it would make her heart rate increase. His subtle touches and whispers made her want to melt.

CHASING DESIRES
by Kasey Martin

They got into the elevator still holding hands. He was unconsciously making small circles with his thumb on her hand. Goosebumps were breaking out on her skin, and she tried to take deep breaths to calm down. The throbbing between her legs was not helping her commitment to fight her attraction.

However, she would stay focused. She would make sure that when they entered the apartment, they would finish discussing Angeletti and she would leave.

Chase took a deep breath as they reached his door. When he unexpectedly tugged her inside, she fell against him, catching herself on his broad chest. Her hands fisted in his sweater, she looked up into his stormy gaze, and she knew they were not going to be continuing a conversation. He pushed her back against the wall with her hands instantly grabbed his bulging biceps. He caged her in with his arms and a deep growl left his throat. His aggressiveness caught her off guard and her eyes widened.

She dropped her arms to her side and she stammered, looking at him in shock. "I-I'm sorry. I lost my balance."

His mouth lifted in a slow sensual smile, and when he leaned in, she placed her hands on his chest. She could feel his torso rise and fall rapidly under her palms. She started to remove her hands when he stopped her. He placed his large, calloused hand over her soft delicate one.

Chasing Desires
by Kasey Martin

"Don't." The one word held so much meaning that she felt herself shiver in response. Chase knew that if she didn't stop whatever was happening between them, they would go past the point of no return. But she couldn't seem to get her body and heart to cooperate with her common sense.

"Lorenzo, I—" before she could protest, he captured her lips in the sweetest kiss she had ever experienced. It was soft and tender and it stole her breath right from her body. They had kissed many times before, and all of them had been breathtaking in their own way, but this kiss was different. This kiss was all knowing, it was soul searing, it was heart-stopping and passionate. This kiss could very well end her resolve.

He made love to her mouth softly, seductively nibbling on her lips until she sighed and opened up for him. Lorenzo took advantage and immediately deepened the kiss. He ravished her mouth as their tongues danced with one another. Every thought went out of her head as her body heated with every pent-up desire she held for this man.

He wrapped his strong, muscular arms around her waist, and they tightened like hard corded elastic bands as he drew her in closer to his body. Chase couldn't help but whimper in response. Her senses were on overload, his spicy scent was surrounding her, and his sweet taste was invading her mouth with every flick of his tongue.

CHASING DESIRES
by Kasey Martin

How could I ever survive this gorgeous specimen? How could I care so much about someone so wrong for me? How could I possibly stop this when it feels so damn good? The questions plagued her mind as she continued to drown in his wonderful exploration of her mouth.

He moaned as his hands wandered down her slender frame to grip her ass in a tight hold. The move snapped Chase out of the foggy, lustful haze. She backed up quickly, putting some much-needed distance between the two of them.

"Lorenzo, we should stop," Chase breathlessly warned. She wanted to be upset at herself because she knew better. She was a professional and she had a job to do even if she wasn't officially on the case anymore. She still owed it to her fallen partner to get him justice for his untimely death. She knew that she had no business being with this man outside of work. However, with all of those things she carried on her shoulders, she still couldn't bring herself to feel guilty about them kissing, or about her growing feelings for Lorenzo Moretti.

"No, we shouldn't stop." Lorenzo closed the distance that she put between them, wrapped his arms back around her waist, and pulled her back against his muscled chest. He looked deep into her eyes before bending down and softly pecking her lips. "But *I* will stop for you."

Chasing Desires
by Kasey Martin

He pulled back from her slightly and released his tight hold on her waist, but he still didn't completely let her go.

He shook his head, seemingly having an internal battle before continuing, "Chase, I know you feel this thing between us. Even with everything we've been through…" He trailed off and ran his right hand through his long curly hair.

Chase felt exactly what he did, and even though she might finally be ready to admit it to herself, she definitely wasn't ready to admit it to him.

"We need to keep things professional between us. Things are complicated enough." She was pleading for him to understand, and cut her some slack.

Lorenzo shook his head vehemently. "No!"

Well, shit! Chase thought as she nervously rubbed her earlobe.

"Things are already complicated, so it can't get any worse. Right?" Lorenzo smirked.

Chase untangled herself from his arms and wrinkled her brows in confusion and frustration. "There are so many flaws in that statement that I don't know where to start."

"Listen to me." Lorenzo paused, seemingly to gather his thoughts before continuing. "I know you feel something. *I know* you do. And believe me when I tell you I know exactly how fucked up this situation between us is. But when it's me and

CHASING DESIRES
by Kasey Martin

you alone like this, I don't want to fight this. Not when it's just *us*."

Chase took a moment to consider his words. It had been so long since she let herself have something. She always followed the rules and always went by the book. She was always the straight arrow. *And just where did any of that get me?*

She was working to avenge her late partner and she had to leave the job she had devoted her life to, in order to do it. Although she had J.C. Inc. to back her up, she was basically alone in the world and she was tired of being alone. She was tired of running from this man. She was just tired. So she decided that she would do something for herself just this once. *I hope I don't regret this.* She smiled mischievously and threw her arms around his neck and kissed him with all the pent-up passion she'd been feeling.

***

Chase must've taken him by surprise because Lorenzo stumbled slightly before he caught her and wrapped his strong arms back around her body tightly. He kissed her back, matching her passionate display with his own.

"Maybe we—" he breathed out, but she cut off his words by thrusting her tongue back in his mouth.

CHASING DESIRES
by Kasey Martin

She was done with talking. She was done with overthinking. She. Was. Done.

"No more talking!" Chase's kisses became more aggressive in her resolve to finally have this man. Lorenzo had been on her mind and in her system since they met. It was time to do something about it.

Chase had pushed down her wants and needs for her job. She had thrown herself into work, and now it was time to take something back for herself, no matter how wrong it may have been. At that moment, she just couldn't bring herself to care about the consequences.

Lorenzo took over the kiss, and her body was on fire. He pushed her up against the wall and pinned her with his body. She was deliciously trapped under his hard, muscular physique, and she thought she would go insane from his touches.

She moaned when he tore his lips away from hers and started to trail nips and licks down her neck and onto her collar bone.

"So sweet," he whispered huskily as he continued to kiss down one side and up the other. He licked her chin, and sucked her bottom lip into his mouth.

Chase couldn't think straight. All she wanted to do was get out of her clothes as fast as humanly possible, so she could feel his heated skin against hers. She tugged at his V-neck

Chasing Desires
by Kasey Martin

sweater, and he pulled it over his head, leaving his curls in wild disarray.

His breathing was ragged, and the fire she saw in the depths of his eyes made her womanhood weep with joy. He peeled off his undershirt before reaching for her and stripping off her top. It left her standing there in just jeans and a purple, lacy bra. More of her hair had fallen from her ponytail, and Chase knew she must look a wanton mess. However, she didn't care because all she wanted was him.

Lorenzo softly tugged the band from around her hair and rubbed his hands through it. He then grabbed it tightly and pulled her head back. He growled out his approval, and she gasped in response to his aggressiveness. She loved a take-charge man. It had been such a long time since she last had an intimate encounter, that she was almost too eager and her raging overheated body was actively reminding her of that fact.

Chase was never really a relationship kind of girl because of her focus on her career, but she did have a date here and there to satisfy her needs. But it had still been several months, so she had to calm herself down before she came off as desperate.

They managed to make it to his bedroom, shedding their clothing along the way. Neither one seemed to want to break the

CHASING DESIRES
by Kasey Martin

connection, so they kissed and fondled each other until they fell naked upon his massive king size bed.

Chase's nipples were extremely hard and almost excruciatingly so. But Lorenzo didn't seem to notice because he slowly rolled her hardened tip slowly with his finger and thumb while sucking the other one in his warm mouth.

Chase moaned her appreciation as she thrust her breasts into his face so that he could take her deeper in his mouth.

He willingly complied, lavishing one breast with attention from his skillful mouth and the other with his sinful touch. She thrashed her head from side to side as her body started to strum from the delightful sensations he was causing.

He moaned when she dragged her nails down his muscular back. She felt his large body shudder as he wedged himself between her thick thighs and began to grind his hardness along her dripping wet slit.

They both groaned long and hard when he thrust his rock-hard steel into her hot waiting passage. He began to rock within her when he suddenly stopped.

"Shit! I'm so sorry, Chase," Lorenzo said breathlessly. "Hold on a second, sweetheart." He pulled out of her agonizingly slow.

Chase was confused at first until Lorenzo rolled over and pulled a foiled package from his bedside table. She was

Chasing Desires
by Kasey Martin

losing it. Chase hadn't even realized that they hadn't been using protection, she was so worked up and ready for action that the last thing she thought about was condoms.

She rolled her eyes at her irresponsible actions. She had never done anything like that before in her life. Lorenzo had her all discombobulated, she was acting so out of character, but she just couldn't seem to stop herself.

It was like she was outside of her body watching another person do things that she knew was wrong. Instead of preventing the inevitable train wreck from happening, she sat and watched helplessly, waiting for the crash to come.

After what seemed like forever, he had the latex rolled down over his enormous erection. He moved back between her thighs and pushed himself all the way to the hilt. They moaned in unison at the connection.

Chase's legs were already trembling as she tried to compose herself. The weight of his body on hers as he moved within her quivering walls was like heaven. She lifted her pelvis up to take him in deeper.

"Shiiiit…" Lorenzo growled as he began to pump into her at a steady rhythm.

The only sounds that could be heard were their pants, groans, and their bodies writhing together, composing a symphony of lustful music.

Chasing Desires
by Kasey Martin

"Oh my Gawd, Lorenzo! Shit…so fuckin' good," Chase panted out between each dominant thrust of his hips.

What the fuck have I gotten myself into? It was the last thought that flitted across her mind before the first powerful orgasm wracked her body.

CHAPTER 15
LORENZO

Chase groaned as her quivering walls sucked him in deeper into bliss. The feeling was heavenly, and Lorenzo wasn't sure how much longer he could suppress the orgasm that beckoned him. He pushed into her body over and over again with mindless recklessness. He fucked her like it was the last time he would ever have sex in his life. He had no idea how he had gotten so lucky. It was just earlier that day, when Lorenzo thought that if he so much as tried to kiss her in private she might castrate him. Now, he was balls deep in the sweetest woman he'd ever had. And the feeling was exquisite.

Lorenzo wanted the feeling to never end, so he slowed down his pace. In fact, he thought he should probably take his time because he wasn't sure if she would wake up tomorrow and regret this, so he had to do his best to make it last.

He bent down and sucked her breast and its hardened chocolate tip into his hot, wet mouth. She tasted so deliciously sweet. He couldn't get enough of her decadent figure, so he kept running his tongue up and down every dip and curve of her body that he could reach. He licked, sucked, and nibbled at her like a man possessed.

Chasing Desires
by Kasey Martin

"Oh shit! Yes! Fuck me, Lorenzo… ugh… umm... Fuck me!" Chase moaned out in ecstasy. Her passionate pleas were making him feel ten feet tall.

Lorenzo knew that he was a good lover; hell, maybe even a great one. He'd had absolutely no complaints in that department. As a matter of fact, women often chased him down just to get a taste. But Chase was different. There was something about the sounds she made, the way she responded to his touch, and the beautiful expressions on her face that had him feeling like the best lover ever.

She was the one woman that he wasn't supposed to have or want. But that's what made it that much more pleasurable. It was the fact that she was forbidden to him that made him long for her. He didn't want to think about any of the other reasons that went far deeper than that. He just kept telling himself that forbidden fruit is always the sweetest.

He no longer worried about trusting her, and betrayal be damned. He was going to keep her in his bed for as long as he could or at least until this whole thing with his cousin was finished. Then when she got what she wanted, and left to go back to her life as a Fed, he would go back to his life as well and not look back. *Yes, that's exactly what I will do.*

Chase's curvy body started to tremble beneath him as her tight cavern squeezed the life out of his now pulsating cock.

CHASING DESIRES
by Kasey Martin

The sensation brought him out of his thoughts and back to the present. He wondered how in the hell he could be so distracted while he was experiencing some of the best loving he had ever had. The thought made him realize just how messed up his head truly was.

She moaned out incoherently and wrapped her legs tighter around his waist, and he thought he was going to have to start reciting baseball stats to keep from orgasming right then.

"Damn, baby, shit!" he groaned loudly as he pushed off of Chase and rolled them over. He had to switch positions to make sure not to blow too soon.

She was now straddling his body, his cock still nestled deep within her dripping wet channel. Chase began to slowly move her hips in a circular motion. She leaned down, and placed her hands on either side of his head. He noticed that she was very conscious of his chest wound, and she kept her hands away from his still sensitive scar.

Lorenzo pumped upwards faster and faster until he was pounding into her like a man crazed. He was very aware that he could possibly be overexerting himself, but the feel of her honeyed warmth was so worth it.

Chase's body started with a light sway, her movements started to get more and more erratic with each surge of his steel rod into her willing heat. Her moans became louder, and the sound of her ass slapping his thighs became more and more pronounced.

She made a wailing sound, and the tell-tale signs of her impending orgasm started with her quivering walls. He knew that she was close and he couldn't hold out his release any longer. It was pure torture to feel and watch her beautiful body come apart around him, and he not able to fill her with his seed.

I mean the condom, not her. No babies are needed between us. Lorenzo wondered why in the hell he was thinking about Chase having his baby when he should've only been thinking about getting his.

Shit! She feels so fucking magnificent!

Lorenzo slowed down again, and turned them over, so that he was back on top. He spread her legs wide as he started to grind into her seductively. With each roll of his hips he rubbed against her hard, throbbing clit. He put one hand between them and pinched her swollen bud.

"Cum!" he commanded.

She shattered beneath him, screaming her release as her body shook almost violently. He ground his teeth together and rode the wave of her orgasm for as long as he could before he drove his massive cock deep into her and held it to the hilt as he pumped the condom full of his seed.

Chasing Desires
by Kasey Martin

"Uggghhh! Hell yeah, Chase!" He roared as his orgasm wracked through his body leaving him spent.

He rolled to the side so he wasn't crushing her as he tried to slow down his breathing. After a moment, he pulled the condom off his softening member. He got up and disposed of the latex, crawled back into the bed, and pulled her close to his body. It was still early evening, and they hadn't had anything to eat. But he figured when they woke from their nap, they could have dinner and finally have a much-needed conversation.

***

When he woke about two hours later, Lorenzo was in the bed alone. He rolled over and looked around, turning on the bedside lamp.

"Shit!" he exclaimed sitting up fully in his bed. He looked around the room, shaking his head. "I knew I shouldn't have gone to sleep," he mumbled, his voice strained with regret.

"What's that? Are you talking to yourself, Love Muffin?" Chase smirked as she came bounding out of the bathroom looking like a wonderfully disheveled goddess. Her ponytail was no more. Her hair was all over her head in wild waves. Her naked body had a wonderful glow under the soft light of the bedside lamp.

He didn't want to explain why it felt as if a giant weight had instantly lifted from his chest with the mere sight of her beautiful, brown, radiant skin, but as soon as he saw her, he sat back against the headboard and immediately relaxed.

He rubbed a hand over the stubble on his jaw, and his handsome face broke out into a wide smile that reached his eyes and crinkled at the corners. He was so glad that she didn't sneak out while he was asleep. If she had, then he knew that they would never get to discuss what was happening between them.

"Are you hungry?" he questioned. He wasn't going to address the fact that he was indeed talking to himself. He would simply pretend that he didn't have a slight panic attack when he thought she was gone.

She narrowed her eyes, and then shrugged her shoulders before replying, "I could eat."

"Good. Let's shower first, and I can order us something."

She nodded, but she didn't comment, or continue to try and push him to answer her questions.

Forty-five minutes and a very sexy shower later, the two were sitting in his living room waiting on the Chinese food to arrive. They were relaxed, but he knew that the mood was about to shift when she took a deep breath and turned to look directly at him. He noticed she did that a lot, especially if what she was about to say was something he didn't want to hear.

Chasing Desires
by Kasey Martin

"How do you want to handle Tommy?" she questioned with a serious expression.

"What do you mean by *handling* him?" he asked with his forehead puckered as he pressed his lips together in a thin line.

"Well, you said you didn't want his girls in your club because you were worried about your reputation, so how am I supposed to get evidence if he's not there?"

"I can call a meeting with him and you can set up some kind of sting operation outside of my club."

Chase nodded. "I guess that might work. We can still keep surveillance going in Premier, but I think it's probably a good idea to set some up at Prime as well."

Lorenzo agreed. His new club wasn't getting the tender loving care it should have. It was open but he hadn't had a grand opening just yet. He was waiting to be back to himself and working full time before he planned one.

"I think we need to get on that ASAP. I can call Jake and have him set something up," Lorenzo responded.

"Okay and I will talk to Mike and see if he can get the technology set up," Chase said.

Lorenzo didn't react outwardly at the mention of Mike's name, but he wanted to snarl, pound his fists against his chest, and tell Chase to stay the hell away from him.

CHASING DESIRES
by Kasey Martin

Mike Thatcher made it no secret that he didn't like Lorenzo, and no matter how much he tried to hide it, Lorenzo knew that he had a thing for Chase. She may have thought that Thatcher was a good friend, but Lorenzo knew better. The man wanted Chase and he wanted Lorenzo out of the way.

When Lorenzo looked up, Chase's eyes were narrowed at him. "What?"

"Don't what me, Moretti. At the mention of Mike's name, you tensed like a snake ready to strike."

Shit. He kept forgetting who he was dealing with. Chase was trained to observe everything around her even if she didn't make it obvious. He definitely had to watch himself more carefully.

"I don't like Thatcher. And you know that he expresses his dislike for me every chance he gets. I'm not going to apologize for my past. I'm not a criminal. I run an upstanding and legal business, and I think it would be wise if he was nowhere near this case."

"I understand what you're saying, but Mike is an important part of our team. He's also a professional and he won't let his personal feelings, no matter what they are, get in the way of helping me close my case."

Lorenzo knew better than that. She could try to sell that bullshit to somebody else. Mike Thatcher would stop at nothing to sabotage him. Lorenzo was no fool. Once he'd found out that Chase was working with Jake's company, he'd had his own private investigator do a check on the members of the Inc. team.

His PI may not have had a whole team of ex-special ops guys, but Marco Bellomi was the best at what he did. Lorenzo knew Marco from back East.

Lorenzo had also contacted Marco about Tommy, but he had some urgent matters he was dealing with, so he wasn't able to immediately get back with him. Lorenzo was hopeful that he would get back with him soon, so his involvement in this whole mess could be minimized.

Marco, however, was able to get him information on everyone else, and the one that stood out from the rest was Mike Thatcher. While everyone else was trying to catch Tommy, Marco found out that Mike was digging into his past.

"I don't trust Mike Thatcher no matter how much you vouch for him," Lorenzo finally answered.

There was absolutely nothing that would convince him that Mike Thatcher had anything but ill intentions toward him. *Nothing.*

Chase sighed and nodded. Then she tensed slightly, and he knew what was coming.

"What a-about this?" she stammered slightly, waving her hand between the two of them.

CHASING DESIRES
by Kasey Martin

"This," he said, copying her gesture, waving his hands. "It stays between us."

She looked at him wide-eyed but relaxed slightly. "Okay, but what does that mean?"

"That means I understand that you're a professional and I know how it may look with us being together. Outside, we pretend. Inside, we don't."

He grabbed her and pulled her close to him. She leaned in and kissed his lips softly before snuggling close to his body.

He was relieved that they didn't have to have a long, drawn-out conversation about feelings and what sleeping together meant because honestly, he just wasn't that type of guy. He wasn't a new-aged man that showed his sensitivity or talked about love. He was old school. Lorenzo was a man of action, and he would continue to show Chase just how he felt with his body.

CHAPTER 16
MIKE

Mike looked at his watch for what seemed like the millionth time since he got off the plane. Showing up unannounced was the only way he would be able to have this meeting. He had to catch the man off guard. If he scheduled a meeting, there would be too much time for him to prepare, and Mike needed to get some real answers.

He'd pulled a lot of strings and cashed in a lot of favors to even get to see him, but he knew it would pay off. It just had to!

"Mr. Thatcher, Agent Worthington will see you now," the female agent who acted as a secretary finally addressed him. She showed no emotion, and she acted like he hadn't been sitting there staring daggers at her for keeping him waiting.

Mike kept his cool because he knew that it was all to show who had the upper hand. The games the Feds played were merciless; they wanted to make sure you knew at all times who was in charge. He'd waited for two hours to get in to see Worthington, but he would be damned if he was leaving before he got a chance to talk to him. He had too many questions, and

Chasing Desires
by Kasey Martin

all of his trails led to one person, Senior Special Agent John Worthington.

Mike strode in with confidence as he came face to face with Worthington. The man stood tall with broad shoulders and a slathering of salt-and-pepper hair covering his head. He had a fierce expression on his tan face, and a no-nonsense stance. Mike knew that this task was not going to be easy. But he hadn't come all the way to New Jersey for nothing.

"Mr. Thatcher. Why may I ask are you here?" Worthington cut right to the point. Mike could respect that, and he was glad he wouldn't have to dance around before getting what he needed.

"I'm here about Agent Chase Johnson, sir."

"I see. Have a seat, young man." Worthington nodded toward a chair located on the opposite side of his massive desk. Mike saw a flash of concern on the man's face before he covered it with a blank expression. He'd seen Chase do the same thing a million times before.

This is definitely not going to be easy. Mike took his seat, and tried to mentally prepare himself for the maze of questions he would have to wade through in order to get the answers that he needed.

Once they were both seated, Worthington took a deep breath, his mask firmly back in place and questioned, "Why are you asking about Agent Johnson?"

"I know that she is under your command, and she's investigating Tommy Angeletti."

"That's classified information, son. And as far as I know, there isn't an agent by the name of Michael Thatcher, so if Agent Johnson is out there giving away classified information, then we have a major problem on our hands."

Okay, so the old man is trying to play hardball. Mike set his mouth in a hard line because he knew that Worthington was bluffing his ass off. He knew that she had gotten special permission to work with J.C. Inc. when the agency told her they didn't have the resources to help her, and Worthington knew it too.

"*We* don't have a problem, sir. I'm sure you already know who I am, so I won't insult my intelligence or yours by pretending you don't. You know how I came to have the information and you know Agent Johnson is not selling FBI secrets."

Worthington didn't say anything, but his mask of indifference stayed firmly in place.

"So again I ask, why you are here, son?" Worthington finally spoke, his voice was full of exasperation.

Chasing Desires
by Kasey Martin

"I want to know where Daniel Reyes is." Mike got straight to his point. Worthington's mask slipped, and Mike knew that he had hit the nail on its head by asking about Reyes. He knew that it would throw Worthington off his game.

"You said you were here about Agent Johnson, so why are you asking about Daniel Reyes?" Worthington's hazel eyes narrowed at Mike and his posture had gone from relaxed to rigid in a matter of seconds.

"Agent Johnson is investigating the death of her partner, and she is convinced Tommy Angeletti had something to do with it," Mike nonchalantly stated. He was watching Worthington closely, reading every tick and tense of his body. And Mike could see that the Senior Agent knew way more than even he initially thought.

"And you're not convinced?" Worthington asked, his body still tense.

Mike shook his head, his shaggy blonde hair slightly falling into his face. "Angeletti didn't kill Reyes."

Worthington leaned in, cupping his hands together and leaning his chin to rest on them. Mike could tell that he was having a hard time fighting his emotions, however Mike didn't understand why that was. He needed to see just how much Worthington was involved in this.

CHASING DESIRES
by Kasey Martin

"I've been telling Ch—" Worthington stopped short of saying her first name. "I've been telling Agent Johnson, that if the evidence wasn't there, then she should stop trying to make someone guilty."

Mike nodded. "I agree, but that's not the reason. The lack of evidence has nothing to do with it. I *know* Tommy Angeletti didn't kill Daniel Reyes."

That seemed to get Worthington's attention. "And just how do you know he didn't if you don't have the evidence to prove otherwise?"

"I *know* just like you that Tommy Angeletti didn't kill him because Daniel Reyes isn't dead."

***

TOMMY

"Putting that tail on Lorenzo was brilliant. He had a lot to report back." Tommy finally saw all of his hard work pay-off. Since Lorenzo had been out of commission, it was easy for Tommy to make the moves he needed, now that Lorenzo was out and about, he wanted to ensure his cousin stayed out of his way.

"The tail gave us some useful information. It seems like your Primo has gotten himself a main chick, and *Mami* is beautiful as hell. I think he's plenty distracted."

Chasing Desires
by Kasey Martin

"Yes, it's the same girl from before. So what did we find out about this woman?" Tommy questioned.

"Her name is Chase Sanders, and it seems your cousin is very taken with her. They've been everywhere together. Even the hot little number I picked up had a lot to say about her."

"Oh yeah, anything useful?" Tommy was intrigued; it wasn't often that the women Luis picked up were good for more than a quick lay, or maybe a trick or two.

"Yeah, she whined all night about how Lorenzo had passed her up for some black bitch. Camilla is cute, but she aint got nothin' on that hot chocolate piece of ass your cousin was with."

Tommy nodded again. "Good. So she should keep Lorenzo busy. Will she be any trouble?"

"Nah, my guys checked her out thoroughly. She works as a consultant or some shit, just moved here. Shouldn't cause any problems," Luis answered dismissively.

"Glad to hear it. The woman can keep my cousin busy while we take his club right from under him." Tommy grinned wickedly.

"Speaking of cousins, have you talked to mine? Is he still comin' or what?" Luis questioned.

CHASING DESIRES
by Kasey Martin

"Yes, I've spoken to your cousin, so I'm no longer worried about him. He will be here; of that, I have no doubt," Tommy responded.

The Salazar Cartel was coming in a couple of weeks, and Tommy wanted to make sure that the girls as well as the drugs were still turning a substantial profit, and he kept his territory on lock. Once Tommy got used to the way things were in Texas, it was easier than he thought it would be to break into business.

The longer Tommy stayed in Texas, the more he realized how much money there was to be made working with the Cartel. The longer he remained down South he also realized that his father had no intention of retiring, and that's when he finally woke up. Tommy needed to be able to control every aspect of all the family business, and needed to be able to do that without his old man looking over his shoulder at every turn. He needed Sal to retire.

It took months for Tommy to get all of his ducks in a row for the Cartel to take him serious. It was easier because of his inside connection he had with them, but Lorenzo being right smack in the middle of the territory he needed to be in, made things more difficult than it had to be.
Justin Russo had jumped the gun and almost fucked up the entire plan by getting caught. But at least he'd managed to shoot

Chasing Desires
by Kasey Martin

Lorenzo in the process and put him out of commission even if he didn't kill him.

Tommy only went to Lorenzo, in the beginning, to check out the territory he would be gaining. He had no intention of letting Lorenzo in on anything. When he told his cousin he had an obligation to the family that was what he'd meant. Lorenzo owed Tommy his loyalty. Nobody walked away from the family. And if Lorenzo didn't want to cooperate, Tommy would just take what he needed; an all-access pass to Lorenzo's club.

Premier was right smack in the middle of prime drug territory. The surrounding properties were all popular restaurants and bars; there were high priced shopping areas and new upscale high-rise apartments. The crowd was young, vibrant, and ready to party. It was just the type of group that had plenty of disposable income for the drugs and girls that Tommy was happy to supply.

Tommy tried for a long time to convince his father that the drug game would increase their money as well as their power, but the old man wouldn't give up his ways. He finally relented when Tommy told him that an associate in Dallas shared how wide open and easy it would be to cash in on the business and expand the Angeletti reach. Just the mere mention of being in Dallas finally made his father see things his way.

Chasing Desires
by Kasey Martin

The old man still had a soft spot for Lorenzo, and he wanted him back in the family.

However, the only thing Tommy wanted from Lorenzo was his property. He had to get control of it somehow, but in the meantime, he would slip in while Lorenzo was unaware and take what he needed for the Cartel to agree to back him. After he did that, he would take care of his cousin once and for all.

Tommy didn't trust his cousin, but Lorenzo was engrained with loyalty to the family since birth, and it would always be there. Tommy was counting on that.

"So, when you spoke to my cousin did he say when he would be in town? You know how my primo is, always so secretive about his shit." Luis asked effectively bringing Tommy back to the conversation.

"He should be here within the week, and you know he has to be cautious. How many times do we need to go over that shit?" Tommy's irritation was evident in his tone.

Tommy could tell that Luis didn't agree because of the frown that covered his face. "Bullshit, Hermano, it's been plenty of time… years. He doesn't have to do any of that shit anymore. He's just fucking paranoid." Luis' Spanish accent was more pronounced when he got upset.

Tommy didn't feel like having this argument again. He had other shit to worry about, and Luis' temper tantrum concerning his cousin was something he was not about to deal with at all.

"As long as he comes through like he did in the past, I don't give a rat's ass about his paranoia," Tommy declared. Luis' didn't understand what his cousin had done for Tommy. He owed him more than what anyone could imagine. If it weren't for his sacrifices, Tommy wouldn't be in the position he was now. As a matter of fact, he would probably be doing a bid in prison without the possibility of parole.

Tommy watched Luis take in a deep breath and relax slightly. He could tell that Luis was letting go of the argument for now. "My cousin always does what he has to do. I'm just saying that sometimes he goes overboard with the covert shit." Luis looked as if he were contemplating something before shaking his head and sitting back in his seat.

"You can never be too careful in this life that we live. You'd do well to remember that, Luis." Tommy sat back sipping his drink.

He learned the hard way that you couldn't take too many precautions when navigating the criminal world. Tommy once thought he was invincible. He'd been young and incredibly dumb, and had thought he was untouchable. However, he soon found out that that wasn't the case.

Chasing Desires
by Kasey Martin

He knew that by getting involved with the Salazar Cartel was a means to an end, and he was past ready. It was his time, and the old man had ruined enough lives and done enough damage in his lifetime.

CHASING DESIRES
by Kasey Martin

CHAPTER 17
CHASE

The talk she had with Lorenzo put her at ease but only for a little while. However, her conscience just wouldn't let her relax, and enjoy the man she had been drooling after since she'd met him. She knew what they were doing wasn't immoral or anything, but she just couldn't help the guilt that came along with all the other hodgepodge of emotions she was feeling about their situation.

Even with the guilt and mixture of emotions, she decided it would be a good idea to take a leave of absence to continue to pursue her case against Angeletti. The four weeks was coming to an end, and she was closer than she had ever been to getting evidence against Tommy Angeletti, but she still didn't have enough for her superiors.

And although she'd taken a leave, she still couldn't focus on the case. And because of that she was riddled with guilt. The guilt manifested itself at night, where she would see Daniel Reyes, in her dreams, or rather her nightmares.

It had been a long time since she dreamt of her old partner. After Reyes died, she'd had dreams for months about the last time they spoke. She finally had to go to a therapist in

CHASING DESIRES
by Kasey Martin

order to let some of the guilt go, but from time to time the guilt would come back, and with it…the dreams.

Ever since she and Lorenzo had gotten involved, the guilt was almost smothering, and the dreams were back. But not even the guilt could stop her from wanting Lorenzo Moretti.

Since she visited the doctor with him, she couldn't help the strong almost gravitational pull Lorenzo had on her. She tried her best to ignore it, but she just couldn't resist him, especially when he let his guard down and just talked to her. They talked about so many things, and in the past several weeks they had gotten to know each other well, and not only their likes and dislikes, but what made the other tick. She could admit to herself that she was way closer to him than she ever thought she could be to any man.

Chase had never truly been in love before. She had undeniably been in lust, and even had a dose of infatuation, but her feelings for Lorenzo went far deeper than anything she had ever felt in her life. She knew that Lorenzo was damaged, but she could see just how much when he finally decided to open up to her about his brother Sergio.

"Chase, what happened to Sergio is my biggest regret in life. He was the one person I loved more than myself. He was innocent, head strong, and so smart," Lorenzo chuckled seemingly playing memories of his brother as he talked to

CHASING DESIRES
by Kasey Martin

Chase. The look in his sad clear blue eyes made Chase's heart ache for the man sitting in front of her hurting.

"When he was killed, I thought I was going to lose my mind." Lorenzo sighed as he ran his hands through his long curly hair, and down his face. At that moment, he just looked so lost, and she only wanted to make him feel better.

"What happened to him?" Chase softly coaxed in her raspy voice. She knew the facts surrounding Sergio Moretti's death because she had looked it up in his files, but she wanted to know from Lorenzo.

"He was at the wrong place at the wrong time." Lorenzo shook his head as darkness filled his eyes.

Chase placed her hand on top of his, lending him her support, but it was like he was reliving it all over again. It seemed like he'd been transported back to when Sergio was killed.

"He was hanging out with people I explicitly told him to stay away from." He paused and looked at Chase, but it was as if he was still in a daze caused by the hurtful memory. "They were a part of Tommy's crew. They were all asshole, only out for themselves. Typical guys in the life. I told Sergio he wasn't cut out for this shit and that he needed to go to college, get a degree, and stay straight. He needed to stay far away from all the bullshit I was involved in and use his head."

Chasing Desires
by Kasey Martin

"He didn't want his big brother telling him what to do?" Chase asked knowingly.

Lorenzo chuckled. "Something like that. I think my punk-ass cousin was whispering in his ear, telling him not to listen to me. Tommy as always denied it, but it makes no difference now."

"What happened wasn't your fault, Lorenzo," she almost pleaded with him to believe her, but she knew this was a deep hurt that he'd been carrying around for a long time.

He smiled, but it didn't quite reach his beautiful, but troubled eyes. "It was my fault. We fought that night. I told him he could do what the fuck he wanted, but if he got himself killed then so be it. That was the last thing I said to my baby brother. If you die, so be it."

Chase scooted closer to Lorenzo and hugged him for a long time. She knew that by him telling her this story he was letting her in and she was so thankful that he was.

"Lorenzo, you were young and upset, and you didn't mean what you said, and it's not your fault that some lowlife killed your brother."

"It is because they thought Sergio was me." The guilt that shadowed his handsome features after the statement had Chase wondering just how she should respond, but he kept talking so she didn't have to. "We looked a lot alike at least

Chasing Desires
by Kasey Martin

from a distance. Same build, and haircut. Sergio even dressed like me, I would tease him sometimes and say he was the uglier clone, but I was proud that my brother looked up to me. Like I said, we looked a lot alike, except he had my father's brown eyes, and I was blessed with the Angeletti blues."

Chase smiled at him. That was one of the first things she noticed about him, was how much he looked like Sal and Tommy, especially his eyes.

"Anyways, my brother was out being a knucklehead, and some gang trying to make a name for themselves, ambushed him and Tommy's crew, and they killed them all."

"What happened to the gang?" Chase honestly had an idea, but the files just said the perpetrators of the crime were never found and Sergio's case went cold and gone unsolved.

"They got what they deserved."

Chase knew then that Lorenzo had taken justice into his own hands and she could see they were more alike than she wanted to admit.

Her doorbell rang, bringing Chase back to the present. She was really tired of her feelings of uncertainty and she needed someone she could talk to about everything. She needed a friend.

Chasing Desires
by Kasey Martin

"Hey, girl, thanks so much for dropping by. You know I could've just come by your house." Chase greeted Charlie with a warm smile and a hug.

"Girl, please. I was already out and you know I'm sick to death being in that damn house. Bear acts like I'm made of glass," Charlie huffed as she walked into the apartment and plopped down on the large sofa.

"You want something to drink?"

"Yes. I'll have some wine please."

"Uh, I don't think I should get you wine, Charlie."

"You asked what I wanted, not what I could have." Charlie sighed dramatically. "Okay, okay, water will have to work."

Chase laughed as she went to the kitchen. After she returned with their drinks, they sat comfortably and chatted about the mundane before Charlie broke through Chase's avoidance.

"So what's up? I can tell something is bothering you."

Chase gnawed on her bottom lip and fidgeted with her earlobe. She really wasn't used to girl talk, so this was all new to her. But she was a strong and intelligent woman, so she could figure it out.

Chasing Desires
by Kasey Martin

She took a deep breath before blurting out, "I've been sleeping with Lorenzo and I feel so guilty, but the sex is so amazing that I think I'm addicted."

Charlie's hazel eyes went even wider with excitement. "Ho-ly shit! I was thinking that you were stressed about the case, but this is some juicy stuff. When you go big, you go all out!"

"I know. I know. It just kind of happened. Well at least the first time did."

"Hold the damn phone. Did you just say the *first* time?" Charlie scooted forward on the edge of the sofa with a look of amazement.

Chase groaned. "Yes, the first time. Come on, Charlie. I know Jake is a handsome guy and all, but you're by no means blind. You've seen Lorenzo. His ass is fine as hell!"

Charlie snickered as she sat back and rubbed her round belly. "I understand completely."

They laughed at their mutual agreement, and tapped their glasses in cheers.

"I haven't told anyone. I hope that you can keep this between the two of us."

It was Charlie's turn to groan. "You can't be serious? Have you met my husband? If he doesn't already know what

CHASING DESIRES
by Kasey Martin

you guys are up to, and that's a big-ass *if*, you know if he asks me about it, he will know I'm lying."

"Why would he ask you about *me*?" Chase asked with a tilt to her head.

"Do you think he doesn't know where I am right now?"

"Good point," Chase mumbled.

"Exactly. He will act all nonchalant about it, but he'll ask what we talked about, and I don't have my normal distraction tools at my disposal."

"Well, maybe you could try to leave out the sex part, and we can talk about something girlie that he won't want to hear about."

"Worth a try, but I'll make no promises. If he figures it out, I can swear him to secrecy. He wouldn't tell anybody your business, Chase. My husband isn't that type of guy."

Chase believed her. She knew that she could've just as easily confided in Jake, and he wouldn't have said a word to anyone else, but she wanted him to respect her as a professional, and sleeping with Lorenzo was anything but.

"I know Jake's trustworthy. I just don't want him to lose respect for me."

"I understand that you being a female in your field is hard, and earning respect even harder, but Bear would never judge you about something like that. You're good at what you do, and he respects that. He wouldn't think you were less of an agent because you have a personal life."

"Yeah, but it's more than just me having a personal life. It's a code that we live by. You shouldn't get involved with men like Lorenzo. It just…doesn't look good."

"I get what you're saying, but Lorenzo is a good man. Do you think I would be working for him if he wasn't? He has a past like everyone else. If that reflects bad on your job, then maybe you need a new one…" Charlie quirked a brow at Chase, and she felt thoroughly chastised.

Chase sighed heavily. "I've just spent so much time, so many years, my entire career, building and proving myself. I just don't want to lose everything because I finally gave in and dared to take something for myself for once."

"You just said it yourself you've spent your entire career proving that you're worthy. And if this one thing erases everything you've done, honey, you need a new career. I'm just sayin'."

"It's not that easy. This is the only thing I've ever wanted to do. I can't just quit because of one thing. That makes no sense," Chase argued.

"Listen, sweetie. I'm not saying it's easy to give up something that you love, but what I am saying is maybe you should ask yourself if your job is the *only* thing you love."

Chasing Desires
by Kasey Martin

With those words, Chase felt like she'd been hit in the chest. It was way too early to be in love with Lorenzo, and she knew that she wasn't. What Charlie was saying was ridiculous. How in the world could she possibly be in love with a man like Lorenzo? *Hell, how can I be in love period?*

The questions that plagued her mind were giving her a headache. She was thinking too hard about this again. The entire reason she had called Charlie was to talk out her confusion, not add to it.

"I don't love Lorenzo," Chase immediately protested.

"Uh-huh." Charlie gave her a pleasant smile. "I'm not accusing you of being in love. I just meant that maybe there's more room to love something other than your job."

"Right, of course, I knew that's what you meant." Chase nervously looked at Charlie. She didn't know why she felt so nervous all of a sudden.

"Okay. So look. You need to relax about all of this." Charlie raised her hands up at Chase's protest. "No offense, sweetie, but you are one of the most uptight people I know."

Chase couldn't even be mad at Charlie's words. She knew that she was a little tightly wound. It was a hazard of the job.

Chasing Desires
by Kasey Martin

"No offense taken. I guess you're right, though." Chase sighed resolutely. "I should just focus on the case, and relax about everything else."

"Well, look on the bright side; at least you won't have to look for a date for Korri's wedding next week."

"Oh, nooo." Chase groaned. "I forgot all about that. I've been so wrapped up with everything."

"I understand. But you know I couldn't forget if I tried," Charlie chuckled. "I've been counting down the days, so my crazy cousin can go back to being normal."

"I thought that she solved that little…uh problem."

Charlie snickered. "Yeah well, she's still driving me insane even if she did finally get the 'D'. Me being pregnant is saving me from some of her wrath, though poor Brandon is about to lose his mind."

Chase smiled. She had gotten so much closer to the group of friends since their first meeting. She'd even attended Korri's bachelorette party, and that night was one of the most fun she had ever had in her life.

"Poor, B. I hope she settles down after the wedding."

"For her sake, she better."

Once Charlie left, Chase felt that her emotions were somewhat settled, and she no longer felt so confused. But the one thing that Chase couldn't seem to get out of her mind was the notion that she was in love.

Oh hell! I'm in love with Lorenzo!

CHAPTER 18
LORENZO

Lorenzo was feeling more and more like himself. He'd started back working out, and all the healthy food he was eating had him back to almost one hundred percent. Both of his clubs, and restaurants were doing well, even though he had an infestation of prostitutes in both places. His assistant, Amber, called him to tell him that one of the girls that was kicked out of Premier was seen at Prime, so he had to have an all-inclusive staff meeting to make sure everyone at all locations was aware of what was going on, and what to look for.

Tommy still wasn't returning any of his calls or messages to set up a meeting, so he wasn't sure just how Chase planned to get her evidence. However, after a lot of reflection and thought, he decided that Jake was right about Tommy. He didn't deserve his loyalty, so he was going to call Marco, his PI, to see if he could help her. He was willing to do things even Jake and his crew wouldn't do. Unlike Jake and his team that did things that weren't exactly legal, Marco did things that sometimes were downright criminal.

And although he really wanted to help Chase, Lorenzo felt a little uncertain about what would happen once she got

Chasing Desires
by Kasey Martin

what she needed. He kept telling himself that everything would go back to the way it was before he'd met her, but he knew that was a lie. He could never go back to not loving Chase.

Oh shit! I'm in love with Chase. How the fuck did this happen? Lorenzo flopped down in his chair like the wind had been knocked out of him. His mama had always told him that love would sneak up on him, but this was fucking ridiculous.

I mean she is one of the only people who genuinely asked how I was even when I was furious at her. She made it her business to call and check on me. I can talk to her for hours about everything and nothing at all. She's the one person that knows how I truly feel about Sergio's death. I can empty my soul to her without judgment. What the fuck am I going to do without her?

Lorenzo knew that he could possibly scare her away with his confessions of love, so he decided he would keep his newfound feelings to himself. He wasn't the romance and candlelight kind of guy anyway, so this was all new to him.

Lorenzo was always focused on coming up. First, it was in the streets and then in the family. Now, he had the same focus as a legitimate businessman. The only time a woman was on his radar was for him to smash and move on. He never wanted a relationship and he never had one. Now, Chase had fallen into his life, and although he never thought he would be

CHASING DESIRES
by Kasey Martin

able to trust her, he knew in his heart that he'd already forgiven her betrayal.

He was glad to have had this epiphany before their date tonight, so he had time to focus and get his shit together. He wanted to take her to a nice place where they could eat and relax, and then enjoy some dancing. Lorenzo absolutely loved the way her body fit so perfectly with his when they swayed together to the beat of any music. He was never really much of a dancer, but to have Chase's tall curvy figure pressed against him, hell, he would damn near compete on *Dancing with the Stars*.

Lorenzo finally had the energy to drag himself from his comfy chair and all of his thoughts to get in the shower to get ready for his date. Hopefully, he would be able to put all these newly-formed emotions to the side and just enjoy his woman. *Yes, she is my woman.*

***

On the way to Chase's apartment, Lorenzo sat comfortably in the backseat of his SUV. He didn't have the overwhelming urge to run away from her or push her away. In fact, the desire to chase her down and claim her for his own was thrumming through his veins.

The SUV pulled up to Chase's place, and Lorenzo smoothly exited. He made his way to get his girl. His heart

Chasing Desires
by Kasey Martin

skipped a beat when she opened her door. Her smooth, ebony complexion had a silky finish that made him want to run his hands all over her. She wore her hair up in a sleek bun at the crown of her head with very minimal makeup. Her plush lips popped with a deep berry lipstick that made him want to kiss it all off.

The long-sleeved suede mocha bustier dress with matching boots made the front of his slacks tighten with desire. The dress clung seductively to each and every one of her curves until he was almost jealous.

"Damn, *Pumpkin*! You did all this for me?" He leaned against the door and openly perused her. *She looks so fucking good!*

"Hey, Pooh Bear." Chase's mouth lifted up on one side as her teeth playfully bit into her plush bottom lip, and he could see the laughter dancing in her eyes. He shook his head in disagreement of the name.

"Okay, uh…how about Baby Cakes?" Chase asked, trying to hold back a giggle.

"No, sweetheart. Baby Cakes ain't it either." Lorenzo's face broke out into a wide grin as he backed her up into her apartment and shut the door with his foot.

Lorenzo pulled her into his strong arms and he took in the delicious scent of vanilla and whipped cream. She smelled like some kind of dessert, and he was about to skip dinner to eat her up.

She kissed him soft and slowly, but Lorenzo wanted more. However, when he went to deepen the kiss, she pulled back and wiped the gloss from his lips.

"So what would you like me to call you instead?" She teased him with a playful smile that lit up her entire face.

He couldn't help but smile back at her, but he was definitely going to make her pay for teasing him later. "How 'bout you call me *Daddy* while I spank you?" He wiggled his eyebrows mischievously, but he was serious. It was his fantasy for her to scream out Daddy while he took her body and claimed it for his own.

She laughed, but he noticed that her eyes had darkened in lust and her breath hitched slightly.

"Yeah, I don't see that happening, but nice try, *Sweet Pea.*" She winked at him and pulled completely from his embrace.

He was definitely going to make her pay for that before the night was over.

They finished their meal and were enjoying dessert along with the relaxing atmosphere of the restaurant when something or rather, *someone* caught his eye.

CHASING DESIRES
by *Kasey Martin*

Camilla Alvarez was sitting at the bar talking with a man. When she saw him, her eyes went wide before she looked away quickly. *That was weird. The last time I saw her, I couldn't pay her to leave me alone.*

"I see your little girlfriend. I hope she doesn't come over here. I'm really not in the mood for her bullshit tonight," Chase leaned in and whispered in his ear.

Lorenzo thought he heard a note of jealously in Chase's tone, and it was absolutely cute and absurd. She had nothing to be jealous about, especially when it came to Camilla, or anyone else.

However, Camilla was acting strange. It was unlike her to back down from a challenge, and Chase was definitely a challenge to her. Although they weren't in competition, honestly, there was no woman that could compete with Chase.

"You're my girlfriend," he leaned in and whispered into her ear. Her brown eyes rounded in surprise, and he couldn't help the smile that broke out on his face.

She didn't say anything. She just leaned in and kissed his lips softly. She nibbled on his bottom lip before pulling back and sighing.

"We need to talk."

CHASING DESIRES
by *Kasey Martin*

Oh shit! The last thing a man wanted to hear a woman say was they needed to talk, especially, after he'd just claimed her.

"*About?*" Lorenzo probed. Of course, he couldn't read her face because the professional mask she sometimes wore was firmly in place.

"I haven't been completely honest with you. And now that this thing between us is more than I ever could've imagined it would be, I just need to let you know the entire story of what's going on."

Fuck! I swore to myself if she lied to me again, I would be done. How could she do this shit again after she promised to tell me everything? Damn! I sound like a bitch. Lorenzo ran his hand through his hair and tried to brace himself for what Chase was about to tell him. He was trying, but failing to keep his anger under wraps because he could feel himself growing redder by the minute.

"Okay, what is it?" Lorenzo asked as calmly as he could.

She sighed heavily, but she looked him in the eyes when she spoke. "I took a leave of absence from the agency. I've been working solo on the case to close it. My superiors didn't support me. So I decided to take a leave and work with my own resources. I'm sorry I didn't tell you sooner. I don't have an excuse." She fired the words rapidly, but he could hear the sincerity.

"Is that everything? Or is there more?" He wanted to make sure that she didn't have anything else to tell him before he got his hopes up.

"Yes. The only other person who knows is Jake. The team isn't aware that I took a leave either. I am officially supposed to be on vacation, but I just needed to get this thing behind me, so that I could move on with my life."

Lorenzo could understand what she was saying, and he wasn't completely blindsided by the information after all. You would only play him for a fool one time.

"I already knew that you were on leave." Lorenzo sipped his wine nonchalantly as he took in the shocked expression on Chase's beautiful face. Her mouth opened then closed, and then opened again, but no words left her luscious mouth.

"Did you honestly think that I wouldn't have you investigated after I found out who you were?" Lorenzo shook his head in disbelief.

"But I was working on the case right after you found out. I just took a leave a little over a month ago."

"You mean right before we started this *relationship*. Look, I became a cautious man after you lied…uh…failed to disclose who you were the first time. So I had my PI investigate you."

"You knew that I was unofficially working the case, but you continued to help me anyway? But why?" Chase had confusion written all over her face, and Lorenzo had to contain his smile. He really wasn't an asshole; he just didn't think he would see the day that this intelligent woman who was always ten steps ahead of him would be so perplexed by his actions.

"Yes, I continued to help anyway."

"Again, I want to know why."

"Because I wanted Tommy out of my business and as far away from me as he could be. I don't ever want to go back to the family and Tommy's presence here made me uneasy. Plus, I just wanted to help you."

Chase nodded, understanding finally gracing her features. "I've felt so guilty about not telling you. I just didn't want you to think it was like before. I never want to betray your trust again."

"Awww, sweetheart, come here." Lorenzo pulled Chase, and she slid closer to his side of their rounded booth. He took her lips in a slow, sweet kiss that showed her his forgiveness. He understood why she didn't tell him, but he needed to make sure that she knew that keeping secrets wasn't something they could afford in their type of situation.

Chasing Desires
by Kasey Martin

"I'm learning to trust you again, and you have to do the same with me. But I'm serious, Chase. There'll be no more secrets or we're not going to be able to keep doing this."

"I know, and you're right."

"You know this is a dangerous situation, so neither of us can afford to be in the dark about anything."

"Again, you're right. I'm sorry."

"I'm sorry too, baby. I should've come right out and told you I'd had you investigated and that I knew you weren't officially working on the case."

"No more secrets…" Chase looked at Lorenzo, and he couldn't help but fall a little harder at the honesty in her eyes.

"No more secrets," Lorenzo replied and he sealed their agreement with a kiss.

Someone clearing their throat gained their attention, and they reluctantly stopped kissing. When Lorenzo looked up into the dark brown eyes of Camilla Alvarez, he knew that his night had just taken a turn for the worse.

"This bitch…" Chase mumbled just loud enough for Lorenzo to hear as she sat up to look at the woman.

"Camilla."

"I didn't come to start anything. I just wanted you to know what was going on around you. Can we talk?" She looked around nervously, and Lorenzo couldn't help but look around as well.

"Whatever you need to say, you can say it now, Camilla." Lorenzo didn't have time for any nonsense, but the way Camilla was acting caused him to become a little worried about her.

"I can't here. There are too many eee…eyes and ears around here," Camilla stammered as she looked around again.

"So where do you want to *talk*?" Lorenzo asked again as he looked around trying to find what had Camilla so spooked.

"Your place."

"Uh…no, ma'am. That shit aint happening. I don't care what boogie man you're running from," Chase snapped, joining the conversation.

Lorenzo smirked. She was so damn sexy, especially when she was acting all possessive.

"Look, Mami, I don't care if you're there or not. I just need to talk somewhere other than here. Hell, we can meet at your place if that'll make you feel better," Camilla said, showing some of the bravado that Lorenzo knew her for.

"Okay." Chase grabbed a pen from her small purse, wrote on a napkin, and slid it to Camilla. "Meet us at this address tomorrow."

Camilla took the napkin, nodded, and walked away.

Chasing Desires
by Kasey Martin

Lorenzo looked at Chase with a mischievous smile. "Are you *jealous*?" he questioned, loving the blush that lit up her high cheekbones.

"Of *her*? Do I have a reason to be jealous?" Chase narrowed her eyes and folded her arms over her chest.

"No, Pumpkin, you have no reason whatsoever to be jealous."

"Uh huh."

Lorenzo smiled as he pulled her arms down and kissed her lips. His woman had a jealous streak, but he would show her she had no reason at all to be envious of anyone else.

"Well, tomorrow should be interesting," she finally commented after he let her out of his kiss.

"Interesting indeed."

CHAPTER 19
TOMMY

Tommy was ecstatic that everything was finally coming together. Luis' cousin had finally reached town, and the ultimate goal of taking over the family was finally within his reach. Just when Tommy thought it was time to celebrate, Luis came slamming into the penthouse suite.

"Stoopid fuckin' punta." Luis' accent was heavy as he cursed and paced the floor without even saying so much as hello to Tommy.

Luis was a good friend and an even better business partner. Tommy owed him a lot, but his dramatics were definitely something that Tommy could live without.

"What is it?" Tommy asked, but he really didn't want to know. Luis was always cursing about some woman or another, and today would be no different.

"That fuckin' Camilla. One of the guys at the restaurant saw her talking to Lorenzo."

"What the fuck do you mean she was talking to Lorenzo?" He narrowed his eyes at Luis. If some stupid whore fucked up his plans after he had worked so hard, he was going to kill both her and Luis.

CHASING DESIRES
by Kasey Martin

Luis ran a frustrated hand through his thick hair. "Yeah, that bitch tried to deny she was talking to him, but Jose saw her. He even got her on video taking something from the bitch Lorenzo was with."

"Do you know what she took or what she said? That bitch better not know shit about what's going on or I will kill the both of you." Tommy seethed as his hands balled into fists.

"I don't know what she took. She wouldn't give up the information, but she don't know shit. That I'm sure of."

"And how are you so fucking sure?"

"I beat that bitch within an inch of her fuckin' life, hermano. There's no way she's lyin."

"After you beat her, I hope you fucking offed her ass."

"Nah, man. She's worth too much money for me to just get rid of her. She won't step out of line again. She's new, so I just had to show her the ropes."

"If she didn't learn her lesson, I'm telling you right fucking now I'm not going down for that shit. You need to find her ass and put her to sleep... *permanently*."

Luis waved his hand dismissively. "You know I've been doing this a long fuckin' time, hermano. The bitch won't say shit. Just let me handle this."

Tommy narrowed his eyes and downed his drink. "You better be fucking right. Or that's your ass, *hermano.*"

CHASING DESIRES
by Kasey Martin

Tommy was serious. Luis was a good friend, but business was business. And if anything or anyone tried to get in the way of him taking over the Angeletti family, he would kill them himself. He had debts to pay, and the price was high. He was running out of time and people that could put him away for the rest of his life were coming to collect.

***

CHASE

Chase paced back and forth before plopping down next to Lorenzo on the oversized sofa in the small café. She and Lorenzo had been waiting over an hour for Camilla to show up for their impromptu meeting. There was no way in hell she would've given Camilla her address, and they already knew that Tommy was watching Lorenzo's place, so the discreet café was the perfect meet up spot.

"Why would she damn near hunt you down to try and *talk* and then not show up?" Chase questioned as she looked at her watch for the hundredth time.

"I don't know, but Camilla is a flake. Maybe she was just trying to ruin our date last night," Lorenzo answered logically.

"I don't know, babe. As much as I don't like her, she seemed really scared last night." Chase absently rubbed her

Chasing Desires
by Kasey Martin

earlobe. "The more I think about last night, the more I realize that Camilla looked terrified, and for her to invite me along to your little rendezvous showed just how much."

"You might be right, but I already called her. Her phone is going straight to voicemail." Lorenzo rubbed Chase's hand, and she instantly felt calmer by the action.

Chase took a deep breath. "I just have a feeling that whatever she had to say to you was important."

Before Lorenzo could respond, a woman sashayed into the café and directly to the back where they were sitting. She wore a form-fitting dress and extremely high heels like she had just come from the club, but it was only eleven in the morning. Her tan face was caked with makeup, and she carried an overstuffed hobo bag. Chase had a feeling she had just gotten off "work." The woman flung her long brown hair over her shoulders and she smacked her gum loudly as she approached them.

"You Lorenzo?" the woman questioned without any preamble.

"Who's asking?" Lorenzo sat up, his tone hard, and Chase immediately went on guard.

"Don't matter. Are you him or not? I ain't got all day for this shit," the woman responded with her hands on her round hips.

Chasing Desires
by Kasey Martin

Lorenzo's posture didn't relax, but he sat back, and the smile that graced his handsome face was one that Chase had never seen before. It was a sinister look, and she had a feeling that the gangster had just arrived.

"I'm him, and like I said. Who. The. Fuck. Is asking?" he questioned, his tone even harder than before.

All of the woman's bravado left and she looked wide-eyed at Chase. Chase's expression remained blank as she gazed back at the woman. *I can't save you, honey, so you better answer his questions.*

"I-I uh…like I said, it don't matter who I am."

Okay, fake it 'til you make it, ma. You got guts. I'll give you that. Chase shook her head at the brazen woman.

"You are absolutely fucking right. It doesn't matter who you are, so if you don't want any problems, you can tell me what you want or you can move the fuck around. The choice is yours while you still have it."

Damn, who is this person? Chase had never seen Lorenzo like this before. He was all business, no nonsense, and really fucking sexy.

The woman rummaged through her handbag before bringing out a crumpled envelope. She placed it on the table and mumbled, "Cami ain't comin'. She's laid up in the hospital and she's in a real bad way."

CHASING DESIRES
by Kasey Martin

"What happened to her?" Chase questioned as she tried to read the woman's body language.

The woman shrugged her slender shoulders. "All I know is she said to bring this here." The woman nodded at the envelope, threw her oversized handbag over her shoulder, turned, and sauntered out of the door.

"What the fuck was that?" Lorenzo's brows were furrowed as he picked up the envelope from the table.

"I have no idea, but Camilla's in the hospital, so at least she's not dead." Chase shook her head. She knew that Camilla wasn't just trying to ruin their date. She had a reason to be afraid.

Chase watched as Lorenzo opened the letter and read it silently before handing it to her.

Lorenzo,

Luis is more dangerous than you know. He is plotting to help your cousin take over your business and his family. I overheard them talking. That's all I know and I won't be around, so please don't look for me.

Camilla

"What the hell is going on?" Chase asked out loud.

What the hell did she mean Tommy is trying to take over the family? Didn't Sal send him here to get Lorenzo to come back to the family? Was everything she thought wrong? Shit!

CHASING DESIRES
by Kasey Martin

Chase knew that she needed to call Jake ASAP and tell him what was going on, but he was getting ready for his cousin's wedding. But it had to be done. She would never go in without backup. Never.

"You should call Jake," Lorenzo stated, but the blank look on his face showed that he was still deep in thought, and trying to process everything just like she was.

"Yeah, I need to let him know what's going on. Are you okay?" she asked, concerned as she took in the expression that made him look harder than she'd ever seen his gorgeous face look.

He let out an audible breath. "Yeah, let's go to your place, or stay in a hotel tonight. I'm not sure what the fuck my cousin has up his sleeve, but I don't trust him."

She nodded in understanding. "Whatever you want to do, babe."

He smiled at her then, and the blank look was replaced with one of admiration. He leaned in to kiss her lips tenderly.

The ride in the SUV was so quiet it was almost solemn as they made their way to Chase's apartment. She was lost in thought trying to examine every detail of what she thought was true. She had wracked her brain to try to figure out why Tommy was in Dallas to begin with. Chase knew that the main money maker for the Angeletti family was their import business, and everything ran through their port in Jersey, so she was thoroughly confused as to why Tommy was here in Dallas working with the Salazar Cartel.

They walked into Chase's apartment, and she excused herself to call Jake. Of course, he didn't answer the phone, so she left him a message giving him the details of what was going on. Once she returned to her living room, she noticed that Lorenzo was still quiet, and held a pensive look on his face that gave her an uneasy feeling. She'd never seen him so hot and cold before, and she was afraid of what he might be thinking.

"What do you think Camilla meant by Tommy was trying to take the family?" Chase faced Lorenzo, finally breaking the tense silence in the room.

"I'm not sure. But I hope he's not planning to do something stupid like kill his own father, although I wouldn't put it past him."

Chase shook her head. "I don't think it's that. He would've already tried it. I don't think he needs the cartel to kill his father."

"No. But he would need the power the cartel possesses to push Sal out."

Although Chase spent a lot of time investigating Tommy, she had no idea about all of the possible inner workings of a crime organization, so she wouldn't pretend she knew anything about how Tommy could push his father out with the cartel's help.

"How would that work?"

Lorenzo paused, and then raked his hands through his hair. "It's simple. It's a numbers game. The more people you have following you, the more power you possess. My uncle has been in the game a very long time. He has associates all over the country, but he's old school."

"I think I get it. Sal keeps all the control for himself. He's the one man at the top."

"Right, but if Tommy were to get the cartel involved, he would be in some type of partnership."

"So why did he have to get you involved in all this? How does your business tie into Tommy's plan?" Chase was trying to wade through all the questions and confusion this mess was causing. The more information she had, the more chaotic everything was.

"That's the one thing I'm not sure about."

"All this is giving me a headache, and I still don't have enough evidence against Tommy."

"You could always go on the little you do have," Lorenzo suggested.

Chasing Desires
by Kasey Martin

"No, it's not enough. It will end up just like before with the evidence missing or being dumped." Chase sighed in frustration.

"Well then, sweetheart, I hate to be the one to tell you that your case has officially gone to shit."

Chase wasn't a quitter, but Lorenzo was right; her case had officially gone to shit. However, that didn't mean she had to stop helping Lorenzo get his cousin out of his life. No matter what she could legally prove, Chase knew that Tommy Angeletti was bad news for anyone that was involved with him.

"So what do you want to do about all this?" Chase asked.

"I'm not sure yet. I probably need to talk to my uncle. Did you talk to Jake?" Lorenzo questioned.

"No, I assume he's busy getting ready for the wedding, but I left a message." Chase paused before hesitantly asking, "Did you uh…still want to go to the wedding? You know with everything that's going on? I would understand if you didn't want to go."

"Of course, we will still go. Life doesn't stop just because the mob and a cartel got into a partnership." She watched him try and smile, but it didn't reach his eyes.

CHASING DESIRES
by Kasey Martin

Chase smiled back at him. At least he was trying to make an effort to lighten the mood, but she knew that he was just as worried as she was about everything that was happening.

CHAPTER 20
LORENZO

Lorenzo didn't like any of the information that he had found out in the letter that Camilla wrote, and he certainly didn't like being played. Again. Tommy was trying to take over the Angeletti family, and he wanted Lorenzo's business…for what? Lorenzo still wasn't sure why his cousin wanted to drag him into his bullshit. He had nothing to do with any of this, and no matter how far he tried to run, they always found a way to try and pull him back in.

The reason he'd come all the way to Texas was to get away from Jersey and the memory of the Angeletti family. He came to the south where the pace was slower and his past was anonymous.

He was lost in his thoughts when Chase entered the room, but he quickly tried to put her at ease. They talked and tried to figure out everything, but it was all so confusing that it made his head spin. He tried to make a joke, and she smiled at him, but it didn't reach her eyes. He needed to get both their minds off the never-ending, problem-causing catastrophe that was his cousin, and on to something that he was even more than sure about. Each other.

CHASING DESIRES
by Kasey Martin

"Come here…" Lorenzo knew that she always protested his bossiness, but he knew that secretly she loved it.

He watched her twist her mouth up in a pout, but she came over and stood between his legs. He pulled her close and wrapped his arms around her waist, kissing her belly. She sighed and scraped her nails through his hair.

Lorenzo couldn't prevent the goosebumps that covered his skin at her touch. He pulled her shirt up and kissed her bare skin. It was her turn to shiver, and he loved her reaction to him. His hands continued to push her shirt up until she got the message, pulled it up and over her head, and dropped it on the floor.

His hands ran all over her smooth, dark brown skin. It always felt like silk and he knew that he would never get enough of touching her. How could he when she was so perfect? His kisses turned into nibbles, and his hands went from her toned stomach to grip her firm, round ass. She groaned, and he tightened his hold as he massaged, and slightly spread her cheeks apart. He couldn't wait to take her from behind so when he pulled them apart again, he could watch himself dip in and out of her sweetness as her globes jiggled and wobbled as he pounded into her. Just the thought had his cock rock hard, and ready. But tonight he would take his time, and make sure that her mind wasn't on anything but the way he was making her body thrum with passion.

Lorenzo tugged at her jeans, and she bent to take them off. She stood in front of him in a little, pink silk thong, and matching bra. She looked absolutely magnificent, and he couldn't wait another second to taste her. He slid his long, thick finger over her panty clad mound, sliding it back and forth, making her moan in anticipation.

"You wet for me baby?" his deep voice questioned seductively. He didn't have to ask because her panties were already soaked with her arousal, but he was a demanding bastard and he wanted to hear her say it.

"Yes."

"Yes, what?" He spanked her pussy, and she mewed with pleasure.

"Y-yes, I'm wet just for you," Chase breathlessly panted out.

The smile Lorenzo wore was wicked. He loved seeing her getting all worked up. Her whole body was covered in a light sheen of sweat and her faced was flushed, and he had only just begun to play.

He pulled her close and inhaled her feminine scent. He stuck his tongue out and took a long, slow lick. The wet spot on her panties increased tenfold, but he didn't stop. He kept on

Chasing Desires
by Kasey Martin

licking her, flicking his tongue rapidly back and forth over her swollen, panty covered lips.

"Take 'em off."

She did his bidding on shaky legs. He could feel her tremble slightly as she lifted one leg and then the other to remove the soaking wet fabric from her beautiful body. She stood in front of him in just her demi-cup bra that pushed her perky breasts up so perfectly, he was almost distracted by them. *Almost.*

Lorenzo focused back on her treasure as he leaned in and lightly pinched her clit. Her body instantly jerked forward toward him. She groaned and spread her thick, toned legs wider so that he could have better access.

"Hands on the shoulders, *Pumpkin*. You know the drill." He smirked at her, and she narrowed her eyes, but he could still see the mirth that danced in them. She still hated that name.

Chase put her hands on his shoulders and spread her legs even wider. He loved when she offered herself up to him without hesitation, and he always gave her a reward. He dove in face first, kissing, licking, nibbling, and sucking on her core like a starving man.

The sweet, musky scent of her arousal always drove him to the brink of insanity. She swiveled her hips, grinding down on his chin, creating more friction against her sensitive spot.

Chasing Desires
by Kasey Martin

"Ride my face, baby. That's it. Fuck my tongue," Lorenzo coached as he stuck his tongue deep within her honey pot. He hummed, and the vibration made the muscles of her canal contract. Her hands tightened with her nails digging deep into his shoulders, and he knew she was close, but he wanted to draw out her first climax. She was always angry at first, but she'd always thank him later.

He stopped humming and withdrew his tongue. Her nails dug in deeper into his shoulders, and he knew she was pissed.

"Why do you do this to me?" Chase whined, her full lips formed into a pout.

"You know why." He rose and took her lips in a long, erotic kiss that had her moaning and her hands gripping his hair almost to the point of pain.

"Up," he commanded in that bossy way of his.

"Are you sure?" she asked tentatively.

"Must we go through this every time? Follow directions, woman. I said up."

Chase jumped up and wrapped her long, toned legs around his waist. They had the same discussion every time, but he was way too horny to get pissed at her right now. The doctor had released him for everything, and although she wasn't at all heavy, she always insisted that he shouldn't be carrying her around. So now he had to prove that he was not only strong enough to carry her, but she was light enough for him to fuck her in this position.

He walked them to the bedroom and lay her down on the bed. He stripped off his clothes and then her bra. He was captivated by her curves, and he ran his hands as well as his tongue all over her body. Her nipples hardened under his touch as he paid them extra attention.

He pinched the rock-hard pebble, rolling it between his thumb and forefinger. He sucked her right nipple while he continued to manipulate her left breast with his hand. Chase's back arched, thrusting her breast deeper into his mouth, and he blew on her wet skin. He watched with fascination as goosebumps broke out over her smooth, ebony body. He absolutely loved how she responded to him.

"Please…" Chase begged, and he knew what she wanted and she never had to beg him, but he loved to hear her say the words.

"You don't have to beg me, baby. Just tell me what you want." Lorenzo never stopped licking and sucking. He continued to roll her nipple between his fingers, increasing the pressure more and more as she squirmed and panted.

"I want you to make me cum. I need you to."

Chasing Desires
by Kasey Martin

"How do you want it, sweetheart? Tell me what you need?" he questioned in a low, husky tone that spoke of all the nasty things he would do to her.

"I don't care how, Lorenzo. Ju-just get me there. Please," she begged again.

Although he would never make her beg, the heady feeling that came over him when she did, made him want to please her in any and every way that he could. He kissed down her body until he was face to face with the sweetest pussy he would ever know. He spread her nether lips with his fingers to find her clit. He flicked the bundle of nerves with his tongue before rubbing it vigorously with his thumb in a circular motion. Her hips lifted off the bed, undulating to the rhythm of his thumb.

Lorenzo kept his thumb on her clit as he reached over and grabbed a condom. He ripped it open with his mouth, and sheathed himself using one hand, all the while keeping up the rhythm on her clit. He blew on her pussy before giving it one last lick. Her body shook slightly from the sensation, and he could no longer tease her. It was time to give her what she wanted. What she needed.

He lifted up, and took her mouth as he thrust into her to the hilt in one hard stroke. They groaned in unison as he kept himself still so that she could adjust to his size. Although they

Chasing Desires
by Kasey Martin

had sex on the regular, every time was like the first time. She was always incredibly tight, and he wasn't the bragging type, but he was way above average in size.

"Move. Give it to me," Chase demanded as she wiggled her hips beneath him.

Lorenzo had to clench his teeth together, and count to ten to regain his control. She felt so damn good that he nearly came with just that little wiggle.

His rock-hard manhood was pulsating with need, and he began to slowly pump into her hot, wet core. Her silky walls had his massive cock in a death grip, and the feeling of her surrounding him so tightly had him on the verge of orgasm with each stroke. Their movements were like a synchronized dance with their bodies flowing together with each deep stroke.

He pumped into her passionately, and she matched him thrust for thrust. *This woman is made for me. So fucking perfect.*

Lorenzo didn't have time to dissect the thoughts that crossed his mind because he was too enthralled in the gorgeous ebony goddess lying beneath him.

"Yes, baby… Just. Like. That," Chase moaned loudly as she continued to move her hips erotically.

"You like that? Tell me how much you like taking my cock, baby. You like the way I fuck you. Don't you?" Lorenzo groaned as his hips moved faster and faster. He could feel

Chasing Desires
by Kasey Martin

Chase's pussy clenching so hard that he knew she was about to cum, and she loved it when he talked dirty to her. The nastier his words, the harder her orgasm would be.

"I like it sooo much, Daddy."

Fuck! Did she just fucking call me Daddy? Shit!

"Wrap your legs around my waist and hold the fuck on. Tight."

Chase followed directions without words, or hesitation. He stood up with her still impaled on his throbbing manhood. Without another word, he began to pound into her like a man on a mission. She screamed out as he moved her up and down on his swollen rod. Her legs tightened around his waist as she caught the rhythm and moved with him. He pushed into her forcefully, and her legs began to tremble.

"I'm about to cum!" Chase screamed her release. Her pussy dripped her sweetness all over his massive cock as she clung to Lorenzo's neck. He continued to pound into her, prolonging her orgasm as much as possible.

He loved to watch her cum, but the overwhelming pleasure he was feeling could not be contained any longer. His body tensed, and he climaxed hard into the condom. He released all of the anger and frustrations of the day. His knees grew weak with his release, and he plopped down hard on the bed with Chase on his lap.

CHASING DESIRES
by Kasey Martin

He pulled out slowly, and they both sighed at the lost connection. She absently stroked his chest, and he rubbed her back lazily as he lay back fully. Neither of them said a word, but he knew that she felt the same calming effects of being in his arms as he did having them wrapped around her.

She yawned loudly, and he knew that they would have to take a nap before he would be able to take her again. He was far from finished with loving on her body, but he would give her time to rest and recuperate first.

"Come on, doll face. Let's go to bed." Lorenzo sat up and pulled Chase with him. He covered them with the comforter and settled in to take a nap.

Chase snuggled in closer to him, clinging to his chest. She was right where he wanted her to be. "You know you called me Daddy, right?" Lorenzo yawned, amusement coloring his voice.

She chuckled. "Is there any way you could just forget that?"

"Hell no! You know how long I've been trying to get you to call me Daddy?"

"Well, all you had to do was spank me, and *voila*. Instant Daddy."

Lorenzo couldn't help the low growl that came from him or how his once softening member was now hardening again.

CHASING DESIRES
by Kasey Martin

"If you want to take a nap, then I suggest you take your sexy ass to sleep before I really spank you and make you call me Daddy for the rest of the night."

Chase giggled. "Hey, you started this conversation."

"And I'm going to finish it," Lorenzo growled as he nipped her bottom lip.

"Okay, I'll call you Daddy *after* our nap."

Lorenzo groaned. "Alright, but just know I'm spanking that ass."

"I can't wait."

Lorenzo couldn't either. And his mind was officially off of his cousin and all of the bullshit. It was now firmly on the woman that he was falling deeper in love with every day.

"I love you," Lorenzo mumbled as he drifted off to sleep.

***

DALLAS AGENT

It took him way too long to make the right contacts he needed to get in the inner circle of the right groups. It was not easy to get to know the type of people that could help further his career. Now he was finally at a place he needed to be in order to make moves that significant people would recognize.

CHASING DESIRES
by Kasey Martin

He was the type of man that would do what he had to do to succeed. And if that meant undercutting someone to further his ambitions then so be it.

The agent impatiently waited while the phone rang. Once the line connected, he didn't even wait for the customary hello before he started talking. "Hey, it's me. We're a go for the plan."

"Great. I'll be there with bells on."

"Make sure you remember our agreement." The agent reminded. Nobody was going to get in the way of his ambitions. So he had to make sure everyone remembered their role, no matter who they were.

"You just do what I asked, and I will make sure you get everything you have coming to you."

The agent disconnected the call with satisfaction. He didn't trust anybody, but on this he would give the benefit of the doubt that his contact would come through. Now it was time to make an appearance at a very important wedding that he bribed and begged to get into.

CHAPTER 21
CHASE

Chase was still reeling from Lorenzo's mumbled confession. There was no way he meant that he loved her. He must've just been drunk off the sex. *Sex drunk... Yep that had to be it!*

At least, that was what Chase kept telling herself. She didn't want to over think it and get herself all worked up. Besides, there had to be some kind of rule about saying "I love you" in the throes of passion. *It didn't count, right?*

She knew without a doubt that she was in love with Lorenzo Moretti, but could he be in love with her too? The question would have to remain unanswered for now because at this moment, she was determined to focus on the love and happiness that surrounded her.

Chase was in a beautiful venue about to watch Korri and Tony get married. She was so excited, and extremely happy to watch her new friends start their lives together. The ceremony location was breathtakingly stunning. The tropical atrium made the winter nuptials feel like it was the middle of summer on an island paradise.

Chasing Desires
by Kasey Martin

Korri picked the perfect place to say I do, and although she didn't have a specific wedding theme, the array of spectacular colors that were spread throughout the space made the event unique and beautiful. The bridal party wore jewel toned gowns, and the groomsmen wore black tuxedos with jewel toned ties. The emerald green, turquoise, royal blue, and purple flattered all the bridesmaids, and the groomsmen looked dashing in their tuxes.

To keep with the color scheme, Chase wore a champagne colored long sleeve gown that was adorned with lace appliqués. Her hair was swept to one side in big barrel curls that hung over her shoulder and her makeup was heavier than normal, but it complimented the beautiful dress she wore, which fit her like a glove. She felt confident and sexy, especially since her date was one of the finest men in the room, and in this particular room that was saying a whole lot.

Lorenzo had on a simple black suit with a crisp white shirt without a tie. It should've looked plain, but the tailored fit on him was simply perfection. His curly hair was tamed in a gelled style that showed off the strong masculine features of his face. Although he had his beard lined and trimmed, he didn't shave it completely. Chase couldn't help but to steal glances at her very own date. He was so handsome with his glittering, clear blue eyes, and no matter how many times she looked into them, she seemed to get lost.

"*Pumpkin,* if you keep looking at me like that, you're going to miss the vows," Lorenzo whispered in her ear as he slung his arm on the back of her chair. She smiled knowingly at him. Chase knew that if she so much as licked her lips, he would pull her out of the venue and to the nearest private space he could find so quick that her head would spin.

"We don't want to miss the vows, now do we?" Chase smiled before biting down on her bottom lip teasingly.

He leaned in, and she leaned towards him anticipating a heart stopping kiss, but before their lips could connect in what she knew was about to be an erotic combustible taking over of her mouth, she heard a loud throat clearing. *Someone is forever interrupting our kiss!*

Chase looked up to catch the inquisitive gaze of Marcus Wright. His thick, bushy eyebrows were raised high on his forehead, and his handsome ebony face held a wide grin.

"I hope I'm not interrupting anything?" He'd posed it as a question, but they all knew that it wasn't.

"Um, nope. Not interrupting a thing," Chase responded, and she knew that nobody would miss the blush that heated her entire face. She felt like a teenager that had just been caught necking by her parents.

Chasing Desires
by Kasey Martin

Lorenzo chuckled beside her. "How are you, man? Have a seat." Lorenzo stood shaking Marcus' hand and gesturing to an empty chair in the same row.

"Don't mind if I do." Marcus gave Chase a big brotherly bear hug before he kissed her cheek. "I saw that almost kiss you know? We will have to talk about that later." He gave her a Cheshire grin and a wink.

He never failed to make her feel like his little sister. Chase looked around and saw that Marcus was alone, which was unusual for him. He always had some sweet young thing hanging off his arm.

"Where's your date, Marc? I'm surprised that *you* came alone." Chase's mouth twisted in a lopsided grin.

"No date today, sweetheart. Family comes first at an event like this." His face was serious, and Chase knew that meant the guys were low-key working today.

She nodded her understanding, and settled in to watch the beautiful ceremony. There were hordes of security, but they were wandering discreetly throughout the venue. Chase saw that some of them blended in with the staff, and others were blending with the many guests. She wasn't surprised in the least. Jake wouldn't have it any other way. And although she had only met Tony a handful of times, she knew that he wouldn't either.

Chasing Desires
by Kasey Martin

There were a lot of high profile people there like politicians, professional athletes, singers, and celebrities of all types. Then there were the normal people like herself and Lorenzo. Well, she wouldn't actually call Lorenzo normal, but he wasn't famous.

Lorenzo and Marcus were engaged in small talk, so Chase entertained herself by looking around the crowd to see if she could spot any famous people. A familiar face caught her eye.

The mischievous glint that was ever-present in his brown eyes was on full display as he sauntered closer with a wink. *Ah hell, I hope he doesn't start any shit.*

"Hello there, beautiful. Fancy seeing you here."

"Lucas, nice to see you too." Chase was barely able to get the response out of her mouth before the chatter around her became eerily quiet. At first, she thought the wedding was about to start, but she knew they were there extremely early because of the crowd and added security, so there was no way that Korri was about to make her grand entrance.

She looked around, and caught two sets of very menacing expressions. Chase sighed to herself. She knew that whatever was about to go down had the potential to get ugly.

CHASING DESIRES
by Kasey Martin

"Franks, how'd the hell did you get past security?" Marcus questioned, but Chase couldn't tell if he was joking or not because his expression was made of stone.

Chase was one of the best agents when it came to reading people, their body language, speech patterns, and even the smallest of facial tics. But once Marcus turned on his special forces training, the gentle giant turned into a terminator robot with no expressions or feelings.

"I was invited of course." Lucas scowled as he looked over at Marcus.

Marcus grunted and stared him down like he was trying to set him on fire with just his eyes.

"Lucas, how are you?" Lorenzo asked the question but Chase suspected it was merely to interrupt the intense stare down. Chase had to admit it was pretty brave of Lucas to stare so boldly at Marcus. Because as gentle as he could be, he was one of the scariest men Chase knew, when he wanted to be.

"Lorenzo, I'm glad to see you guys still going strong."

Chase knew shade when she heard it however, normally it came from a female, so this was new to her.

It was like Lucas had done a one-eighty since the last time they saw him. He was staring inappropriately, but he wasn't so bold in his disrespect. It seemed like Lucas may have wanted to start some shit after all. Lorenzo smiled in that special way of his that gave Chase the willies. She knew that Lucas better tread lightly.

"I didn't know you had a death wish, Lucas." Chase turned to look directly into Lorenzo's darkened eyes, she knew that he didn't take too kindly to anyone trying to flirt with her, but threatening this man was a little overboard in her opinion. *Surely, it's not that damn serious.*

Lucas didn't respond, but the smug expression slowly faded from his face. And if Chase wasn't mistaken there was a flash of animosity before it was replaced with a blank expression. Lorenzo moved his arm from the back of Chase's chair, and he leaned forward and placed his large hand high upon her thigh. The heat from his palm radiated from her thigh straight to her core. At that moment, she was really glad that the ceremony wasn't in a church because the nasty thoughts that flashed through her mind would surely send her directly to hell.

Lorenzo squeezed her thigh, bringing her back to the tense moment, but he was still looking at Lucas. "The last time we spoke, I thought it was understood that disrespect is not something that I tolerate especially when it comes to this very special woman beside me."

Chase had to turn her head away from the raw emotion coming from Lorenzo. His voice had a low gravely quality that was making her overheat. She was doing her damndest not to

Chasing Desires
by Kasey Martin

squirm. When she happened to catch Marcus' eye, his brow raised in question. Now she knew for sure that they were going to have a long conversation, she was just glad that Mike wasn't there to see what was going on.

Lucas mumbling some half assed excuse brought Chase's attention back to his and Lorenzo's conversation. "Now, this isn't the time nor the place for me to make sure you understand the level of respect you need to show my woman, so for now, I'll just tell you to stay the fuck away from us, and I better not see your ass in the street."

"There's no need for threats. I got you."

"I sure the fuck hope so," Lorenzo said in a no-nonsense tone.

Lucas scowled but walked away without saying anything else. Chase was sure that all of his macho bullshit was just that—*bullshit*. She didn't understand why Lucas was acting like such a jackass. When she first met him, he seemed to be an alright guy, nice even. She thought that he and Lorenzo were actually pretty cool with one another, but she couldn't have been more wrong. But one thing was for sure, she knew that they would never have another problem with Lucas Franks again.

***

Chasing Desires
by Kasey Martin

When Lucas left, everyone immediately became more relaxed.

"So do either of you want to tell me what that was about?" Chase asked the two men sitting beside her.

"What?" Marcus had a totally unbelievable innocent expression on his face, and Chase couldn't help but laugh at him.

"You know what…you guys treated him like he was an enemy of the state or something. What gives?"

Marcus shrugged his colossal shoulders. "He's an asshole."

"That's it?" Chase asked incredulously as she looked from Marcus to Lorenzo.

It was Lorenzo's turn to explain his behavior. "Listen, sweetheart, I know the first time you met Lucas I was real cordial, but like I told you before and you need to please believe me when I say, we are *not* friends."

"But you seemed genuinely happy that night." Chase was legitimately confused by the hostile display between the two of them.

"Baby, you make me genuinely happy. I was having a good night and it was nice to be out. Plus, Lucas is an associate I've worked with on occasion. We've always been friendly, but as soon as he disrespected you, our cordial association came to an end."

Chase could understand that, but she still felt like the threats, and the aggression were a little too much. However, she knew that trying to argue that point with Lorenzo would be like banging her head against a brick wall. There would be no point and she would end up with a massive headache.

"So when did you two stop pretending, and start actually being a couple?" Marcus asked out of the blue, effectively changing the subject.

Lorenzo quirked a thick brow at Chase and laughed. That was the clue that she would be the one explaining to Marcus what was going on.

"It's been a while, but if you could keep it to yourself, I would really appreciate it."

Marcus nodded. "You do know that you work with a team of ex-special forces members, right?"

Chase did know, and she understood what Marcus was saying. She may have tried to keep her relationship with Lorenzo's private, but she worked with a team of people that was well trained in observation, and if they caught a glimpse of the two of them together, they most likely already knew what was going on.

Marcus smiled at her, "Don't worry, CJ. If it's none of our business, then it's *none* of our business… got me?"

"I got you Marc," Chase smiled back at him. He wouldn't tell anyone her business, and neither would anyone else on the team that may have figured out what was going on.

Lorenzo kissed her cheek, and squeezed her thigh in support and she felt herself relax. She didn't have to worry about losing respect from the team, and it just made her love them that much more. Maybe she could find a permanent place in Dallas after all.

CHAPTER 22
CHARLIE

Charlie was so excited that today was her cousin's big day. She couldn't be more proud of the woman Korri had become. She knew that she wasn't her mother, and she was only a couple of years older than her, but she felt protective over her younger cousin. Korri had been through so much in life, and Charlie just felt like she deserved to finally find happiness and love. Tony was the perfect man for Korri, and she was proud to be her maid of honor for their big day.

Charlie was getting ready when she felt another sharp pain, and she knew that she was having contractions and real ones this time, not the Braxton Hicks that she experienced two weeks ago. They were far more painful, but far enough apart that she figured she could manage, as long as they started the wedding on time that is. Now if she could just make it through the ceremony and her toast at the reception before her giant baby made his debut.

"Are you ok?" Brandon whispered with a look of worry covering his handsome light brown face. "You've been trying to hide that grimace all day. Are you in labor?"

CHASING DESIRES
by Kasey Martin

"Shhh. Keep your voice down." Charlie waved her hand at him frantically. "It's just a little pain here and there, I will not ruin Korri's day."

"So if your water breaks during the damn ceremony then what?" Brandon put his hands on his hips, and narrowed his eyes at Charlie.

"It will be fine. They are only coming about fifteen minutes apart. It will be fine," she repeated unconvincingly. "Active labor is not until they're about three minutes apart, so don't worry your pretty little head. Just go help Korri get dressed, so we can get this show on the road."

"I swear before the sweet baby Jesus, if your big, giant-ass husband comes in here, I'm telling on you." Brandon pointed at her wildly. "I will not be the one to have to tell him why I let his precious Heart walk around in pain all day," Brandon huffed with irritation, his eyes narrowed even more into thin slits.

"You are so damn dramatic. Bear will not come in here. He's busy with Tony. Just keep Korri happy, and I'll be fine. I promise."

"You better be!" Brandon whisper-shouted before he turned and sauntered away.

Chasing Desires
by Kasey Martin

Brandon started fussing over Korri's makeup, so it gave Charlie a minute to take a few deep breaths and get herself together.

The contraction finally passed, and Charlie was able to resume preparation. Her royal blue dress complemented her dark, ebony skin to perfection. The empire waistline still showed off her baby bump but in a very elegant way. Lauren's dress was royal purple, which also complimented her skin as well. It was a one-shoulder chiffon dress that flowed freely when she walked and it accentuated her long legs.

Then there was Korri. She adorned a bright, white mermaid trumpet style dress with a lace overlay, and sweetheart neckline. Her gown was enhanced with a rhinestone embellished belt that cinched in her tiny waist. Korri's hair was styled in a low side chignon bun with a side swept bang. She wore large diamond studs with a matching diamond bracelet, and she looked absolutely stunning. Charlie felt the tears well up in her eyes for the millionth time that day.

"Don't you dare start!" Lauren yelled across the room at Charlie.

"I'm sorry. You know I can't control these pregnancy hormones," Charlie hiccupped as she tried to catch the tears before they fell and ruined her makeup.

Chasing Desires
by Kasey Martin

"Yeah, well, if we wait any longer, you won't be able to claim it's your hormones because the baby will be here," Brandon responded with pursed lips.

"What are you talking about, B?" Korri questioned with an inquisitive gaze directed at Charlie.

"He's just being dramatic as usual." Charlie waved him off dismissively. "He knows we need to get you to the altar in less than five minutes to stay on schedule. You know we are not on CP time."

"You're right! Let's get moving divas!" Korri squealed in excitement, and everyone laughed and clapped.

Charlie narrowed her eyes at Brandon and mouthed, "You better keep your big mouth shut!"

He pursed his lips and sighed, but he didn't say anything else.

The wedding ceremony was beautiful. Although the crowd of people was huge, Charlie could see that when Tony laid eyes on his bride, it was like they were the only two people in the room. The expressions on both of their faces radiated the true meaning of love. Their vows were simple but traditional, and Charlie could barely see to hold Korri's bouquet for the exchange of rings because her eyes were flooded with emotion.

The kiss that Tony and Korri shared when they were pronounced husband and wife was so erotic that Charlie felt her

Chasing Desires
by Kasey Martin

face heat with a blush. She was pretty sure that the two wouldn't be making it through the entire reception without sneaking off to consummate their marriage.

During the reception, the drinks were flowing and the food was plentiful. Charlie didn't realize how many celebrities Tony and Korri knew. It made her slightly nervous about giving her maid of honor speech. However, before she could hide, it was her turn to talk, and she was glad because from her last count her contractions were about seven minutes apart. She was glad that her overbearing husband was busy with his best man duties to notice his wife was about to give birth.

Charlie cleared her throat before she started talking. "I want to say how proud I am of my dear sweet cousin. She's more like a sister to me, and I'm especially glad to have her in my life." Charlie paused to wipe the tears from her eyes before continuing, "I knew that these two were made for each other the moment that I saw them together. The light in Korri's eyes and the glow he put on her face made me…ohhhh."

The agony that shot through Charlie was like no other pain she had ever felt in her entire life. She doubled over, and before she knew it strong arms were swooping her up, and carrying her out of the room.

"Heart, baby, how far apart are your contractions?" Jake's emerald green eyes were filled with worry.

CHASING DESIRES
by *Kasey Martin*

"Seven minutes, may…be less…now," Charlie let out between choppy breaths.

Charlie could hear that Brandon was speaking in the microphone, but both Korri and Tony were in the hall with her and Jake. As a matter of fact, the whole crew was there, Marcus, Chase and even Lorenzo were all in the hallway.

"I need to get her to the hospital, now!" Jake picked her up, and was headed to the car.

Although she was in a horrible amount of pain, Charlie was extremely excited to finally get to meet the little guy that had been sitting on her bladder for the last seven and a half months.

***

JAKE

Jake couldn't believe he was about to meet his first child. He was so excited that his son was about to be born, and in true Cameron fashion he had to make the most dramatic entrance. With the celebration that was taking place around him, he felt a little guilty about his wife giving birth in the middle of everything. He was pissed at Charlie for not telling him that she was in labor. She had to have been having contractions for a

CHASING DESIRES
by Kasey Martin

couple of hours for them to be so close together now, but she never said a word.

Jake understood who his wife was, so he knew that she wanted to keep from interrupting Tony and Korri's wedding day, but she should've let him know what was going on, so that he could've been there to take care of her.

Jake was damn near running full speed while carrying his wife. He could tell that she was doing her best not to cry out in pain, but she was squeezing the life out of his neck.

"Bear, stop running so fast, you're going to knock the baby loose," Charlie breathed through clenched teeth.

He slowed down a fraction, but he was still running quite fast. He parked in a private lot close to the venue so that he wouldn't have to valet, but someone had boxed in his big truck. Jake knew that he could just get in, and run over the little car because the lift on his Ford F150 made his pickup look more like a monster truck.

"Shit! Somebody has me blocked in! Shit!"

"Don't worry, I have a driver," Lorenzo said from behind him. For the first time since he grabbed Charlie, he noticed that the whole crew had followed him out to the car.

"He's coming now."

Jake nodded. He had been in numerous dangerous situations throughout his career, and he was always able to keep

CHASING DESIRES
by Kasey Martin

his cool. That was one of the things that made him the best at what he did. Now, however, his heart was beating so hard he felt like it was going to come right out of his chest. All he could hear was the sound of his blood pumping through his veins. *I have got to get my shit together!* Jake took a deep breath to gather himself, and he looked at the love of his life. As soon as he looked deep within her big hazel eyes, calm like he had never felt before engulfed him.

Jake saw that she was excited, but he could tell that she was also very afraid. This was their first baby, and she was looking to him to be her rock. And he was going to be just that.

"Just do your breathing exercises, Heart. I promise we will get you to the hospital in time. I love you so much, baby. You are doing such a good job."

Charlie smiled, but she followed his directions and kept up her breathing.

"Hee-heehooo, hee-heehooo. I told you we…hee-hee… we shouldn't have had… hee-hee… sex last night… hooooo… shiiiit!!" Charlie yelled out with the last contraction.

"Baby, I'm so glad we did. Because it will be another six weeks before I can get that sweet pu—"

"Uhh, yeah…do *not* finish that sentence," Marcus groaned loudly. He treated Charlie like the rest of the women in their tight knit circle, like a little sister.

Chasing Desires
by Kasey Martin

"The car's here!" Chase yelled as everyone proceeded to clear the way from the nosy onlookers that started to gather around the commotion.

Jake put Charlie in the back of the SUV, and everyone started to pile in when he stopped them. "Korri and Tony, don't you guys fuckin' think about leavin'. You enjoy the rest of your reception. Come by the hospital tomorrow. I'll keep you posted."

Tony shook his head. "We will stay, but we'll be there tonight. If you think I would miss my Godson being born you're insane." Tony gave Jake a quick hug, and kissed Charlie on the top of her head.

The couple went back inside with a slightly hesitant pouting Korri. He knew she was torn between wanting to be there for Charlie, and wanting to celebrate their special day. Jake was glad that Tony pulled her away. They had gone through so much as a couple, and they deserved to celebrate their love.

Marcus was making calls to everyone on the team, letting them know the situation while Lorenzo directed the driver to the hospital. Chase called ahead letting Charlie's OBGYN know that they were on the way.

Chasing Desires
by Kasey Martin

Jake was reassuring his terrified wife that he was proud, and she was doing such an amazing job. In no time at all, the driver pulled up to the emergency room entrance.

Jake barely waited for the SUV to stop completely before jumping out and scooping Charlie into his arms again before he rushed into the hospital frantically looking around for her doctor.

Just when he was about to yell for someone to get their ass in gear, a plump nurse ran up with Dr. Andrews right on her heels. The nurse got Charlie in a wheelchair and they all rushed through the ER doors into a room. Dr. Andrews wanted to examine Charlie to see how far she had dilated since her water hadn't broken yet.

Dr. Andrews was an older, African-American woman with a smooth, pecan complexion. She had a motherly, nurturing presence about her, and Charlie took to her immediately. Dr. Andrews was conducting her examination when she did a double take at the monitor.

"Nurse Fredrick, can you come here a sec?" Dr. Andrews and the nurse were talking rapidly in hushed tones, and Jake was just about to lose his shit.

"Is my wife alright, Doc?" Jake was trying to remain calm, but the expressions on the nurse and the doctor's faces was giving him a bad feeling.

CHASING DESIRES
by Kasey Martin

"Well, Charlie is doing great, but it looks like in our haste we overlooked something. What we thought was a very strong heartbeat was actually *two* heartbeats."

"You mean Charlie and the baby's heartbeats?" Jake was confused. *What the hell is she talking about?*

"Nooo. I mean there are *two babies*. It looks like we have a little one hiding under the big brother here. It's not a normal occurrence, but it does happen."

Jake couldn't believe what he was hearing. How in the hell did they miss the fact they were having twins! He looked at Charlie, and her eyes were even wider.

"That's why I'm so damn big!" Charlie sobbed out a laugh, and Jake kissed her on the lips. He was going to be a father of not one but two boys!

***

After another four hours of not dilating any further and her water not breaking, they decided it would be safer for Charlie and the babies if they did an emergency C-section. Just as they suspected, their son, Jacob Antonio Cameron was a little monster, and his baby sister Journee Korrine Cameron was a tiny little thing that had stayed hidden under her brother for the entire pregnancy.

CHASING DESIRES
by Kasey Martin

Jake knew that he was truly blessed beyond belief. He got his son, and a precious little girl all in one go. And he vowed to protect them and their mother for the rest of his days.

Later that night while his wife was resting, he took a walk to the nursery and just stared at his babies when he heard movement behind him. His cousin came in looking tired, but excited. They gave each other a warm, brotherly embrace.

"Two babies, huh? You two would be the ones to have a baby hide from you for nine months."

Jake chuckled at Tony. "First off, it wasn't nine months. They came early, and besides, her brother was just protecting her. Might as well get used to that."

Tony laughed. "Yeah, that poor kid won't have a chance with a big brother, and you as her dad…"

"And you as a Godfather…"

Tony nodded and smiled. "Poor kid." They said in unison as they watched the precious babies sleep peacefully.

There's no way I could be more blessed.

CHAPTER 23
MIKE

Mike had been in New Jersey for almost two and a half weeks. Worthington had been giving him the run around, and Mike was still convinced that he knew exactly where Daniel Reyes was. He found evidence that Reyes was very much alive at the same time the FBI claimed his body was being discovered at the warehouse. He hacked into several files at the agency, and although it had been almost a decade, he was able to find where the footage was stored. Daniel Reyes was seen on an ATM camera at midnight, and it was significant because the report Mike was able to pull from the FBI server claimed Reyes was killed at around seven P.M.

If Reyes was alive, then all of Chase's efforts had been for nothing. Chase said that Worthington was always trying to convince her to let go of the vendetta she had against Tommy Angeletti, and just accept the fact that her partner was dead.

Mike had to ask himself why Worthington would work so diligently to keep his best agent from solving the murder of their fallen brother. As her superior and mentor, he should've been bending over backwards to make sure she had the

Chasing Desires
by Kasey Martin

resources needed to take down the perpetrator of such a heinous crime, especially against one of their own.

Ever since the day Mike had bum rushed Worthington in his office, the old man had done a remarkable job at avoiding him. If he ever wondered how Worthington got into his position in the FBI, he now didn't have any doubt that he'd earned it by being the best at evasive tactics.

Mike had called back to Texas several times, and hadn't gotten any answers. Mike knew that Tony and Korri's wedding was the day before, and he couldn't bring himself to go. He wasn't really close to either one of them, and seeing everyone so in love bothered him.

He didn't want to accept the fact that he and Chase were arguing over Lorenzo Moretti. He just wanted her to see what type of person she was getting so involved with. He wanted her to see the type of man she really needed; a type of man like him.

However, at the moment, he couldn't focus on Chase and her decisions because Jake should've been free to answer his call after the wedding, so he was starting to get worried. He hated being out of the loop, but this was important to him.

Mike needed to find out what happened to Daniel Reyes for Chase's sake. He hated that she had spent the majority of her career chasing ghosts. She was a damn good agent, and her potential was being wasted, and as her friend and somebody who loved her he was determined to make sure that came to an end one way or another.

Mike decided to give up calling the Inc. for now. He made his way to sit outside of Worthington's office, something he had been doing on the regular since he arrived on the East Coast.

"Mr. Thatcher, it's such a surprise to see you here," the female agent said dryly as she eyed Mike warily.

After the first couple of days, there'd been a change in agents manning Worthington's office. The uptight, silent mannequin had been replaced by an energetic spitfire, Agent Lidia Burgess. She had something smart to say to Mike every time he walked in the door.

Mike really was there to see Worthington and get some answers, and he was not just stalking this man's office because of a beautiful FBI agent he couldn't wait to see. He had his fair share of beautiful sassy women with smart mouths. At least that's what he told himself.

"Agent Burgess…" Mike's tone was just as dry as hers, but he couldn't help the wicked smile that graced his lips. "You're looking rather beautiful today. What's the occasion? Let me guess. You were waiting on me?" He liked to tease her. In fact, he looked forward to their back and forth banter while he waited.

Chasing Desires
by Kasey Martin

She didn't smile, and her facial expression remained impassive. But he saw the twinkle in her deep, dark brown eyes. He knew that she enjoyed their little exchanges just as much as he did. But he had to admit to himself, Agent Lidia Burgess was indeed looking stunning today.

Her hair was pulled back into its usual bun. However, today she wore her bangs pulled out of her face, so Mike had a clear view of her high cheekbones and cute button nose. Her naturally long lashes were thick and luscious, and they made her eyes look sultry. Her bottom lip was slightly fuller than the top that gave her a natural pout. She had gorgeous brown skin that, as cliché as it may have sounded, reminded him of toffee candy. Every time he was there, he often found himself wondering if she tasted just as sweet.

"You should know by now that flirting with me will get you absolutely nowhere," she smirked at him, and he couldn't help but smile even wider.

"But it can't hurt... right?" he flirtatiously questioned with a wink.

Agent Burgess leaned in closer, as if she was about to tell Mike a secret. Her face now held a serious expression. "Look, I don't know why you're here so often, but Worthington has given explicit instructions not to let you anywhere near him. I'm surprised you keep getting this far inside the building to begin with, which makes me wonder who the hell you really are…"

"I knew he was trying to avoid me, but I didn't know he was giving orders to not let me in." Mike's hackles really rose with that information.

He now understood why his credentials were revoked after the first visit. However, Worthington gave himself way too much credit while at the same time underestimating what Mike Thatcher was actually capable of. *No wonder I had to hack my way into the system again.*

Mike had a suspicion that Worthington had his access to the building denied, but he couldn't prove it. Now, Burgess was essentially confirming his suspicions. Worthington had something to hide, and he was doing his best to keep it from Mike.

"As much as I love seeing you almost every day," Burgess rolled her big doe eyes, and gave him a small genuine smile, "I have to tell you the truth. Worthington went to Dallas. That's why you haven't caught up with him."

What the fuck is he doing in Dallas! Mike barely had time to say goodbye before he was making his way towards the exit, and calling the airport for a flight back home.

***

CHASING DESIRES
by Kasey Martin

LORENZO

The day before had been extremely long and tiresome, but Lorenzo had to admit that they had enjoyed the ceremony. And the small portion of the reception that they got to attend was great. Then Charlie went into labor, and chaos ensued.

Once they got to the hospital, it was a waiting game. They actually stayed until Charlie gave birth to the twins and they got the news that both babies and mommy were doing great. After they gave their well wishes to Jake, they went back to Chase's apartment to relax.

Lorenzo was so happy for Charlie and Jake. They were so in love, and with the addition of their new bundles of joy, they both seemed to be floating on cloud nine. In all his years, the thought of having a family of his own had never crossed his mind. He was all about making money, having power, so building a family had never occurred to Lorenzo. He never even considered having a relationship, so having a wife and child was foreign to him on so many levels.

Now after seeing his friends start a family, he had to admit to himself that he wasn't just satisfied with being in love; he also wanted what they had. Everything seemed possible. The wife, kids, the family life he never considered before, was exactly what he wanted now. *I just have to find out how Chase feels about all of this.*

He wanted to wait to bring up their relationship after they rested because after the day they had, having an emotional discussion wasn't something he was looking forward to. Lorenzo wasn't sure how she was going to react, and the uncertainty had him hesitant to bring it up. He hated talking about feelings and emotions, but he knew that he had to do it.

Although Chase was comfortable working with and being considered "one of the guys," Lorenzo knew that she loved to be pampered and loved on, like every other woman. Just because she had a harder outside shell than most women, didn't make her insides any less soft. In the months that they had been together, Lorenzo learned that Chase held a lot of her emotions in, but she was really sensitive. Being raised by a military father, and going into the FBI, she knew how to cope with hardships, and keep everything bottled up. But she was one of the sweetest, kindest, and most loving individuals he had ever met in his life.

She was also extremely private and very protective over her career, which Lorenzo could appreciate. However, Marcus showing up, and asking questions made Lorenzo realize that their "secret" relationship wasn't that big of a secret after all.

CHASING DESIRES
by Kasey Martin

He knew the team she worked with was ex-Special Forces, and he should've known that they would figure out what the two of them were up to. Chase should've known as well, but his only guess was that at the agency people were too busy trying to get ahead in their careers to notice what their counterparts were up to in their personal lives. But Jake's company was like a family, so of course they would notice.

He had to smile at the thought of her flushed face when Marcus asked if they were together. And although she wanted to keep her business private, she didn't hesitate to claim him as her man, and that made Lorenzo fall in love with her that much more.

The thought of her being proud to be on his arm made him extremely satisfied. Especially when dicks like Lucas Franks kept trying to push up on her. Although he had nothing to prove to anyone, he hated the thought of assholes thinking he was weak because of his injury. He was healed enough to whoop a motherfucker's ass if they disrespected him or his woman, and if he saw Lucas Franks in the street he was going to do just that.

Chase interrupted his thoughts when she came out of the bathroom with a bottle of lotion in her hand. He found out the reason she was so soft and smooth was because she lathered herself in the best smelling lotions every night. He watched her walk to the bed, and sit like she was going to put the lotion on her body. *If she thinks she's going to tease me, she's got another thing coming.*

"You need some help with that?" He posed it as a question, but he took the bottle from her hand before she could reply. He squeezed a generous amount in his hand and started massaging into her calf.

She moaned when he worked his way up one leg, and down the other, and the sound made his cock harden in anticipation.

"That feels so heavenly, babe," Chase moaned again. He put the lotion aside and began rubbing on her stomach. He was making his way up to her breasts when his cell phone rang.

Normally he would have ignored it, but the special ringtone told him that he couldn't. It was the phone call he had been waiting weeks for. His PI, Marco, was finally calling him back. He knew that the information Marco told him could potentially help break Chase's case.

"Hold that thought, babe." Lorenzo reached for his phone. "I gotta take this."

"As long as you finish what you started, Moretti."

Lorenzo smiled and kissed her smirking lips as he answered the call.

CHASING DESIRES
by Kasey Martin

"Marco, it's about damn time you called."

Marco simply chuckled. "You better be glad I even called you at all with everything I've got going on."

Lorenzo heard the amusement in his voice, but he could also hear the seriousness. "Everything okay?"

"Yeah, you know I handled it. Anyway, I've got what you need, and it's amazing how your cousin could be so smart and an idiot simultaneously."

"I wouldn't exactly use the word amazing when referring to my cousin, but idiot… definitely."

Marco chuckled again. "Well, your cousin has been mighty busy since coming to Texas."

Marco went on to tell all of the details he had found out about Tommy and his plans. He let him know that Tommy was meeting up with a contact within the Salazar Cartel. Lorenzo would never know or ask how Marco came about his information but he would be forever grateful that he knew him.

Once Lorenzo hung up with Marco, he turned to a curious-looking Chase with a bright smile on his handsome face. "Pumpkin, looks like you got your chance to finally set up your sting operation."

CHASING DESIRES
by Kasey Martin

Her brown eyes lit up, and he was glad that he was the cause of that look. It took Lorenzo a while to accept that Chase loved her job so much, but he realized that she was just passionate about what she did, and that made him fall for her even more.

"It's about damn time!"

CHAPTER 24
TOMMY

It was finally time to get what he came all the way to Texas for. The meeting with Luis' cousin, the Salazar Cartel contact, was tonight. Tommy strolled into the crowded restaurant, and was immediately shown to a private room by the Maître d'. He was ready to get this shit over with. This deal was important, but the time it took to get everything together was killing him. All of the plotting and planning had Tommy ready to commit murder.

At least in a couple of days I will finally get what I deserve. He thought to himself as he ordered a glass of bourbon from the waiter who was promptly at his side as soon as he was seated.

Tommy had just received his drink, when he saw a familiar face headed his way. He smiled broadly; it was good to see his old friend after so many years. Both of them were very aware that they had to limit the contact after the cluster fuck at the warehouse so many years before. They couldn't have anyone putting any of the players that were there that night together. Although it was virtually impossible to connect them, it wasn't completely unimaginable.

CHASING DESIRES
by Kasey Martin

However, they were in a different state, and it had been almost a decade, so the likelihood of anyone recognizing them was slim to none.

The men smiled at one another, shook hands, and gave each other a brotherly embrace followed by pats on the back. "It's good to see you, man. You look well. Mexico has done you some good." Tommy smiled as he reclaimed his seat.

"You look good too, *hermano*. Maybe you should consider staying in the South. The slower pace might be what you need."

Tommy shook his head as he laughed. "No, thanks. I'm an East Coast type of guy. Shit's too slow down South for me," he replied before he sipped his drink.

"You really ought to consider setting up shop here. The business that you and Luis are doing is remarkable. The girls are making money, and your mules are moving more product than any of our other operations," he smiled and nodded. "You've done all this in just a few short months and you've just landed some of the biggest territory in North Texas. Think of what you could do if you were here on a permanent basis."

Tommy nodded. He may not have been one to brag, but he always kept track of his business, so he was well aware of all his accomplishments since he'd been in Dallas. Even with

CHASING DESIRES
by Kasey Martin

Lorenzo being shot, which drew more attention to him than he wanted, he was still able to make major moves in Texas.

"I understand where you're coming from, but our home base is in Jersey, always has been and it always will be. But Texas is uncharted territory for the Angeletti family, so with the Salazar family backing, we can continue to expand and do great business here."

"I agree." He nodded. "That's why Jesus has agreed to all your terms and he's ready to move forward with your plan."

Tommy felt like the weight had been instantly lifted from his shoulders. Jesus was the leader of the Salazar Cartel. It was his family, and he didn't do business with just anybody. So Tommy knew that he'd proven himself without the backing of his father. Now, if Sal didn't want to retire, he'd have enough power to convince him otherwise.

However, Tommy knew that the power he held may not be enough, so he had some information to blackmail his father with. The blackmail and the backing of the cartel would finally be enough to push the old man out, so that he could take his rightful position as head of the Angeletti family. His father had been in charge long enough. He was damn near seventy years old, and had driven Tommy's mother to an early grave, so he felt like his father owed him this. And if Sal didn't agree, he would have to be taken care of.

CHASING DESIRES
by Kasey Martin

Luis' booming voice brought Tommy out of his musings. He always knew just the right time to show up for the celebration.

Luis and his cousin shook hands and hugged in greeting and Luis sat and looked expectantly at the two men. "So what's the deal? Are we doin' this or not?" he questioned, his Spanish accent thick.

"We are definitely doin' this. You've done a good job here, so we would be stupid to overlook this opportunity."

"You sound so damn stiff, primo. Loosen the fuck up! We got shit to celebrate!" Luis smiled widely at his cousin.

Tommy finally felt himself relax. It had been a long time since the three of them, Tommy Angeletti, Luis Castillo, and Ruben Castillo had been able to sit and shoot the shit with each other. Ever since that dreadful night so long ago when everything changed.

"Look, Tommy, the fellas from the block are up to no good. You helped me out, so I'm just trying to warn you. You need to stay off the streets tonight Hermano." The phone call from Luis' cousin Ruben warning him of a gang hit surprised Tommy. A few months prior, Tommy had helped Luis and Ruben with some gun deals, and it looked like the cousins were thankful, and paid their debts with information.

CHASING DESIRES
by Kasey Martin

However, he'd never really dealt with Ruben before, so he didn't know how much of his word he could take. He and Luis had done some business here and there, so he trusted him, but Ruben was new to the equation.

Ruben Castillo had been trying to make a name for himself, so Tommy was weary of the warning. He had business to take care of tonight, but just in case Ruben wasn't totally full of shit, he called his father to get some advice. Sal told him to send his cousin Sergio to do the grunt work for him because he was disposable. Although Tommy didn't agree with Sal's reasoning, he went along with it because it was short notice and it was better if he covered himself.

"Okay, man, I'll stay clear, but if nothing happens and I lose out on some money, it's gonna be your ass, comprende?" Tommy was serious about his cash. The more he made, the more power he had, and he loved having the power. He loved being in charge, leading his men to success beyond their wildest dreams. It was a hedonistic feeling that he chased on a daily.

Tommy called his younger cousin, Sergio Moretti, and told him to go with his crew for a quick pick-up. Of course, the kid jumped at the chance to prove himself, he had been Tommy's shadow lately wanting to be a part of his crew. He knew that Lorenzo didn't want the kid to be a part of the "family business" but Tommy felt like it wasn't Lorenzo's

Chasing Desires
by Kasey Martin

decision. Sergio had every right to take part in the Angeletti family just like Lorenzo did. So Tommy gave the kid a chance.

That was one decision he would forever regret. Ruben had been right about the hit and Sergio along with his crew were dead. Now Ruben had to lay low because his old gang was looking for him because he snitched to Tommy.

Ruben came to Tommy in a panic, so he decided to repay the favor, and save his life. "My cousin is looking for revenge, he thinks the hit was for him and his brother was killed by mistake. So all we need to do is put the word out in the street telling who did the hit, and your problem will take care of itself."

Ruben seemed to relax at the prospect of not being hunted down, but Tommy knew he still owed Ruben big time for saving his life.

"Good. Without having backup, the Ninth Street gang could cause problems for me," Ruben replied nervously.

"Well, you won't need to worry about that." Tommy waved his hand to dismiss the comment. "Speaking of backup," he said after a moment, "since I'll need to rebuild my crew, I'm going to need your help. I have a major deal going down at one of our warehouses. I don't have time to get enough people in that I trust, so I'm going to need you to stay low and cover my back. I'll give you five stacks for your troubles."

CHASING DESIRES
by Kasey Martin

Ruben's light brown face broke into a bright smile, and Tommy knew that he had him. All you had to do was flash a little cash, and people will be willing to do just about anything.

The warehouse deal was another way that Tommy was trying yet again, prove himself to his father. He had a knack for business, but Sal Angeletti refused to give him any credit for all the business he brought in. Hell, Sal even gave his precious Lorenzo a hard time when it came to money.

Tommy wasn't jealous of his younger cousin, because he had no reason to be. He knew that once his father stopped being so stubborn, the family would be his to run. But the way Sal treated Lorenzo bothered Tommy for some reason that he just couldn't quite put his finger on. But it always seemed like he was in competition with Lorenzo to be bigger and better, so he had to take more and more risks. And this time, they caught up with him.

What Tommy hadn't counted on was that Lorenzo didn't get all of the gang members, and Tommy was ambushed at the warehouse before the deal even went down. Thanks to Ruben hiding in a secret room, he was able to sneak up on the assassins, and get the upper hand. It was another brush with death that Tommy had survived because of Ruben Castillo.

Ruben happened to have a contact at the FBI, and he helped with the clean-up.

CHASING DESIRES
by Kasey Martin

It wasn't like Tommy to trust a dirty cop, but the special agent had guaranteed that nothing would come back on him, so Tommy left the warehouse and never looked back.

Since it was extremely heated, Ruben thought he should leave for Mexico. He felt safer with his cousin at the cartel, and he would work to build a name for himself. They parted ways, and decided it would be best if they kept contact to a minimum.

Those memories often came back to Tommy. He owed Ruben a lot, and as dirty as the FBI agent was, he was a good asset to have throughout the years. Anytime the Feds were getting close to him, his contact would warn him in time. Although the agent would never tell him who was investigating him, he never let Tommy get caught up.

Lately, there'd been some shake ups at the bureau, so his contact always wanted more and more money, or information on drops and deals. It was beneficial to Tommy at first, and the agent would keep him informed about when he was being watched or followed and even when raids were supposed to happen. However, Tommy felt that the bad was starting to outweigh the benefits, so with the power that came with running the family, he could finally give the agent everything he needed to stay content and quiet.

CHASING DESIRES
by Kasey Martin

Tommy's phone chimed with a message notification, but it was too late to read it because all hell had broken loose and all of a sudden, the place was crawling with federal agents.

***

MIKE

Mike knew that Chase would be pissed when she found out that he knew about Worthington's plan to arrest Tommy Angeletti without her. When Agent Burgess told Mike that Worthington was headed to Dallas, it took all of his hacking skills to find out everything he could about his trip. Mike was able to head off Worthington at the local Bureau in Dallas. Worthington didn't seem all that shocked that Mike was waiting on him when he got to the office. As a matter of fact, he had invited him along on the operation to catch one of the high-ranking members of the Salazar Cartel that was meeting with Tommy.

Apparently, someone at the local bureau owed Worthington a favor, so when Ruben Castillo made his way across the border, Worthington was notified.

Now Mike along with a dozen or so local agents were busting in on what looked to be a meeting between the Salazar cousins and Tommy Angeletti.

CHASING DESIRES
by Kasey Martin

The scene was chaotic with people screaming and running. Tables were being knocked over, glasses crashed to the ground, men pulled out their weapons, but to Mike's surprise there weren't any shots fired.

As he took in the room around him, he noticed that although the cousins as well as Angeletti, had men with them, they were all being subdued. That's when Mike knew that Chase wasn't just going to be a little upset she was going to be highly pissed off.

Mike wasn't sure how Chase and the guys knew about this meeting, but since they were there too, it was obvious that he was going to have a lot of explaining to do.

"Mike, I can't believe you would do this to me." Chase's beautiful face was lined with anger.

Mike held up his hands in surrender. "I didn't do anything to you. I only followed Worthington to help you."

As soon as the words left his mouth, a smug-looking Worthington approached them followed by a man he didn't recognize.

"Worthington! How could you undercut me like this? And Lucas, what the fuck are you doing here?"

The blonde man stepped around Worthington to look at Chase with a sleazy grin. Mike wasn't sure who this guy was, but he already didn't care for him.

"You didn't think I was just hanging around these people for the hell of it, did you?"

"So you're an agent? Did you know who I was, and if you did, why didn't you say anything?" Chase accused him with her brown eyes blazing.

"I knew you were an agent, but the way you were acting I just thought you were another of Moretti's whores."

Chase stepped towards him with her fists balled, but before she could move any closer, Marcus, who came out of nowhere, was in front of her.

"I've warned you once, Franks," Marcus growled.

"Easy, big guy. I got this," Chase replied as she gave Marcus a look. He instantly backed up but not too far. Mike could see that they had gotten much closer while he was off chasing down the whereabouts of Daniel Reyes.

"Yeah, easy boy. I thought you left your guard dog at home?" Lucas questioned as he looked around.

"Fuck you. Once this shit is done, I got somethin' for your bitch ass." Marcus growled and the smug expression slowly slipped from Lucas' face.

Mike noticed that Worthington was awfully quiet during the exchange, and he was surprised to see the man not coming to Chase's defense.

Chasing Desires
by Kasey Martin

"What are you even doing here Chase? You're on vacation remember?"

Mike could see the anger in Chase's eyes, but Worthington was right. She wasn't officially supposed to be working any case.

"You're right, Senior Special Agent. I'm no longer working for the bureau. I'll meet you in Jersey to hand in my resignation."

Chase turned and left the scene without saying another word to anybody. *Shit, she will never forgive me for this!*

CHASING DESIRES
by Kasey Martin

LUCAS / DALLAS AGENT

Lucas had been double crossed. He slammed his fist against his desk. Worthington reneged on his deal, and took the credit for the bust. All of Lucas' hard work had gone down the drain just that quick. He knew not to trust Worthington, but all he could see was the recognition he would gain from the take down of a major player like Angeletti.

Lucas paced the length of his cramped office. He had to think of a way to get credit for his undercover work. He had to act fast while Angeletti and the Castillo cousins were still in Dallas. He couldn't think of anything and just when his level of frustration was reaching an almost unbearable level, his office phone rang.

"This is Franks," Lucas answered gruffly.

"Franks, you sound a little upset."

"What… did you call to gloat? You fucking double crossed me you son of a bitch!" Lucas seethed. He couldn't believe the audacity of this man to call him after what he did.

"No, I called to give you some good news. Angeletti is mine. I can't let Dallas have the credit for his arrest. My office has been sitting on this guy for way to long, and my superiors aren't having it."

"Yeah, so what's the good news?" Lucas inquired cautiously.

"The Castillo cousins are yours. We want no parts of the Salazar Cartel, and all of the extraditions would cost too much, Jersey won't have it," Worthington stated.

"Ahh, I see now. The Castillo's would take up too much of your precious time." Lucas now understood why Worthington had done a complete one-eighty. The Dallas bureau had jurisdiction over the Castillo's. All their evidence was for crimes they committed in Texas, and it would take too much effort for Worthington to steal his arrest of the cousins. Tommy Angeletti on the other hand was a wanted man in Jersey, and extraditing his charges from Texas would be much easier.

"Well, at least that's something. Do you want the credit or not?" Worthington sounded smug on the other end of the line. If he didn't have Lucas by the balls, he would tell Worthington where he could go and how to get there, but Lucas needed this to advance his career so he would take what he could get.

"I'll take it. And Worthington?"

"Yeah?"

"I no longer owe you shit…" Lucas disconnected the call. He wouldn't ever have to deal with John Worthington again. He could no longer hold over his head that he helped Lucas cover up an incident when he was in Jersey.

When Lucas was caught in a hotel with an escort, his career could've been over before it got off the ground, but John Worthington stepped in, and Lucas had been doing favors for the man ever since. Now, he could finally be done with the favors, and his career was not only intact it was still on the rise.

CHAPTER 25

CHASE

Chase couldn't believe the betrayal. Both Mike and Worthington had gone behind her back to make the arrest she had been working her entire career to get. She had worked her ass off for nothing. Worthington had swooped in from Jersey and stolen her collar. He also got to take down both Ruben and Luis Castillo who were totally caught off guard by the arrest. Both men were waiting in a Dallas jail waiting for extradition to Jersey.

When she got back to the J.C. Inc. offices, she gave Marcus the third degree. He admitted that he knew that Lucas was an agent, but he also knew that he was undercover, and as much as he despised the creep, he would never give up someone's cover.

Chase understood his position but she really wished she would've known that Lucas was not only an agent, but he worked for a close friend of Worthington's. Lucas had been investigating the Salazar Cartel and their sudden emergence in North Texas. His cover as a club promoter got him into the same locations without being obvious. Chase had to admit that he did well as a sleazy club promoter.

If she would have known that he was such an ass, she wouldn't have given Lorenzo such a hard time about threatening him.

She walked into her apartment and was welcomed by a pacing Lorenzo. He stopped cold when she came in. They hadn't had an argument before she left, but he strongly disagreed with her going to the restaurant for his cousin's meeting without him. They were only supposed to be doing surveillance when Worthington and a dozen agents showed up.

"Hey." Chase gave Lorenzo a small smile.

"Hey. Are you alright?" Lorenzo asked as he closed the short distance between them. He hugged her close to his body and kissed the top of her head tenderly. She had to admit to herself that there was no other place she would rather be.

"I'm fine. It's been a long day."

"Why don't you come tell me all about it, *Pumpkin*." He smirked and led her to the couch where he proceeded to slip off her shoes and massage her feet lovingly.

As Chase relaxed, she told Lorenzo all about the disastrous night.

"So, they arrested Tommy?"

Chasing Desires
by Kasey Martin

Chase nodded. "They took him along with the Salazar cousins into custody. I'm not sure what they're even holding him on. I've been kicked out of the loop by my own mentor."

Lorenzo hugged her warmly. He kissed her lips softly at first then he deepened the kiss, his tongue caressing hers with masterful precision. This was exactly what she needed. He was her cure all. She moaned into his mouth and he slipped his hands down her body.

When his phone rang, she sighed heavily.

"I'm sorry, Pumpkin, it's my mom…"

Chase shook her head and reached for his cell that was on her coffee table. She handed him the phone, "Don't apologize, sweetheart. Here."

Chase left the room so that he could have some privacy to take the phone call. She was exhausted but at least everything had finally come to an end. Worthington had stolen her case out from under her while she was on vacation, but at least Tommy Angeletti would finally go to jail.

She still felt betrayed by Worthington, but none of that mattered anymore. She'd quit right on the spot and she meant it. Mentor or not she would not be able to work under someone that she couldn't trust to have her back. Worthington more than proved that she would never be able to trust him again, and she wouldn't work like that.

Chasing Desires
by Kasey Martin

Chase decided to take Jake up on his previous job offer and stay in Dallas. She needed a new start. She wanted to be far away from her old life as possible, but she did have to go to Jersey to tie things up first.

Lorenzo coming into her bedroom brought her out of her thoughts. The look of distress on his face had her instantly on alert.

"What's wrong?"

"It's my mom. She took a nasty fall."

"Oh no! Is she okay? What can I do?"

Lorenzo gave her a small smile. "You can go to Jersey with me."

She nodded. "Of course. When do we leave?"

***

The next day Chase made all of the arrangements for the two of them to go to Jersey. She was glad that she would be able to be there for Lorenzo when he needed her and she could also hand in her resignation in the same trip.

"Hey, *Pumpkin*, you ready to go?" Lorenzo called out from the living room. Chase chuckled to herself. Their little inside joke about the nicknames had actually stuck. He hardly ever called her anything but *Pumpkin*. And although she told him she hated it, she secretly loved to hear the cutesy name that she swore up and down irritated her.

CHASING DESIRES
by Kasey Martin

"Yes, Zaddy, I'm ready." Chase walked into the living room pulling her luggage behind her. Lorenzo had a strange look on his handsome face.

"What the hell is a *Zaddy*?" Although his face held confusion, Lorenzo's eyes were dancing with laughter.

Chase started to laugh at the look on his face. "Hell if I know. I saw it on social media, so I thought I'd try it out." She shrugged her delicate shoulders with a smile. "What? You don't like it?"

Lorenzo laughed as well. "No, *Pumpkin*. I don't like it. Zaddy isn't going to work for me either. I thought we had established you were going to call me Daddy?" The wicked twinkle in his eyes instantly made Chase's panties wet. That look that he gave her always led to him doing and saying the naughtiest things, and she would end up calling him Daddy every single time.

She knew how much he loved when she called him Daddy. The reward was always worth it. However, it was only fun if she pretended like she didn't want to say it.

"No. That's a bedroom nickname, not an in the streets nickname." Chase smirked at his now frowning face.

"Says who?"

Chasing Desires
by Kasey Martin

"Says me," she laughed. "My grown ass will NOT be calling you Daddy outside of the bedroom." She shook her head. "You are such a freak."

"I am. And you love it." He smiled and winked.

"Yes, I do love you." Chase laughed, and then stopped when she heard Lorenzo's laugh cut off.

Oh shit, did I say that out loud?

She turned slowly to look at him, and the heat in his blue eyes was unexpected. For some reason, she expected him to be panicked, but if she wasn't mistaken, she thought she saw love reflecting back at her.

"What did you just say?" he questioned as he stalked towards her.

"I uh…" Chase's brain stuttered, and she couldn't think. When she opened her mouth to speak again, his phone rang with his mother's ringtone.

"Saved by the bell," she mumbled thankful that she didn't have to have the, *I love you,* conversation just yet.

"Don't think we aren't going to talk about that little slip," Lorenzo smiled, "and I love you too." He pecked her lips, and turned to answer the phone.

How the hell? He's just going to say it like that, and turn away from me? She was thankful that they could skip the awkward conversation about being in love, but what did this

Chasing Desires
by Kasey Martin

really mean for them? Chase had no idea where they would go from here. However, she couldn't help the smile that graced her beautiful face.

He loves me too.

CHASING DESIRES
by Kasey Martin

CHAPTER 26
LORENZO

The flight from Texas to Jersey seemed like it took forever, even sitting in first class. Although he had been given several updates on his mother's condition, the anxiety that Lorenzo felt was through the roof. He just wouldn't be able to feel comfortable until he was able to see her for himself.

Chase had been a trooper, making all the travel arrangements for them, especially after all the shit that had gone down with her case. He couldn't believe how convenient it was for Worthington to show up and make the arrest. He was also shocked that his uncle hadn't contacted him, but he couldn't worry about any of that; he had to make sure his mother was alright.

They arrived at the hotel, and checked in. It was already late, so they decided to get room service, and stay in for the night. He called the hospital to check on his mom, and her condition hadn't changed, so he decided that they would go to visit her early the next day.

He walked into the bedroom of the large suite where Chase was meticulously hanging clothes on hangers and placing them in drawers. He thought it was funny, considering that he hardly ever unpacked.

Lorenzo walked up behind her and placed his arms around her waist in an intimate embrace. He leaned down and nuzzled her neck before he placed a kiss on the top of her head.

"You know we will be here for at least a week, and you don't have to hang everything up at this very moment."

Her sigh was uneasy, "I know, but I'm just nervous, and I needed something to do."

"Aww, *Pumpkin,* what are you nervous about?" Lorenzo question as he turned her around to face him.

"Being here with you… like this. I would never hesitate to be here to support you, but it's dangerous for us to be in Jersey together. Although I keep a tremendously low profile, people still know me here…" Chase took a deep breath, "I'm just worried and stressed."

"I understand your concerns, baby. But please believe me when I say… Nothing will happen to you or me… Nothing."

Lorenzo cupped her face and looked deeply into her eyes, which had the suspicious sheen of unshed tears. "I love you and I would give my last breath before I would let anything happen to you. Do you understand?"

CHASING DESIRES
by Kasey Martin

Chase nodded her head, and a tear slowly descended from her eye. He had an idea why she was crying; the case finally being over and the stress of everything that had happened was finally breaking her outer shell, but seeing her tears was not something he wanted to get used to.

She hastily wiped her face, and smiled a watery smile. "Okay," she answered finally.

"Don't cry, sweetheart."

"Nobody has ever said anything like that to me before. I love you too, so much."

He took her lips in a passionate kiss that spoke of all the love that he felt for her. When she kissed him back, he could feel all of the love they shared. This thing between them may have started out as her cover, but it was far more than that. It was genuine. It was raw. It was real. It was love.

Lorenzo meticulously pulled her heavy sweater and t-shirt over her head. Then he continued to take off the rest of her clothes, leaving her in just her little red lacy panties. He pulled them down her long, toned legs, and threw them over his shoulder.

She lay down on the oversized bed, and he stood over her to enjoy her beautiful body. She was a Nubian Goddess, and he was going to worship every dip and curve of her gorgeous ebony physique.

CHASING DESIRES
by Kasey Martin

Lorenzo slowly undressed and he watched as Chase's eyes filled with lust. He was proud of the progress he'd made at the gym. He had lost too much weight following his accident, and he had finally put it back on, and then some. His muscles were bulging, and he was in the best shape of his life, and his woman was getting her fill.

He watched her pink tongue run slowly over her pouty bottom lip, and then she sank her teeth into it, she was a damn temptress. He groaned as he crawled slowly over her body. Lorenzo kissed her stomach, and licked her belly button. He kissed up her body but skipped over her breasts because he knew how sensitive they were, and he wanted to savor those later. Lorenzo knew that she would be frustrated and it would just heighten her anticipation more if he kissed all around them. So he focused his attention as well as his tongue on her collarbone, and the sensitive part of her neck behind her ear.

When Chase groaned in frustration, Lorenzo kissed his way back down her body, finally paying her glorious breasts some much needed attention. He sucked one into his mouth, hard. She moaned and her back arched feeding more of herself to him. He groaned and flicked his tongue rapidly over her nipple. She tasted so fucking sweet. He couldn't get enough of her.

CHASING DESIRES
by Kasey Martin

He continued to move down her body and he sat up. Lorenzo grabbed her hips and pulled her toward him. Chase wrapped her legs around his waist, and before he could even think twice about it he sank his rock-hard shaft into her warm, waiting, pulsating pussy.

"Shit, *Pumpkin*, you feel so fucking good." He moved into her with long firm strokes.

"Ummm, yes, Lorenzo…go deep, Daddy," Chase moaned as she thrust her hips up to match his rhythm.

Fucking temptress! She knew what that shit did to him; calling him Daddy and moaning his name. He was going to go soft and slow. He was making love to her now, but he was going to fuck the shit out of her before it was all over.

"You know what that shit does to me. Don't you?" Lorenzo questioned as he flipped her over, and pushed himself back inside of her. He wrapped his hand around her pony tail, and pulled her head back making her arch her back in the process. He smacked her ass with the other hand as he continued to thrust inside of her over and over again with powerful strokes. Her pussy was soaking wet, and the sound of their collective moans was starting to fill the room.

Lorenzo played with her clit as she gyrated her hips in a circular motion, her hot canal had him in a death grip, and her arousal was coating his shaft and dripping down his balls. He started moving faster and faster, as he spanked her firm round globes harder and harder.

"Yes, baby! Right there, Daddy… ooooh, yeah!" Chase shouted out as her whole body tensed and then trembled with her release.

"Damn, sweetheart! Yeah. Come on my cock! Call me, Daddy…" Lorenzo growled as he completely lost control, he wildly pumped into her.

"Daddy, yes Dadddyyyyy!" Chase continued to orgasm on a loud long moan that made Lorenzo's climax rush forward. He felt his balls draw up, and his cock went rigid, right before he pumped his seed into her waiting body.

Her sugar walls pulsated around his manhood which prolonged his orgasm. He had never in his entire life felt something so good, and so right. He collapsed onto her body, both of their naked bodies drenched, and covered in sweat. They both were breathing tremendously hard, and they were connected intimately with his manhood still buried deep inside of her body.

Lorenzo knew in that moment that he was incredibly lucky to have found a woman like Chase Johnson. A woman made just for him.

"I love you, babe," Chase sighed contently.

CHASING DESIRES
by Kasey Martin

"I love you too, *Pumpkin*." He kissed her lips, and pulled from her body slowly. They groaned in unison at the loss of their connection.

Lorenzo rose from the bed slowly, and after getting a towel and cleaning them both up, he got back in bed, pulled Chase close to his body. He would never take for granted what they had. He'd spent too much time resenting her, and denying his feelings. He would never go back to not loving Chase. Never.

***

Early the next morning, the couple got up, got dressed and headed to the hospital. Lorenzo was ready to see his mom, even though the circumstances weren't the best. He felt guilty about not seeing his mom as often as he should, but he prayed that God would see fit to give him the time he needed to redeem himself. It was just hard for him to watch the once vibrant and fun loving woman deteriorate right before his eyes. Her not remembering him, and always thinking he was her brother, calling him Sal every time he went to see her, hurt his heart.

But Lorenzo had to accept the fact that it wasn't about him, it was about his sick mother, and he needed to be a better son. He was determined to start today.

They walked into the hospital hand in hand, and Lorenzo could feel the nervous energy radiating from Chase.

CHASING DESIRES
by Kasey Martin

She fidgeted the entire way to the hospital, and he wasn't so sure why she was so on edge.

He stopped walking before they made it to his mother's room and pulled her to the side. "Chase, Pumpkin, what is the matter? You've been moving nonstop since we got in the car."

Chase visibly sucked in a deep breath. "I know your mother isn't well. And she doesn't know who you are, and she won't know who I am, but..."

Lorenzo cut her off, he cupped her face and looked deep into her dark brown eyes. "I get it, and I love you. There's no reason for you to be nervous and even if she wasn't sick..." He paused to make sure she was listening. "She would've loved you just as much as I do."

He watched her visibly relax, and it just made him realize how lucky he was to have a woman care so much about him that she was nervous to meet his mother.

They kissed slowly before going into the room. He was surprised to see his mother awake, and looking somewhat alert. She was gazing out of the window like she usually did when he visited at the home, the only difference was the absence of the blank stare she normally had. She turned toward them, and a smile brightened her lovely face.

"Ma, how ya' doing?" Lorenzo approached her slowly to make sure she felt comfortable with him.

CHASING DESIRES
by Kasey Martin

"You always looked so much like him, ya know?" He was surprised that she was aware enough to ask questions even if it didn't make sense to him.

"Like who, Ma?" Lorenzo stood at the edge of the bed. He couldn't tell if she was actually talking to him or reliving some memory that she was stuck in.

She shook her head and smiled again. "Who's your friend, son?"

Lorenzo's eyes widened in shock. Although she would remember him from time to time, it happened so rarely that he was always caught off guard whenever she was lucid.

"This is my girlfriend, Chase Johnson, Ma. Chase this is my Ma, Theresa Moretti."

Chase came over and clasped his mother's hand in a warm greeting. "It's very nice to meet you, Mrs. Moretti."

"Likewise, Chase." Theresa smiled warmly.

"So you kids came to check on your old Ma, huh?" Theresa turned her attention back to Lorenzo with a motherly nod and smile.

"Yeah, Ma, you took a nasty fall. I had to come make sure you were okay."

"You should come to see me more often."

He nodded. "You're right, and I will. Maybe you would want to come to Texas?"

Chasing Desires
by Kasey Martin

"No, son. Your Ma is too old to be moving around. I'm fine just where I am." She smiled at him and then turned to gaze out the window again.

They sat in silence for a while, and Lorenzo was content with that. Chase stepped out to take a phone call, but he knew she was just giving him some alone time with his mother. He was still so surprised with how alert she was. This was one of the longest conversations he had with his mother in a long time. He would savor this moment because there was no telling when he would get this chance again.

"Where's Sergio, Sal?" Theresa questioned. And just like that she was gone again. The return of the blank look in her eyes made Lorenzo's heart sink.

"Sergio is away, Theresa." Lorenzo learned to just go along with the conversation. Denying he was Sal and trying to make her remember him just made her upset.

"You know, Sal, I still feel guilty about not telling Lorenzo everything." The fact that her face held so much worry along with the mention of his name made Lorenzo sit up and pay attention.

"What do you feel guilty about?" Lorenzo questioned. He wasn't sure why his mother would be remorseful because she was such a genuinely good person.

"You know that I love that boy like he is my own."

CHASING DESIRES
by Kasey Martin

Wait! What the hell did she just say? Lorenzo was confused by this odd conversation. Maybe his mother was sicker than he thought. Maybe she wasn't just losing her memory; maybe she was creating a whole other world.

"I know you don't agree because it could make you lose everything. But he should know he's your son, Sal." She continued talking and Lorenzo was absolutely floored.

"What do you mean he's *my* son?" Lorenzo questioned, still unable to get his mind to catch up to this very real confession his mother was obliviously making.

"Come on, Sal. I know I promised that I would never tell. But he's so rebellious, so much like you. He's fighting all the time with my husband. He needs to know that *you're* his father."

"No..." Lorenzo croaked out. *This can't be true. This isn't real.*

Theresa must've mistaken his denial for an answer because she went on to plead her case. "Sergio is getting older and he follows Lorenzo like he's his shadow. I'm afraid of what might happen to my baby if he does the things that you all do."

Lorenzo's broken heart felt like it had been ripped from his chest at her words. His mother had been afraid of the inevitable, just like he was, but for totally different reasons. Sal wasn't his uncle; he was his *father*.

CHASING DESIRES
by Kasey Martin

What the fuck is happening?

CHASING DESIRES
by Kasey Martin

CHAPTER 27

CHASE

Chase was pleased that Lorenzo wanted her to come with him to visit his mother. It showed her that what they had was real. She was really happy that Lorenzo's mother seemed to be lucid enough to know who he was. He'd previously told her how he had a hard time dealing with the fact that she didn't know him when he came to visit. So it was wonderful that he could enjoy a conversation with her, and she was excited that she was able to meet her when she was coherent, even if she may not remember her later. Chase wanted to give them some alone time, so when her phone rang she took the opportunity to do just that.

Her phone had gone silent once she stepped into the hall, but she used the opportunity to just think about everything that was happening.

The past week had been totally exhausting, and Chase was being shut out of everything that was happening with the bust, and it was all because of her mentor. She just couldn't believe that a man that she looked up to as a father figure would betray her like that. But she was finally back in Jersey and she would deal with her failing career later. Right now she wanted

Chasing Desires
by Kasey Martin

to be there for the man that she was head over heels in love with.

Chase was on a natural high and feeling special. She'd never thought that spending time with Lorenzo could feel like this. He treated her like a queen, and showered her with love and affection in ways that she didn't even know existed. With every single whispered word, soft caress, and passionate kiss, she fell deeper and deeper in love with him. And although she felt worried about them being in Jersey together, because she was technically still an agent, she knew that she wasn't willing to give him up.

She had given up too much of herself to her job over the years, and she almost made the mistake of giving up on Lorenzo before they even had a chance. She was so busy chasing after what she thought she wanted that she almost let what she needed go. Chase decided that she would never do that again. It was past time that she chased what mattered most in life, and that was the love she shared with Lorenzo.

Her cell rang again and the screen displayed a familiar number, it brought her back to the present. She didn't know what to expect from the caller, but it couldn't have been anything good.

"Hello?" Chase finally answered after taking a deep breath.

CHASING DESIRES
by Kasey Martin

"Hi, is this Agent Johnson?" the female voice asked. Chase pulled her phone away from her ear to look at the screen. It was Worthington's office number, but it definitely wasn't her mentor on the phone. She wasn't expecting to hear anything from him or the bureau since she'd been basically cast aside, so the call was definitely shocking.

"Yes, this is she. Who's calling?" Chase suspiciously questioned.

The female caller sighed heavily. "Thank goodness. This is Agent Burgess. I've had a helluva time trying to track you down."

"And just why are you looking for me?" She'd seen the young agent around, but she hadn't been there long before Chase went to Dallas, so she didn't know the other woman very well.

"I think a friend of yours may be in some trouble."

"What friend and what kind of trouble?" This woman wasn't making any sense whatsoever and her talking in code was really wearing on Chase's nerves. She understood why the agent may have been cautious, especially after everything that had gone down. But she still didn't have the patience to deal with it.

CHASING DESIRES
by Kasey Martin

"Look, you know where I am, but I couldn't take the chance and not call you immediately. Mike Thatcher has been here, and I really think he's going to do something crazy.

"We need to meet. Immediately!"

Chase set-up a meeting time with Agent Burgess, and quickly called Marcus. She knew that Jake was still at the hospital with his wife and babies, and had no time to deal with this cluster fuck that was unraveling around her.

Marcus answered on the first ring, and Chase began speaking before he had a chance to say hello. "What the hell is Mike doing back in Jersey?"

"Well, hello to you too, CJ," Marcus stated in dry tone.

"I just got a call from an agent from my home office here in Jersey. She was trying to warn me to help Mike. Marc, what the hell is Mike doing?" Chase questioned, her impatience and irritation for the situation growing by the second.

She heard Marcus groan and then take a deep breath. "Thatch found some evidence and he went back to Jersey to follow a lead."

"What are you talking about? Evidence on what?"

"Thatch had been working on some things. He wanted to make up for what happened—"

CHASING DESIRES
by Kasey Martin

Chase cut Marcus off mid-sentence. "He made his bed when he betrayed me. Marc. He helped Worthington undermine all the work I did. He should've told me and you know it!"

"He wasn't trying to undermine your case. He went about it all wrong, but he was trying to help you Chase. You know Thatch better than that." Marcus sighed heavily.

Chase grunted but didn't comment.

"He's been working on something that he knew was a sore subject for you, but he got caught up in the Angeletti bust, and everything went to hell."

"Stop beating around the damn bush, Marc. What the hell is he working on?" The irritation Chase was feeling was almost overwhelming. She could feel the beginnings of a migraine coming on.

"He's following a lead that Daniel Reyes is still alive."

"What…what the hell did you just say?" Chase slumped against the wall like she'd been punched in the gut. At that moment, she was extremely happy that she was in a hospital because she just might die of a heart attack.

"Thatch thinks Reyes is alive. He found evidence recently that leads him to believe it. He also thinks that Worthington knows all about it."

The punches just kept coming, and she crumpled to the floor. *What the hell is going on around me?* Chase tried to take deep breaths, but she couldn't seem to breathe. *Why would Worthington let me think Daniel was dead? This man's betrayals just keep coming.*

Chase could hear a distorted voice calling her name, but her head was spinning, and she couldn't get her bearings. She was a highly-trained agent that knew how to handle combat. She was taught to act quickly, and make judgment calls on a dime. She was trained to not hesitate, and to keep her cool. However, all of her training had gone out of the window when she heard those words… Daniel Reyes is alive!

***

Chase woke with a start. She sat up quickly and a sharp pain ran through her arm. She looked down and noticed an IV attached to her. She moaned when she whipped her head around and the pounding almost knocked her back down.

"Hey easy, *Pumpkin.* Lie down before you hurt yourself." Lorenzo was beside her in a flash. He rubbed her hand, and assisted her in relaxing back on some pillows.

"What happened?" Chase croaked out.

"I'm not sure. I heard a loud thud, and when I came to check on you, you were passed out in the hall. Marcus was yelling your name on the other end of your phone, which you were still holding by the way."

Chasing Desires
by Kasey Martin

Chase sighed and ran her hands through her disheveled ponytail. She took the band out and tried to detangle it with her hands. "I had a panic attack and I couldn't catch my breath. I must've fainted. I've never done that before."

"Well never do it again, because you scared the shit out of me!" Lorenzo leaned down and lovingly kissed the top of her head.

"How long was I out?" Chase asked. She wondered if she missed the meeting with Agent Burgess. She really needed to get her shit together, so that she could find Mike.

"It's only been a couple of hours. Marcus didn't want to tell me what you guys were discussing." Lorenzo ran his hands through his long, dark curly hair. His blue eyes were more tired than she'd ever seen them.

"Babe, what's wrong?" Chase rubbed his hand like he'd done her moments before. She knew that he wasn't just worried about her. She merely fainted, the strain that was etched across his handsome face told her something more was going on that she wasn't aware of.

"We can talk about it later. It will hold, believe me," he mysteriously answered with a sigh. Chase would make sure they did indeed talk about what was bothering him later.

"Okay, but we will talk about it."

He nodded and gave her a small smile. "So what's going on with your case that you fainted?"

Chase took a deep breath and told Lorenzo all about Mike and his side investigation. She was still having trouble wrapping her head around the fact that after all these years, Daniel could still be alive.

"So why wouldn't he just tell you what he thought? Why the big secret?" Lorenzo almost angrily questioned.

"I don't know. Mike has always been the type to come with solid proof. Maybe he thought I wouldn't have believed his theory."

"Well, do you… believe him? Do you think your partner is still alive?"

Chase shook her head. "I don't know what to believe. Mike is a genius at what he does. If he thinks he found something that says that Daniel is alive then I don't doubt that."

"But you still have doubts."

"Yes, a lot doesn't add up, and I need to meet with Agent Burgess, and Mike, to find out what the hell is going on. And I need to do that before he gets himself killed."

"Well, I will be going to this meeting with you and so will Marcus. He's on his way here now."

Chase just agreed. There was no reason why she needed to argue with him about it. Meeting with Agent Burgess and

Chasing Desires
by Kasey Martin

Mike wasn't a dangerous situation, but the information she would find out could potentially be devastating to her emotionally, and for that she was glad Lorenzo wanted to be there for her.

Chase had spent the better part of her career obsessed with making Tommy Angeletti pay for the death of her partner, now she finds out that Daniel Reyes might be alive. But where was he all of these years, and why was he hiding? There were so many questions that she needed answered.

It had already been a long day, but upon her release from the hospital, she decided to meet with Agent Burgess. Marcus was arriving around ten that night, and because all of her calls to Mike had gone unanswered, they would try and get in touch with him later, so that they could meet up with him the next day.

When there was a knock on the hotel suite's door, Chase went to answer it. Of course, it was Agent Burgess. "Hi, Lidia. Come on in." Chase didn't want to call her agent because she wanted to be cautious about everything; even something as small as that.

"Hi, Chase," Lidia responded with a nervous smile.

Chase led her to the sitting area of the hotel suite where they sat down and were swiftly joined by Lorenzo. Agent Burgess wasted no time telling them what she suspected Mike was up to. She told them all about him coming into the agency and damn near stalking Worthington, but she didn't know why.

"Worthington had been avoiding Thatcher since I'd started working at his office, so I had a friend look into who Mike Thatcher really was, and not the bullshit profile anyone could find either."

"Okay, so you found out who Mike was." Chase hoped the woman would get on with the story.

"Worthington had left for Dallas, but Thatcher was still showing up at the office. I broke protocol and told him where to find Worthington. I thought that would be the end of it until a couple of days ago when Angeletti was arraigned and Thatcher was back stalking Worthington."

"Okay, so—"

"There have been some things left out of the media. I know what Worthington did to you."

Chase nodded. Everyone knew that the Angeletti case was hers. For Worthington to take the credit was a shit thing to do, but it happened all the time.

"Angeletti was only charged with some flimsy misdemeanor shit. That's how he made bail. Worthington basically got him off."

"What the fuck!" Chase was even more enraged than before.

CHASING DESIRES
by Kasey Martin

"I'm sure Mike knows because he didn't see me, but I saw him at the office following Worthington from a distance and I'm pretty sure he wasn't looking for a friendly chat."

"Mike knows something. We need to track him down and figure it out. Do you have Worthington's schedule?"

"He has a meeting in the morning at the office, but after that his schedule is clear."

"We need to make sure we monitor his movements tomorrow. We find Worthington, we find Mike."

"Ok, and I will monitor him from the inside and keep you posted." Burgess got up to leave. "I will see you guys tomorrow."

"I can't let you do that Burgess." Chase stopped her from leaving. "This thing could get messy real fast, and you have your whole career ahead of you. There's no need for you to get involved in this."

"I'm already involved. And there's no way in hell that I can just sit back and wait for something to happen. No, I'll be there with you guys, even if it's unofficially." Lidia nodded and reached for the door. "See you guys tomorrow."

Chase took a deep relieved breath. She was more than happy to be done with this whole thing. She just hoped they made it in time to save Mike even if it was from himself.

CHAPTER 28

MIKE

Mike was paying for not being around for over two weeks. Apparently, Chase and Lorenzo were in a relationship, and she had run off to Jersey to officially quit her job. He had to give it to Worthington; he'd managed to screw Chase and him at the same time.

Evidently, the sting operation had been put into motion months before Chase had taken a leave of absence and Worthington never said a word. He let her think his superiors were freezing her out when it was actually him the entire time.

Mike found out too late that Worthington had used Chase and the sting to distract him. He was getting too close to the root of all this. John Worthington knew where Daniel Reyes was, and exactly why he'd been hiding for all of these years.

Once the dust of the sting settled, Mike had more questions than answers about everything that had gone down. Mike was like a dog with a bone when he had unanswered questions. He had to find out what had happened now more than ever, especially if he ever wanted Chase to forgive him.

CHASING DESIRES
by Kasey Martin

After looking through all of the files he had previously hacked into, Mike still hadn't found the positive identification of Reyes' body that should've accompanied the initial report. There also was the missing autopsy report which made Mike question the validity of his death. Why would an Agent who worked so hard undercover disappear? Mike knew that there could be any number of reasons, but the angle he was working on was that Reyes was dirty.

He didn't want to tell Chase about what he suspected, because she was so invested in catching Tommy Angeletti that he knew she wouldn't have taken him seriously. He wanted to have solid proof of everything. Now that Angeletti was out of the way, he would take his evidence to her. The last thing he had to do was actually get the proof, and he would do that by following John Worthington.

***

Mike hadn't talked to any of the team since he left Dallas. He left a message letting them know what was going on, but he wasn't up for trying to explain himself anymore. They were all pretty pissed at him for not letting them know that Worthington was on his way to undercut Chase, but he was just trying to help close her case. Now he was all the way back in Jersey chasing Worthington yet again to prove to Chase he was only trying to help her.

Chasing Desires
by Kasey Martin

Mike's phone rang yet again, and this time it was Jake. Mike hadn't heard from him since he'd left the voice message, so he decided to answer the phone instead of letting it go to voicemail.

"Hey, Cameron. What's up?"

"*What's up*? That's all you have to say to me, Thatch? After you left the message telling me about what you've been doing, you go radio silent?" Jake sounded extremely pissed off, and Mike knew that he would have to smooth things over with the big guy. Jake didn't like for his guys to go silent no matter what was going on. It kept everyone safe.

"I'm sorry, man. I don't have any excuse." Mike knew that trying to explain his reasoning to an angry Jake was an exercise in futility. Jake would never accept it, and it would only piss him off that much more.

"You know protocol, man. It's not just for your protection, it's there for everyone involved." Jake let out a long deep breath.

"I know. I told you where I was and what was going on. I don't know why everyone is panicking over me not answering the phone for a couple of hours." Mike said exasperated. He knew not to make excuses but damn, it wasn't like he fell off the face of the damn earth. It was only a few hours.

CHASING DESIRES
by Kasey Martin

"You know damn well that things could change in a few hours!" Jake yelled into the phone.

Mike had heard enough. He didn't need a lecture from Jake, or anybody else. That's why he stopped answering his phone, and checking the messages. He knew that telling Jake what was going on in a voicemail had the potential to backfire on him. However, he knew that he had to tell someone what was going on.

"Look, Jake. I have to go. I'll call you when I get out of this meeting."

"Mike…Thatch…wai—"

Mike hung up the phone, and turned it off. Whatever needed to be said could be said once he finished confronting Worthington.

He pulled up to a spot where he could see the front entrance to the building. He wanted to wait to see who Worthington was there to meet first, and then he would try and ambush him to get what he needed.

Mike waited for about twenty more minutes for anyone else to show up. Whoever Worthington was meeting with, was either really late or they weren't coming. So Mike took the opportunity to go in and see what was going on, and confront Worthington on his findings.

CHASING DESIRES
by Kasey Martin

Mike made sure both his weapons were locked and loaded. He had a Glock in the small of his back under his shirt, and a small caliber weapon strapped to his ankle. He also made sure to have his knives strapped to the side. It always came in handy to have multiple weapons especially when you were going into an uncertain situation.

He cautiously approached the building. On one hand he was glad that it was daylight and he could see what the hell was going on around him, but on the other hand it made his job of being covert that much more difficult.

He looked through a couple of windows as he slipped silently into the entrance. Although the windows weren't covered, there was nothing to really see. The place was sparsely decorated with desks and chairs spread around here and there. He still couldn't figure out why Worthington would be meeting in a place like this, but he was soon going to find out.

Mike made his way inside the building, and the silence was deafening. He didn't hear anyone talking or moving around, but he knew that Worthington was there.

He crept his way to the back silently where an office was located. He was assuming Worthington was in there since he didn't seem to be anywhere else. Mike slowly approached the door, and opened it cautiously.

Chasing Desires
by Kasey Martin

"I was wondering what was taking you so long." Worthington gestured to the vacant chair, and Mike sat down. Unlike the rest of the building, this room was completely furnished with a large desk, chairs, book shelves, and tables. The entire room was completely out of place.

"So you were waiting on me to show up?" It wasn't like Mike to be a step behind, but Worthington's actions had him thoroughly confused.

"I've been waiting on you. I couldn't have you coming to the office anymore. Too many people were starting to notice."

"Where is Daniel Reyes? I've told you my theory, so you need to tell me what the hell is going on…"

"Daniel Reyes is dead," Worthington stated so simply that Mike had to wonder if the man had any heart at all. This was one of his men who had supposedly been brutally murdered, and he acted like he was talking about the weather.

"I have evidence to suggest otherwise. I know he was alive when the massacre was happening at the warehouse. The records were falsified, and I want to know why."

Mike could see that Worthington was getting agitated, and he was glad. The old man had too much practice at holding in his emotions Mike had to knock him off his game if he was going to get any real answers.

CHASING DESIRES
by Kasey Martin

"You're barking up the wrong tree, Thatcher. Daniel Reyes is dead.

***

WORTHINGTON

"I knew I couldn't trust you. What the fuck are you doing here?" Worthington's voice was hollow. When Reyes called him about the deal, he told him not to go in without back-up. However, the real reason was, so Reyes didn't find out about him working with the mob.

"Of course, I can be trusted." Reyes held up his hands.

But Worthington wasn't persuaded, he knew Reyes, so he pulled out his gun with a silencer attached. Daniel was always sticking his nose where it didn't belong. It was really too bad. If he would've just followed directions and stayed away from the warehouse, Worthington wouldn't have to kill him.

"I have knowledge of something that will bring down everyone. Especially you."

"What the hell are you talking about?" Worthington pointed the gun directly at Daniel's head. "You little shit! You stole the fucking ledger! Where the fuck is it?" He seethed still pointing the gun.

There was a book that Tommy Angeletti kept, it had everyone he dealt with listed; there were many powerful people

CHASING DESIRES
by Kasey Martin

in that book. Worthington never understood why he would keep such detailed accounts of all his criminal activity, but anybody that got a hold of that ledger would have the criminal world at their fingertips.

"We can both get what we need," Reyes responded his hands still raised.

Worthington cocked his gun. "Or you could die right here?"

"Or... we can make a deal." Reyes lowered his hands slowly.

"What deal could you possibly want to make?" Worthington's voice was cold. He didn't take Reyes as being a sniveling coward, but it looked like he was mistaken.

"I want out of this life. I'm tired of being undercover, and you know as well as I do that I can't just retire."

Worthington didn't get into the position of a Senior Special Agent because he was stupid. Daniel Reyes was a lot of things, but he wasn't a dirty cop. It was too bad that he really couldn't make that deal. Worthington was always looking for a few good men to help him with his extracurricular activities.

Worthington shook his head. "You should've listened." There wasn't a sound when the bullet pierced the skull of Daniel Reyes. His large body dropped to the ground with a hard thud.

# CHASING DESIRES
by Kasey Martin

Worthington hated the extra work he would now have to do to dispose of the body, but it was worth it. He had no idea what Reyes did with the ledger, but he was confident nobody else knew of its existence because he definitely would be in jail.

Worthington would make it his mission that nobody ever found out what happened to Daniel Reyes, and the knowledge of the ledger would die with him.

***

CHASE

They pulled up to the nondescript building, and parked in a semi vacant lot. There were only a few cars there, so Marcus parked the SUV towards the back and out of sight. The four of them exited the vehicle with a clear plan in place.

Marcus and Agent Burgess would go in the main entrance, and Lorenzo and Chase would go through a side entrance. They didn't know what to expect when they got in the building, but they knew that Worthington was up to no good. He had sabotaged her case and let Angeletti off, so they knew not to trust him.

Chase and Lorenzo made their way to the side entrance, where they came into contact with two heavily armed men. Chase snuck up behind the smaller man, and using all of her

CHASING DESIRES
by Kasey Martin

body weight she was able to put him into a choke hold that knocked him unconscious. Lorenzo punched the larger man in the back of the head putting him out as well. They quickly disarmed both men and made their way inside.

Once they were in the building, they crept to the back where they heard voices. Chase pulled out her weapon when she peeked through the cracked door, and saw Worthington pointing a gun at Mike's head. She wanted to be shocked, and appalled, but she had come to the realization that she had no idea who Special Agent John Worthington actually was.

She heard Mike pleading with Worthington to tell him why he was doing all of this.

"Why would you kill your own agent?" Chase heard Mike ask. Her hand wavered slightly. *Did Worthington kill Danny?* She looked wide-eyed at Lorenzo who was behind her with his own weapon drawn. The confusion on his face told her he had heard the same question.

"He was in the way just like you are now." She heard Worthington sinisterly respond.

She had no idea who this man was. He had been such an influence over her life; all the decisions she'd made over the years, all of the things she did to make him proud, and he was not only dirty, but a murderer. Worthington wanted her to drop the case then stole it from under her because he was afraid that she might stumble upon the truth. He'd killed her partner. He'd killed Daniel Reyes.

Before she knew it, her feet had a mind of their own and they were moving forward. She entered the room with her gun drawn, and she knew the exact moment that Worthington realized he was no longer alone with Mike.

His hazel eyes grew wide, and his mouth formed a disapproving thin line. "You just couldn't stay away. Always have to be the hero." Worthington shook his head.

Chase was disgusted at the audacity of Worthington. He was the one who taught her to stand up for what she believed in, and make sure to get the guy. Now he was upset that she never gave up, and found out who he really was.

"I would've never given up looking for Daniel's killer."

"Oh, tsk, tsk, Chase." He shook his head again, a smirk breaking out over his face. "You weren't looking for Daniel's killer. You were looking to put Tommy Angeletti away. And I was making too much money to let you do that."

Chase hated to admit it, but the son of a bitch was right. She had her mind made up that Angeletti had killed Daniel and she'd never looked for any other possible suspects. That was a mistake that she would rectify. John Worthington would not get away with his crimes. He had spent years blocking her progress and running with the criminal world. Now, he was going to pay for every single one of his misdeeds, including Daniel's death.

"Put the gun down, John. You will never get away with this. Too many people know about you now." Chase tried to coax him to give himself up, but she knew that Worthington was not the type of man to go to prison, he was the type to go down in a blaze of glory.

Right on cue, Worthington swung the gun on her, but before he could get a shot off, Chase ducked and swept her leg out knocking Worthington's feet from under him.

He fell to the ground with a loud thud. Chase scrambled to get on top of him to get the upper hand, but before she managed to subdue him, there were gunshots fired through the single window of the room.

Chase dove out of the way taking cover behind the desk, before she knew it both Lorenzo and Mike were at her side returning the gun fire.

"How many guys do you think he has surrounding the place?" Lorenzo questioned.

"Couldn't be many because there wasn't anyone here when I arrived," Mike responded.

Chase could barely focus on what they were saying because her sights were set on her sleazebag, dirty ex-mentor trying to slither his way out of the only exit in the room. Like

Chasing Desires
by Kasey Martin

the snake he was, he was on his belly crawling as quickly as he could to get away.

Chase wouldn't let him get away, so among the throng of bullets, she chased after the snake. When she exited the room, she stopped short when she came face to face with the barrel of Worthington's gun.

"Come on now, Chase. Don't make me do this. I can disappear and be out of your life forever or I can kill you right now and I will still disappear."

"I will never let you get away with this!" Chase seethed through clenched teeth.

Worthington shook his head. "I taught you well. But I can't let you do that."

Worthington's finger was on the trigger, but before he got off a shot, a knife hit his hand that made him drop the gun then a shot hit him in the shoulder. He fell to the ground with a loud wail in agony.

Although Chase would've put a bullet in her mentor, she was glad that she didn't have to. She was also glad that the two men she cared most about didn't let her down in her time of need. They both had her back.

Marcus entered shortly after and secured Worthington, putting him in cuffs while Burgess called everything in. Worthington would go away for a long time, and Chase was

CHASING DESIRES
by Kasey Martin

both ecstatic and saddened by the prospect. She'd gotten the bad guy, the man who had killed her beloved partner, a man who'd been like a brother to her. Unfortunately, the man who had killed her brother was the surrogate father that had mentored her to be the best.

Chase's thoughts and emotions were all over the place, and she was glad that she had already made the decision to leave the Bureau because she wanted as far away from her old life as possible.

CHASING DESIRES
by Kasey Martin

CHAPTER 29
LORENZO

Lorenzo was glad that he insisted on going with Chase to find Mike. John Worthington was a sneaky bastard that had spent years manipulating Chase. He knew that what she heard outside of that office had rocked her to her core. The look on her beautiful face almost broke his heart. She had lost so many people in her life, and to have the man she looked up to as a father let her down in such a way, was devastating.

He knew that the news would throw Chase off her game, and he had to have her back. And although Mike was quick to react by throwing his knife, Lorenzo's shot to Worthington's shoulder, made sure the man was incapacitated. He didn't want him to get to his gun and get a shot off. Because if anything would've happened to Chase, they wouldn't have to worry about putting Worthington on trial because he would've been six feet deep.

Lorenzo was back at the hotel, doing his best to relax, but his thoughts were keeping his anxiety level at an all-time high. He didn't know how Chase was going to handle all the information that she now knew about her mentor. It would've been a blow to anyone, but now that her case was closed,

CHASING DESIRES
by Kasey Martin

Lorenzo had to face the fact that he would now have to focus on his own fucked up situation. He had to confront his Uncle Sal with what his mother had unknowingly confessed to him because it wasn't in him to let this go. Lorenzo had to know what the hell was going on.

He always knew that he looked more like his uncle and the Angeletti side of his family, but he never once suspected that he was Sal's son. Although in his teenage years, he had a rebellious streak and fought constantly with his father, he never treated him anything but like his son. And his uncle never treated him any differently than he did his younger brother, Sergio. He treated them all like the family they were. He never gave him any special treatment, and Lorenzo always worked to gain any position he had in the family business.

Lorenzo just wanted to know why he was kept the family secret for all these years. Why was he the son that was hidden in shame? He wondered if his father knew that he was Sal's son and not his. *He had to know, but he loved me anyway.*

Chase brought him out of his thoughts as she came sauntering into the bedroom looking glorious as usual, but the slump in her shoulders told him that his *Pumpkin* would be dealing with Worthington's betrayal for a long time. Maybe they could take a vacation to somewhere tropical and get their minds off all of the bullshit, and back on each other. These past few months had been filled with hardships, but he was glad that they managed to make their way to each other.

He pulled her to his side as soon as she climbed into bed. He cuddled her close and kissed the top of her head. She snuggled in even closer, wrapped her toned arms around his torso, and lay her head on his chest. He tightened his arms around her and breathed in her soft vanilla scent. Holding her like this was just what he needed. He needed to feel the genuine love radiating from someone who truly knew who he was. He needed to be reminded that he was the same person; that Sal being his father didn't erase who he was as a man, it didn't erase the truth.

"You know, I'm glad to be moving to Dallas permanently and to take that job with Jake."

He wasn't at all surprised by her revelation because she had been considering leaving the Bureau for some time. He was glad that he didn't have to try and influence her to stay in Dallas. Now, all he had to do was convince her to move in with him.

"I'm glad that you will be staying in Texas." He hesitated before asking, "So your case is closed. What now?" He had to ask because there was still some uncertainty to their situation. Now that she was no longer investigating his cousin, would she even want to continue what they had? Did she truly love him like she'd said she did?

"Well, I'm going to let the justice system handle it from here. I just can't believe that all this time I had exactly what I needed to take down the entire Angeletti family."

Lorenzo nodded. Apparently, Chase had a ledger that belonged to Tommy. The book had all the evidence she needed to take down his scheming cousin. But Lorenzo didn't give a damn about what would happen to Tommy or Worthington. All he wanted to know was what was going to happen with them.

Chase sighed again before she continued. "I know we don't have to continue what we have because I'm no longer working a case, but I honestly love you Lorenzo. I'm in love with you, and I want to be with you."

Lorenzo couldn't have been more relieved. "We may not have gotten together under the best circumstances but you're it for me. I'm in love with you too, I can't be without you."

He kissed her softly on her plump, succulent lips. He was so in love with this woman that it drove him crazy just to think of not being with her. Lorenzo had to lock her down ASAP.

"So now that all of that is out of the way, what's been bothering you?"

CHASING DESIRES
by Kasey Martin

Lorenzo could only smile; she would always be able to read him. Chase didn't miss a thing, and he loved her even more for her concern.

"It's a very long story that can wait until another day." He kissed her slowly savoring her sweet taste, and her kiss swollen lips. She moaned into his mouth, and he knew that relaxing was out of the window. Lorenzo was going to make slow passionate love to the woman he planned on making his wife.

***

Lorenzo finally told Chase about his mother's confession, and it was like a weight had been lifted from him. She was sincerely supportive, but she didn't want him to go meet with his uncle. However, he had to go and see him, he had to know the reasons he had been kept in the dark. Chase wanted to come with him, but he wouldn't let her. Even though she was no longer an FBI agent, he still didn't feel like it would be safe for her in that type of environment.

Lorenzo confidently walked into his uncle's large mansion where he was immediately shown into his uncle's office. Lorenzo nodded at Jimmy, his uncle's longtime body guard, and went to greet his uncle.

"My boy, I'm so glad you came to see me, son." His uncle's words made him cringe. He never noticed how much his

Chasing Desires
by Kasey Martin

uncle said those words, but now he could remember every conversation that his uncle called him *son*.

"Uncle Sal, I'm glad you're doing well," Lorenzo automatically responded.

"Have a seat, son. How's Theresa doing? When I checked, they said she'd fractured a bone."

Lorenzo was glad that he had brought up his mother. It would make it easier for him to dive into the conversation. "She's doing just fine. In fact, she was quite clear-headed when I last talked to her. She knew who I was, and we were able to have a very long and informing conversation."

Lorenzo saw Sal's smile fade slightly, but he nodded and sipped his drink. "Good. It's always good when your Ma remembers you."

"It is. That's the reason why I'm here. She told me she's not my mother."

Sal's face grew pale, and Lorenzo watched him visibly swallow. "Your mother has dementia, son. The things she says sometimes are just unfortunate ramblings of a very sick woman."

He knew that his uncle would try to pull this shit. His mother may have been sick, but that conversation was real. She was reliving a memory like she so often did, and if it was the

Chasing Desires
by Kasey Martin

last thing he did, Lorenzo was going to get a confession out of this man before he left this house.

"No, you see. I don't think they were ramblings at all. As a matter of fact, it was more like a confession. She couldn't bear to keep living knowing that you were my father and you two kept that a secret for all of these years."

"Son, listen. I—"

Lorenzo slammed his fists against the desk, knocking over glasses in the process. "Don't you fuckin' call me that! You sit here and deny me to my face like you've done all my life. The least you could do now is admit it!"

Sal nodded and waved his hand toward the door. Lorenzo noticed for the first time that Jimmy had re-entered the room. Jimmy looked between the two men, and when Sal motioned again, Jimmy left with a soft click of the door behind him.

"It's a very long story, son…Lorenzo. Please sit down."

Lorenzo ran his hand through his hair and slid his tall muscular frame back down in the chair. He wanted to hear this story. He needed to.

"I was young and already married. Sylvia and I already had Tommy, and I was making a name for myself in my wife's family. She was Henry Cicero's only child, so I was to take over the family when the old man retired."

Chasing Desires
by Kasey Martin

Lorenzo nodded for him to continue. This story was long overdue, and he wanted him to get on with it.

"I met this young lady as sweet as candy, but she had bad habits." Sal shook his head, seemingly remembering the young woman he spoke of. "She was beautiful with long dark hair and crystal blue eyes. Everyone always thought you had inherited the Angeletti blues, but you have your mother's eyes. Janice and I had been having an affair for years when she became pregnant with you. She wanted me to leave Sylvia and start a family with her."

"So, what happened?" Lorenzo asked the question, but he had an idea of what could've happened to Janice.

"I couldn't leave Sylvia. I was about to inherit the family. Janice wouldn't just play her position, and Theresa had just lost her baby."

"You killed my mother and gave me to your sister to raise? What kind of fucked up world do you live in?" Lorenzo couldn't believe what he was hearing. How could he try to justify his actions? This man was a monster.

"I didn't kill your mother, son. She died because of the drugs. Like I said, she had her bad habits, and when I wouldn't leave Sylvia, she started to do drugs again. The drugs sent her into early labor and she died. I've done a lot of things that I'm not proud of, but I didn't kill your mother."

Chasing Desires
by Kasey Martin

"You only killed his father." Tommy strolled into the office with narrowed eyes, and an evil grin on his chubby red face.

"Tommy, what are you doing here? Now is not the time for this. You've just been released," Sal responded between clenched teeth.

Tommy chuckled without humor. "I'm here because I had to go to jail again. Now, I'm here to see my old man and catch up with my cousin. Or is it *brother*?" Tommy's smile was sinister.

"Like I said, now is *not* the time for your shit! You've caused enough heat to come to this family. You need to be in the city lying low." Sal seethed at Tommy.

"Oh, no, I'm done with laying low. It is way past time for this conversation. Just like it's way past time for you to retire."

"What are you talking about, boy?" Sal questioned in confusion. The frustration was clear on his withered face.

"I had the backing that I needed. But you threw a wrench in my plans, didn't you?" Tommy boldly questioned his father.

"You little shit nobody questions me! I'm the bo-"

Tommy cut his father off by laughing in his face. "Your time to reign is over old man. The Salazar Cartel knows it was you that sent the Feds in. They are still going to back me. Do you think Worthington was going to let me go down alone?"

"Worthington is in jail. He can't protect you anymore. And who do you think let me know what you were up to in Dallas? Never trust a dirty cop." Sal smirked.

Lorenzo found all of this information fascinating. All of the double crossing and backstabbing was beyond his comprehension, but all he really wanted was to know his role in all of this.

"I don't give a fuck about Worthington, the Salazar Cartel, or any of this bullshit! What did you mean he killed my father?" Lorenzo pointed at Tommy in anger.

"Well I guess it's time to finally pay for your sins Pops especially since you just tried to set me up to be killed. Now as I was saying, he may not have directly killed your mother, but he definitely killed your father. Or I guess, he wasn't actually your father after all."

"You don't know what the hell you're talking about. You need to keep your fuckin' mouth shut!" Sal threatened as he pointed his shaking finger at Tommy.

Lorenzo wasn't sure what was happening, but he knew that it wasn't about to end well. "My father died of a heart attack." Lorenzo looked between the two men and watched as

Chasing Desires
by Kasey Martin

the brewing war heightened in both their eyes that was so much like his own.

"Your father didn't die of a heart attack. He died of a needle full of sulfuric acid." Tommy seemed to be willing to tell every secret his father had.

"Shut the fuck up Tommy!" Sal shouted as the door swung open and Jimmy stepped inside again.

"How do you know that?" Lorenzo questioned both men again.

"I was there when good ole' pops stuck it in his neck, only I didn't know why, but I helped bury the secret, like always."

Lorenzo couldn't believe the shit that was happening. All of this time he thought he knew these people, but everything he thought was a lie.

"So you let my mother die, and killed the man I thought was my father, so you could what?"

"So I could keep what I worked so fucking hard for! And you think you're going to take it from me?" Sal shouted as he slammed his hands against the desk. "Do you think I would be head of this family with a pregnant mistress? Do you? I did what I had to do, and I won't apologize for it."

"So why did you kill my father?"

CHASING DESIRES
by Kasey Martin

"He found out that you weren't his son, he threatened to tell you. It would've jeopardized too much." Sal's face held a resolved expression before he continued with his crazy tale. "Then Tommy fucked up and Sergio was killed. I thought it was best for you to leave, and we could bring you back later."

"What do you mean Tommy fucked up?" Lorenzo words were menacing as he narrowed his eyes on Tommy.

"It wasn't me that got Sergio killed. I didn't fuck up. You did," Tommy said pointing at Sal. "You told me to get the job done, and get Sergio to do it."

Lorenzo shook his head. He always had so much loyalty for his family. He was a ride or die soldier, and did everything possible to make sure to put the family first. And his family didn't give one flying fuck about him.

"So you came here to divulge all your father's secrets?" Lorenzo's question broke the argument up.

"No, I came here to let him know it's time for him to retire. I have what I need to take over the family." The smug look on Tommy's face made Lorenzo want to punch him.

His cousin was certifiable. Did he actually think that he was going to walk away scot free with all the shit that was going on?

"I'm not retiring. Fuck you… you fucking ingrate! You think a fucking Cartel is going to save you? Give you any power… huh? With all the charges against Worthington, none of his arrest will stand. Yours included!" Sal yelled his face growing red with emotion as he stormed towards Tommy. Sal pushed his son and knocked him off balance.

Tommy regained his footing and punched his father, knocking him to the ground. Before Jimmy could move, Lorenzo jumped up and lunged at his cousin. They pushed and punched each other before Jimmy broke them up.

"I didn't want to bring you back in the family by the way. That was all Sal. He wanted you back but I wanted you to stay out. I needed you out of my way, and I tried to make that clear, but Russo royally fucked that up. I told him to kill your ass, but what's done is done. But I will take your business when all of this is over, for all of the trouble that you've caused." Tommy's lip was busted but he still managed to get out an evil laugh.

"You must be out of your got damned mind." Tommy didn't have time to react and neither did anyone else because before he knew it, Lorenzo had pulled out his Glock and was beating Tommy with it. This son of a bitch had gone too far. He stood by and watched his father die, he could've stopped his brother's death but didn't, he wanted him to hand over his business, and he tried to have him killed!

Chasing Desires
by Kasey Martin

Lorenzo could feel the blood splatter up onto his face, but he couldn't control himself. He wanted this asshole to die, and by his hand. Before he knew it, he was being pulled away from Tommy's blood soaked body.

He had no idea that old Jimmy was so strong. However, when he looked around he noticed it wasn't Jimmy who had pulled him off of his cousin, it was Marcus.

That's when he knew that Chase hadn't done what she'd promised she would. She didn't stay behind. She had followed him to the meeting. He had blacked out when he was beating Tommy, so he didn't hear any of the chaos of the house being invaded by people.

Before he knew it, Chase was in front of him with her small hands on his face. Her soothing touch brought him back to the present. "I'm here. I will always have your back."

Damn! I love her.

CHAPTER 30
CHASE

Chase never thought she would be glad to get back to Dallas. She handed in her resignation and left the Bureau and New Jersey without looking back. They'd been back for just under a month and things still weren't back to normal. When the story broke that Worthington was in bed with the mob, and all the pertinent players in the Angeletti family were being charged with multiple felonies, the proverbial shit hit the fan.

There were so many Fed's involved with the Angeletti family that the whole division had to be cleaned out. Worthington had been working with Tommy for years, and of course he was the one making her evidence disappear. But she had no idea that he had so many other agents working with him. Worthington had double crossed Tommy and started working for Sal when Tommy started to miss payoffs.

Once Chase heard Worthington's sordid tale, she finally looked in the duffel bag that Daniel had left at her apartment. Chase went to the storage unit and read the ledger from cover to cover as soon as she pulled it out of the bag. Tommy had kept records of every payment, debt, and dirty deed that he had done for years.

Chasing Desires
by Kasey Martin

Chase found out that Daniel had actually made a copy of the ledger, so Tommy never suspected that anyone knew of its existence. Chase wished she could've seen the look on his face when they presented him with the warrant, and arrested him for the second time. He was held without bond, and the case was plastered all over the news.

Since the Castillo cousins were arrested, the Salazar Cartel hadn't been seen around North Texas. Chase figured since there was so much snitching and disloyalty, the Cartel didn't want to take the chance in getting caught up, and cleared out back to Mexico.

Chase was still dealing with the betrayal, and the loss of her mentor. But she had a whole new group of people that loved her and treated her like family. She was so thankful to Jake and his guys for making her feel so at home, especially after everything she'd just been through.

The only lingering problem was between her and Mike. She wasn't upset anymore with his part in the Angeletti bust, but he still wasn't able to accept the fact that she and Lorenzo were an actual couple. He treated her with a disdain and hostility that she wasn't used to. Lorenzo threatened to kick his ass on several different occasions but every time he'd brought it up, she'd distracted him with sex.

CHASING DESIRES
by Kasey Martin

After weeks of not speaking, Mike finally agreed to have lunch with her, after Jake threatened him. They were meeting in Chase's favorite little coffee shop. She had already ordered her drink and was sitting on a comfortable sofa when Mike walked in.

His blond hair flopped carelessly into his face, and his eyes twinkled even though his mouth was held in a tight line. He walked over and sat down across from her.

"Hey, Mike, how are you doing?" Chase cautiously questioned. She tried to feel him out because if he started with his bullshit today, she was going to curse him out and give it to Jesus because there was no way she was going to continue to let him treat her like she was nothing.

"What's up, Chase? Why do you want to talk to me so bad now?"

"And just what the hell do you mean by that?" She asked her anger starting to rise.

"You spent months avoiding me, and not telling me the truth about you and Lorenzo, and now all of a sudden you want to talk?" Mike's voice rose with every accusation.

"I didn't spend any time avoiding you. And what I do in my personal time has nothing to do with you. What Lorenzo and I do is none of your business!" She would not back down like she normally would. He had no right to be upset because she'd fallen in love.

"But everyone else knew except me!" he shouted, pointing to himself. "You're my friend, Chase, and I was doing everything in my power to help you. But as soon as I turned my back, you ran off with the nearest criminal!" Mike's face was now flushed red, and his chest was heaving like he'd just run a marathon. Chase didn't understand why he was so mad at her.

"You didn't know because you weren't here and it wasn't your business," Chase said in a calm tone. "I can't help that I fell in love with Lorenzo, but he's not a criminal. It's unfair that you keep bringing up his past when he has been nothing but good to me. You've never given him a chance, and he's helped me when he didn't have to."

Mike shook his head. "I didn't need to give him a chance."

"I don't owe you a damn thing, Mike. You're my friend, but you have treated me like shit for too long. Whatever your problem is with Lorenzo, you better fucking get over it! You're my family, and I love you, but I won't let you treat me like shit!"

Mike's eyes grew stormy and he shook his head, resigning. "I'm sorry, Chase. I didn't mean to treat you like shit I jus-just didn't want you to make a mistake by being with

Chasing Desires
by Kasey Martin

someone like Lorenzo. I loved you, Chase. Why couldn't you see that?"

Chase was shocked by his confession. Lorenzo had always told her that Mike wanted more than friendship, but she didn't believe it.

"I love you too, Thatch, but just not in *that* way." Her eyes were full of sorrow for the love that could never be. "I'm in love with Lorenzo. He is one of the good ones."

Mike nodded. "I know you're in love with him because you have been for a long time. I just thought that we could've been a better match. I knew once I saw you two together, it wasn't meant for us."

Chase grabbed his hand and made him look at her in her eyes. "We are meant to be best friends. I do love you, Mike."

"It's ok, Chase I've accepted things for what they are, but I was still upset that you shut me out. Like you said we are best friends, and best friends don't hide things from each other."

Chase nodded and smiled. "You're right and I'm sorry."

Mike nodded his acceptance. "I'm sorry too. Nothing but the whole truth from now on?"

"Nothing but the truth." They hugged tightly, which was a start.

CHASING DESIRES
by Kasey Martin

They ordered lunch and quickly settled into comfortable conversation, catching up on all of the things they had missed in each other's lives.

"So, how's Lidia doing?" Chase smiled knowingly at Mike whose face had turned red for a whole different reason.

"Agent Burgess is doing fine. She's been buried under paperwork with everything that's been going on, but I've managed to talk to her a couple of times."

"Agent Burgess... please don't act like you two aren't on a first name basis. I like her for you, she's cute."

Mike's handsome face held a look full of longing, "No. She's beautiful. I'm going to Jersey in a few weeks to see her." He smiled boyishly and his blue eyes were bright, "You're right though, we are definitely on first name basis."

Chase noticed the blissful look on Mike's face, and she knew that he was a goner for Agent Lidia Burgess. She was glad that her friendship with Mike could be saved. Things weren't the same with them fighting. Chase knew that it wouldn't be an easy road for them, but they finally seemed to be back on the same page.

***

After she had lunch with Mike, she went back to Lorenzo's apartment. Since they'd gotten back from Jersey she'd only been back to her apartment to get clothes. They had settled into a routine, Lorenzo was back working full time, and getting Prime ready for a grand re-opening while making sure Premier was surviving without Charlie being there.

She'd been working at J.C. Inc., and settling in with permanently living in Dallas. It was a smooth transition considering she'd spent so much time there, but now all of her things from Jersey were here.

"Man-Candy, I'm home!" Chase snickered when she heard Lorenzo groan at the nickname. She still got a kick out of calling him the most random things that came to her mind.

"*Pumpkin*, could you please just call me something normal like, babe, or sweetie?" He questioned as he sauntered into the room wearing basketball shorts and running shoes.

She stopped in her tracks. Lorenzo had bulked up even more since they'd been together, and the sight of him without a shirt on with sweat dripping down his tall muscular frame had her almost drooling. *Who am I kidding, I am drooling!*

"Damn! Honey smacks, you sure are looking good." Chase whistled appreciatively as she stalked toward him and kissed his lips.

He groaned and wrapped his arms around her waist and picked her up.

Chasing Desires
by Kasey Martin

Her feet dangled in the air and she squealed and giggled. "Put me down! You're all sweaty." She laughed and slapped his bare chest.

"But I want to make *you* all sweaty." He stuck out his bottom lip in a fake pout and she couldn't help but suck it into her mouth.

"I think I will let you get me all sweaty." She smiled deviously with a wink as he put her down. She led him into the bathroom. "But first, I think I'll let you get me all wet."

Chase turned the water on and waited for it to heat up. They stripped down and walked into the spacious shower. She poured a generous amount of fresh scented shower gel onto a loofah. She lathered it up, and started washing his chest. She smoothed it over his scar slowly, and down over his stomach. She continued moving the loofah all over his torso, and down to the V that led to his rock hard manhood. However, she would skim over his shaft without really touching it. His arousal was standing straight up and pointing at her, and he was holding himself stalk still, like he was waiting to pounce on her at any second, but she knew he wouldn't.

Lorenzo loved when she pampered his body, and she knew that with her every touch his control was slipping. She rubbed over one nipple and then the other. She took her soapy hand and ran it down to his cock that was hard with his arousal.

CHASING DESIRES
by Kasey Martin

She grabbed it with her hand, and moved it up and down in a firm grip.

He groaned and placed his hands against the wall behind her head. He leaned down and kissed the top of her hair, but he didn't move his hands. His body rocked back and forth with the motion of her tugging. Chase was so turned on that she could feel her thighs slick with her own arousal. She dropped to her knees and took his massive cock into her mouth. She sucked the mushroom shaped head while she rubbed his thighs. She hollowed out her cheeks and sucked the rest of him into her mouth as far as he could go.

Lorenzo moaned as he continued to thrusts his hips to the rhythm of her sucking. He finally lost control, and his hands went to her hair as he pumped in and out. He pulled her head back and forth and fucked her mouth. She hummed and she knew the vibration would send him over the edge.

"Aww shit! Chase, fuck! Your mouth feels so fucking good!" he shouted and groaned in agonizing ecstasy.

All of a sudden, he pulled her off her knees, and he popped out of her mouth with a loud plop. He turned off the water and stepped out of the shower pulling her behind him.

He wrapped them in towels and quickly started to dry them off.

CHASING DESIRES
by Kasey Martin

"I wasn't done yet; you know?" Chase quirked a sassy brow at him as he continued to rush to dry her off.

"Who said anything about being done?" His brow raised at her in question as a broad smile broke out over his handsome face.

His smile alone could make her wet, his straight white teeth and kissable lips surrounded by the dark stubble made her knees weak, and he knew it.

Once he was finished drying her off, he carried her to the bedroom and finished what she'd started. He made love to her for the rest of the afternoon. She was so thankful to have this man in her life and she didn't know what she would do without him.

***

The next day, Chase pulled up to Jake and Charlie's house. They were having a girls' day in because the twins were just over a month old, and Charlie was still healing from her C-section.

Chase knocked on the door, and was let in by an exhausted-looking Jake. "Hey, big guy. You look like you need a nap."

Jake ran his hand through his thick beard and chuckled. "We're the first ones of our friends to have kids, so there was nobody to tell us how exhausting this shit is."

CHASING DESIRES
by Kasey Martin

Chase patted his back in sympathy. "It will get better. At least I've heard it will."

He chuckled again. "Yeah, I sure hope so. Heart's in the living room."

Chase headed to the living room and heard loud laughter as she got closer. When she rounded the corner, she saw Charlie holding one baby and Korri holding the other. Everyone else was sitting around laughing and talking.

"Hey, everyone," Chase greeted as she walked further into the room.

"Hey, girl." Charlie smiled at her.

Chase gave everyone hugs and went to see the babies. They were so gorgeous with their butterscotch complexion and dark green eyes. They were a perfect combination of Jake and Charlie. As a matter of fact, baby JJ was huge, and baby Journee was tiny. They were a mirror image of their parents.

"My goodness, Charlie. How much does this child weigh?" Brandon grimaced dramatically as he took baby JJ from Korri.

"Hey, don't you talk about my little giant. He can't help it. You've seen his daddy." Charlie chuckled.

"Well, his big behind better not be taking all the milk from my sweet little Journee pooh." Brandon cooed at baby Journee as she lay sound asleep on her mother's chest.

Chasing Desires
by Kasey Martin

"Oh, no worries. My little princess is getting plenty of milk. It's their daddy that's a little salty about not getting any."

"TMI, Charlie!" Korri rolled her eyes.

"Hey just 'cause you're getting it on the regular, *newlywed*, doesn't mean everyone is. I still have two more weeks, and I think my husband is having serious physical withdrawals at this point. Poor guy."

"His giant A-S-S will be fine." Brandon whispered spelled as if the month old babies knew what he was saying. Everyone laughed at him, and continued talking.

"We can still have grown-up conversations. They're only a month old. It's when they start learning to talk where I'll need a babysitter to have a conversation." Charlie rolled her eyes dramatically.

"Well, if they're as nosy as you and your cousin, then you will most definitely need a babysitter for them not to learn what S-E-X is before they're two." Brandon laughed.

All the women laughed as well, and Charlie waved her hand dismissively, "Whatever. So Chase, how's everything going with you? I've hardly seen you since you've moved here." Charlie stated as she patted her fussing baby and gently rocked her back to sleep.

"Everything is good. Thanks." Chase broadly smiled.

CHASING DESIRES
by Kasey Martin

"By the looks of that smile, things are better than good," Eden responded with a smile of her own.

"I know right. You must be getting some good loving," Farren added with a laugh.

Chase couldn't help the blush that crept over her ebony complexion. She was getting good loving and she had never been happier in her life. She now had a great job that she loved, good friends that treated her like family, and the love of her life. Everything was perfect.

EPILOGUE
TWO YEARS LATER
LORENZO

Lorenzo looked out at the beautiful turquoise ocean. The breeze was heavenly, and the weather was wonderful. It was the perfect day. The giggling laughter made his heart warm with joy as he watched the toddlers frolic and play in the water.

"Jake, you're a lucky man." Lorenzo smiled at his friend as Jake watched his growing children play.

"Man, you have no idea how lucky." Jake smiled back at him.

"I still don't know how you do it with two kids at once. I'm surprised you're still standing. I would be somewhere asleep," Tony said as he joined the conversation.

"Believe me it took damn near a year before they started sleeping on a regular schedule. The little cock blockers."

The men laughed at Jake's disgruntled comment. "How are you just going to call your own kids such harsh names?" Lorenzo questioned with a chuckle.

"Listen, man, I swear they knew every time I got their mama worked up and ready to go. One of them would cry bloody murder. Usually, it was JJ." Jake shook his head and sipped his beer.

CHASING DESIRES
by Kasey Martin

Lorenzo couldn't believe how his life was now. He was on a couples' vacation on a tropical island. In the past, he'd barely taken a day off, so taking a week-long vacation to Jamaica was unheard of. But his beautiful wife could get him to do anything she wanted.

All she had to do was bat those long thick lashes and smile, and he would ask how high she wanted him to jump. And he didn't give a damn what anybody said about it because a happy wife made a happy life. Those were words to live by.

It only took Lorenzo four months to get Chase to marry him. She didn't want a big wedding, so they had a small ceremony and reception with their friends. Now, they were enjoying their last few months with just the two of them, so they decided to take a vacation. Chase called it a babymoon or something. He didn't care as long as he got to spend some alone time with his beautiful pregnant wife.

If it was anything like Jake and Tony complained about, once the baby arrived, sex could be hard to come by if you didn't get creative.

Tony and Korri had a fifteen-month old baby. Korri didn't realize that she was already pregnant before the wedding because of all the stress she had been under. They were ecstatic that their little boy, Anthony Cameron, had made an early appearance.

CHASING DESIRES
by Kasey Martin

Now, it was Lorenzo and Chase's turn. They were having a little girl, and he was both excited and nervous. If she was as beautiful as her mother, then he was going to have to buy stock in Smith and Wesson. *Hell, who am I kidding? I'm definitely going to have to buy stock.*

Jake was already cleaning his gun on a regular basis, but at least he had help with JJ. The little giant hardly let anybody near his baby sister, and Tony's lucky ass had a boy. He didn't have the same type of worries when it came to his little man.

"So you guys are still out here moaning about your kids?" Mike chuckled as he walked up holding more beers.

"Hey, just because you and Lidia haven't started yet, it doesn't mean you get to make fun of us." Lorenzo smiled as he grabbed a beer out of Mike's hand with a nod and a smile.

"That won't be happening. Lids has threatened my life if I knock her up before the wedding. She says she worked too hard to get in her dress for me to ruin it with a baby in her belly," Mike chuckled.

"Why do I have the feeling you're still trying to ruin her wedding dress?" Marcus questioned with a smile.

"You know me too well." Mike smirked as he and Marcus clinked their bottles together in cheers.

"So where's Lo? I didn't see her on the beach with the other ladies," Mike mentioned.

CHASING DESIRES
by Kasey Martin

"She had a long night, so she'll be down later." Marcus nonchalantly sipped his beer.

Both Jake and Tony groaned their disgust. Nobody had any idea that Marcus and Lauren were dating. But apparently after Korri's brush with death, the two had been discreetly seeing each other. They didn't want any interference from their family, so they didn't say anything until they became exclusive. Now they were going on three years of happiness.

Lorenzo laughed at their dramatics. He'd never in a million years thought that he would've been here with these guys. That he would be close friends with all of them, especially Mike Thatcher. It took a while for the two of them to become cordial, and eventually friends. Chase had a lot to do with that, though. She would never let her husband and one of her best friends remain enemies.

And he would never do anything to make Chase unhappy, so as much as he didn't want to have anything to do with Mike, he sucked it up for his wife. Now, they were all one big happy dysfunctional family.

Lorenzo smiled as he watched his beautiful wife with her belly round and full with his child, waddling toward him. She had no idea how sexy she was to him, especially pregnant. Or maybe she did because he couldn't keep his hands off of her.

CHASING DESIRES
by Kasey Martin

"You okay, *Pumpkin*? You need anything?" Lorenzo fussed over her as he helped her sit under the large umbrella on the sun lounger.

"I'm okay, Sugar Pops." She grinned at him, and he shook his head and laughed. He would never get tired of her creative nicknames for him.

"How's my precious baby girl?" Lorenzo leaned down and kissed her stomach lovingly. He found himself talking to her belly a lot, especially when he felt the baby kick.

"Your precious girl is kicking Mommy's butt today. I think I must be growing a gymnast in here because I'm pretty sure she's doing cartwheels." Chase smiled at Lorenzo, and he couldn't help but take her mouth in a passionate kiss.

There was nothing in this world that could make him happier. Here with his extended family and his beautiful wife. He was so extremely thankful that Chase Johnson was such a dedicated agent that she had chased her desires right into his life.

THE END

CPSIA information can be obtained
at www.ICGtesting.com
Printed in the USA
LVHW080029211022
731175LV00013B/471